31 FIELDS

Matea Čvagić Prašnjak

4-U-Nique Publishing
Breaking the Status Quo, One Book at a Time.™

4-U-Nique Publishing
A Series of VLB/VBJ Enterprises, LLC

31 Fields

4-U-Nique Publishing books may be purchased for educational, business, or sales promotional use. For information, please email: info@4-U-Nique Publishing.com

First American English Edition

Cover Design By: 4-U-NiquePublishing

ISBN-13: 978-1088036327

To My Husband,
(who remain my greatest crush)

Thank you for playing me that corny James Blunt song while leaning on my iron bed frame and so becoming (with the humming and the cookie chewing) the fundamental motive of this story.

31 FIELDS

	Prologue	**15**
Chapter 1:	**Wings**	**21**
Chapter 2:	**Cradle**	**29**
Chapter 3:	**Mirror**	**37**
Chapter 4:	**Eyes**	**45**
Chapter 5:	**Clock Hands**	**51**
Chapter 6:	**The Boy**	**67**
Chapter 7:	**Olympia**	**89**
Chapter 8:	**Lost Compass**	**111**
Chapter 9:	**Metamorphoses**	**127**
Chapter 10:	**Zair**	**149**
Chapter 11:	**Chameleons**	**159**
Chapter 12:	**Suitcase**	**173**
Chapter 13:	**Fairy Godmothers**	**185**
Chapter 14:	**Iris**	**199**
Chapter 15:	**Limits**	**213**
Chapter 16:	**Touches**	**227**
Chapter 17:	**Curtain**	**241**
Chapter 18:	**Mailbox**	**255**
Chapter 19:	**Shadows**	**265**
Chapter 20:	**Lullaby**	**277**
Chapter 21:	**Golden Tooth**	**289**
Chapter 22:	**Carousel**	**295**
Chapter 23:	**Faked deaths**	**305**
Chapter 24:	**Daughter**	**311**
Chapter 25:	**Estuary**	**319**
Chapter 26:	**Silhouette**	**325**

Chapter 27: **Chocolate Complexion** **339**

Chapter 28: **Boomerang** **347**

Chapter 29: **Wounds** **355**

Chapter 30: **Tango** **365**

Chapter 31: **Snow** **371**

Dear Reader,

I reduced some parts of my sweet and pleasant reality. I added a few new fragments to it and then gathered all those lovely pieces of the real and the unreal in an entirety that I named *31 Fields*. *31 Fields* is a very ordinary story about ordinary people that always have been and always will be an inseparable part of my imagination. Let me ask you a question: what is more magical than ordinary people and ordinary things intertwining at the right angle? Truly nothing, I'd say. All those ordinary things always find their place in the alchemy of magic.

If you decide to give me the pleasure, all these characters will also come alive in your imagination – in a magnificently changed and unique way. I'm giving you a small part of my universe as a gift and the complete freedom to do with it as you wish. I wrote this story out of my pleasure and for very selfish reasons. However, I finished it for a completely different and unselfish one – to please you and provide you with the illusion you thirst for. While you enjoy that illusion, my dear Curious Reader, try to keep one thing in mind; every illusion is born into reality.

I created this story following several characters. Each part of the book follows one specific character and period. Many things will be unclear at first, seeing as one chapter takes place in the 70s, and the next possibly in the 40s. I implore you, Dear Reader, to read my words carefully and pay attention to the years and events. Please don't lose hope that everything will, in time, become apparent.

Trust me on this - life transcends the concept of time, and everything is but an oddly rounded entirety in the world... Let's say the world is much smaller and more magical than you'd hoped.

Naturally Yours,

Matea Čvagić Prašnjak

In every real man, a child is hidden that wants to play.
(F. Nietzsche)

Croatian Names' Pronunciation Guide

In order of appearance:

Nadja (Na-dee-ah)

Zrinjevac Park (Zree-niye-vah-ts)

Ilir (Eel-eer)

Osijek (Oss-ee-yek)

Žanet ('Ž' is pronounced like 's' in 'vision', 'g' in 'mirage', 's' in 'pleasure'; Ž-anette)

Tabita (Ta-bith-ah)

Zair (Zai-eer)

Patrik (Patrick)

Marko (Marco)

Karla (Carla)

Petar (Peter)

Franjo Bošnjak ('š' is pronounced like 's' in 'sure'; Frah-niyow Bosch-niyak)

Oto Gamulin (Otto Gam-mou-leen)

café Trica ('c' is pronounced like 'c' in 'cease'; Tree-tsa)

Ante Starčević square (Ahnt-ay Star-che-vitch)

Lončar (Lonch-arr)

Lea (Leah)

Franjo Krežma (Frah-niyow Kray-ž-mah, 'ž' is pronounced like 's' in 'vision', 'g' in 'mirage')

Ema (Ema)

restaurant Breskvica (Bress-kwee-tsa)

Ivan Gundulić (E-van Goon-dou-litch)

Prologue

SEPTEMBER, 1972
OSIJEK

Once upon a time, there was a little girl. Her mother's soft voice read out loud. Out of all the wishes a person could have in this world, the little girl had but one – to see a thousand shining orange lanterns fly into the night sky. Lanterns so bright that the stars would scarcely be needed. The magic of those flying lanterns would be perfect enough to adorn the sky and illuminate anyone who gazed at them.

The girl would often close her eyes to revive that image. The image of herself sitting on a boat, looking up as the bubbling background in the sky performed its magic on her. She was never alone in that thought of hers. A pair of glowing green eyes were always right across from her. In one blink of an eye, gazing at her, and in the other, at the lanterns. However, she could only keep the greenness of those eyes in her mind for a mere second. It was more of a feeling, like something innate, somewhat incomplete.

Her wish was compelling and strong. She alone was often unaware of the strength a wish could have. She would think about it every night before sleep, before she'd put out the shimmering candle on the creaky loose cupboard next to her bed. Then the little girl would fall asleep, always dreaming about her only wish.

The girl lived in a poor family. Not only did they have little money, but they had no other children either. For the little girl, that's what being truly poor meant – not having a brother or a sister. They'd often ask her: "How would you know, silly girl, that poverty meant having no brothers or sisters if you've never had them?" She would ever so patiently answer: "How does a poor man know he'd be much happier if he had more money? Simply because his stomach aches for food. That's how my heart aches for a sister or a brother."

The only wealth that her parents possessed was a lake not far from their small estate. A clear, almost glassy lake. During the summer, the girl would always go there at the day's end. She would stare at the smooth surface of the lake and the moonlight scraping at its bare consistency. If she sat there long enough and watched closely enough, she could see the reflection of a thousand magical lanterns on the lake's surface.

The evenings she would spend there did not differ much from one another. One night, however, something was different. The little girl was not alone. A strangely beautiful woman sat next to her. She had unusual, decaying wings on her back, her hair had a greenish glow, her irises were utterly yellow, her teeth separated, and her cheeks entirely pale – as if she wasn't alive. Her figure was downright skinny, and the thin threads of her dress – as though made from frozen sunbeams – dangled around her. Just like the little girl's coat dangled from the wooden hanger next to her rotten doorway at home.

The strangely beautiful woman started gazing into the little girl's eyes assertively, with a peculiar smile on her surreal face. Assertively and ambiguously, just the way all creatures from our imagination and dreams look at us. Or rather, all the creatures that don't really exist. The little girl turned around fearfully and looked right at the woman. Then she glanced at her dead wings and her completely ruffled green hair as chills overtook her whole body. Yet, the girl didn't run away for some deep (but seemingly unknown) reason.

"I won't harm you," said the strange creature. She had a clear, a bit hoarse, and quite masculine voice.

"Are you a fairy?" the little girl asked.

"Yes, I am," she answered.

"Can you fly?" The girl glanced once again at her decaying wings.

"I could," the fairy ran her fingers over her wing somberly.

"You can't anymore?"

The fairy shook her head, widened her eyes, and sighed deeply.

"But I can do something else," she uttered.

"What?"

"I can grant a wish," she replied.

"Grant a wish," the little girl's eyes held a peculiar shine.

"Yes, grant a wish," the fairy answered. "But only one."

"That's how many I have," the little girl uttered melancholically and lowered her gaze toward the palms in her lap. "But how do I know I can trust you?"

"If you don't try, your wish will never be granted, will it?"

The little girl gawked at the fairy, fidgeting with her tiny, dirty hands.

"I want to see flying lanterns, a thousand of them, the ones from my dreams," stated the little girl with a great but fearful excitement in her voice. "Flying towards the sky. That is all," she bowed her head.

"Alright," the fairy answered.

The little girl continued fidgeting her fingers more anxiously now as if she were expecting something. But, from all that vigorous hope she nurtured inside, a few stars seemed like lanterns.

"I knew you couldn't grant wishes," the little girl again lowered her head.

"I can grant wishes," said the fairy. "But to notice that your wish has been granted, you must do something as well."

"That's nonsense," the girl shook her head. "Of course, I'd notice if my only wish were granted."

"I'll make you a promise," the fairy touched the little girl's round chin with her finger and turned her head, "If you promise me something in return."

The little girl gasped from the sheer excitement and fear.

"Then your wish will surely come true," added the fairy.

The little girl perked her ears and tilted her head like a puppy waiting for the tastiest treat.

"Exactly seven years from this day, two choices will appear before you," the fairy's yellow gaze penetrated the little girl's eyes. "Pick the one where you can see the reflection of a thousand orange lanterns."

The fairy paused for a second, possibly to ensure the little girl understood her words.

"Then," she proceeded, "And only then will my task be easy, and you will truly see the light of those lanterns above you."

"How would I know if I made a mistake?" the little girl asked.

"The lanterns will go out," replied the fairy.

The little girl looked up at the dark sky above them.

"And I," the fairy went on, "I will never be able to fly again."

Wings

SEPTEMBER, 1972
OSIJEK

Nadja was drifting off to sleep. Her cheek was already a bit bruised from the weariness. She lays reclined on the cold pillow engorged from its freshness. Then, finally, she extended her small, sweaty palms over it and let out a clear and satisfied exhale. She had spent the whole previous day running around the Zrinjevac Park, casually plucking the freshly mowed grass, climbing the old and worn-out playground apparatus, walking on the giant concrete benches – even though she'd been strictly told not to – and, from time to time, swiftly entering a café that was part of the Zrinjevac Sports Hall to ask for a big glass of water with ice. She was astounded by the fact that the water was free.

After all, she quickly fell asleep with the images from a carefree day etched into her mind. Her golden blonde hair spread all over the whiteness of the pillow as nimbly as silk, twinkling under the dimmed light of the night lamp her mother sat next to and read to her every night before her dreams caught up with her. Nadja didn't care what her mother read to her, be it fairytales, words arranged in verses, or simply an ordinary newspaper article – the solitary act of reading was far more important.

Above all, Nadja adored everything uttered by her mother. To be fair, her mother had read a newspaper article to her only once. It was about a ten-year-old boy that sold books at a

Christmas fair. But she didn't really remember it that well because she fell asleep before the end of the story, just like she does now.

Her big, smooth eyelids covered her exceptionally green irises, and her breath slowed significantly, letting her mother know that slumber had finally taken over. She gently kissed her low forehead and turned off the night lamp, trying remarkably hard not to produce a sound. Finally, she tiptoed out of Nadja's purple room, leaving the door slightly ajar.

***

All that fatigue she felt made it seem like the night flew by in a single moment. Nadja's dreams were so sweet – almost edible – that they rushed through the night, flashing through her small room like little sparrows jumping from branch to branch. She felt like she had conjured her dreams and immediately switched them off with a simple closing of her eyes. And just like that, as though with a blink of an eye, the morning was already there on her white wooden window. The sun smuggled its rays through two green curtains covering the high window like two guards watching over a door. In a swift movement, she rubbed her eyes and squeezed her eyelashes with her soft fingertips, leaving a shell-shaped dent of her beautifully formed head on the pillow. Her locks, having been playing around the nape of her head throughout the night, ended up out of order. She had her slumber to thank for that. After rubbing her eyes, she headed towards the bedroom.

She ran lethargically and loudly. Like an elephant in a China shop, her mother would say. Her legs danced anxiously and delightedly through the thin corridor – which to her seemed far too long and serious – that separated her room from the master bedroom. She settled down only when she stepped in front of the bedroom door, feeling like she had won an important, unbeatable marathon. Then she'd lay her hand on the cold round door handle at the height of her nose and peep inside the room very quietly, gritting her baby teeth.

Upon entering the room for the first couple of moments, her thieving gaze would usually examine how her mother slept. The way her distinctly black hair diffused all over the pillowcase, her somewhat irregular lips covered in lichen, one soft hand that hung from the bed, a foot that shyly stuck out from under the covers, and finally, the side of the bed that has been empty for a long, long time. Nadja would then get ready for a running leap onto the bed. At that precise moment, her mother's slumber would indisputably end. Then, after a couple of jumps with Nadja's feet ending up in the air and staying in that position as if she were flying, she would curl up around her mother's head and start whispering.

"Mommy," she uttered sweetly, "We have to get up."

"Nadja," her mother replied in a tired voice as her eyes remained closed, "You're jumping again; I have told you a hundred times...."

Her voice got lost in the intensity of Nadja's jumps until she finally got off the bed.

"If you don't come," Nadja put her hand on the latch, "I'll make my own breakfast."

As her mother gasped widely, intending to warn her not to do that under any circumstance, Nadja interrupted her.

"We know you don't want that."

***

Their mornings were always rushed. But no matter the pace, the room Nadja and her mother shared always had a sense of peace and bliss. The corner of the well-lit small kitchen echoed with the cheerful voice of the Jutromlat radio host. His purpose was mainly to awaken the children and cheer them up so that the process of leaving them in schools and kindergartens would run smoothly, without tears and protests on the ever-so-current topic: Why can't a parent bring their kid to work?

Her mother warmed up Nadja's milk every morning – it had become their tradition. She would loudly place the pot on the stove as Nadja listened to the crackling of the fire striker. After that, her mother would leave the milk on the stove until the milk skin appeared on the surface. From a wooden drawer – whose creaking was the highlight of Nadja's morning – she'd pull out a round spoon (Nadja loved those specifically) and place the breakfast on the table in front of her. Nadja would then skim through the morning newspaper she had grabbed from the doorstep earlier. At the soft sound of the bowl being placed on the table, she would stop skimming through the newspaper, flick her golden hair back, and, with a joyful gaze, immerse herself in the bread soaking in the milk. She loved observing the way the whiteness of the milk engorged the bread pieces while listening to the ringing noise of the spoon hitting the sides of the ceramic mug. That was the sign of her mother stirring her first and her favorite and most aromatic coffee of the day.

Twenty minutes before departing, they would stand in front of the mirror that reflected the orange and green bathroom tiles. Nadja would stand on a wooden stool that her grandfather made so that she could reach her mother's height, and her mother would fix her hair and adjust the collar of her stiff white shirt. Sometimes, Nadja would observe how the darkness of her mother's blue eyes almost cut the glass before them, cracking it with its gaze. She would then grab Nadja's golden locks with her dry palms and swiftly but devotedly braid her hair in a thick pigtail, licking the redness above her lips. Then, like every morning, her mother would tap her shoulders upright and exhale.

"Alright, now bugger off and put your shoes on!"

In that instant Nadja would, usually without saying a word, run off towards the cramped hallway, put her shoes on, and wait readily next to the door with a red leather backpack while her mother grabbed her purse and car keys. The car ride was probably one of Nadja's favorite parts of their mornings together. Her mother let her play her favorite tape they'd sing along to like no one else existed. In all fairness, they'd usually close their windows so no one else could notice their singing. They did the same thing that morning. They sat in their car as Nadja opened the brown leather compartment and took out the tape. The Moody Blues – Nights in White Satin. It was a tape with only one song that her father recorded for her after a series of strenuous naggings. The drive, as usual, lasted the length of the song precisely. Her mother took an extra 30 seconds to park the car.

Her mother worked in a bakery. Her working hours started very early –5:30am – because the schoolchildren were always hungry and thirsty early in the morning, and the kindergarten Nadja attended opened at 7am. That is why Nadja came to the bakery with her mother every morning. She would sit on a tall wooden cupboard behind the glass counter that served no purpose other than accommodating Nadja.

Mister Ilir, the owner of the bakery Studen, adored watching Nadja blissfully sit there and skim through all sorts of picture books that her mother kept for her in the bakery's storage. He was grinning widely as he observed how she bowed her head towards the round letters, carefully and meticulously going over each and every one of them with her big eyes. Every now and then, she'd put the long and thick strands of her hair behind her ear whenever they nimbly escaped the clutches of her braid. And when she completely immersed herself into the simple world of the picture book, she'd start moving her tiny feet, her heels bluntly tapping the cupboard doors, echoing throughout the bakery. Whenever Ilir arrived, Nadja would run towards him with her backpack running after her and plunge her cheeks into his fat belly, to which he'd usually respond by patting her on the head and picking her up.

"Why are you so dear to me?"

He brought her to the wooden cupboard and sat her there. He had noticed the way she passionately read all those picture books, newspaper articles, and verses from her mother's poetry collection, which is why he was, for quite some time now, planning to give her a notebook to write her first stories or poems in. He visited Zagreb six months earlier and saw a brown notebook at a book fair. It was lined with smooth brown leather and carved with sloppy handwriting, and a skinny red bow was used to close the notebook covers tightly. The moment he laid his eyes on it, he couldn't help but imagine Nadja's first stories—her first free words. And so, that expensive but valuable notebook had already been sitting there for some time, in a hidden nook of his home, gift-wrapped in green, waiting for her seventh birthday, lurking around the corner.

In the hour Nadja would spend at the bakery before kindergarten, she loved – other than the fantastic smell of chocolate donuts – going outside, to the front of the bakery, especially when it rained. In those particular moments, when her mother was around the oven and had no clue about what was going on outside of the bakery, she would go out and bounce in the rhythm of heavy raindrops, spin around her axis, and reach out for the distant sky, hardly keeping the smile off her face. Ilir would grin at her with his dull snaggletooth.

Right beside the bakery door, tight against its glass window, sat Ilir's wife in a wheelchair. Unlike him, she was extremely skinny, her face hollow, and her hair a strange, quite inexplicable brown tone. Some exceptionally dry grays sprouted all over her glum brown hair. She always had a red blanket covering her lap, a scarf around her neck, and a cigarette perpetually hanging between her lips, almost as if it were an essential part of her whole existence. Her hands were shaking, and that was why – as Nadja figured it – she only preferred to hold the cigarette with her lips. She would rarely hold it between her fingers due to her hands trembling so severely, which would, in turn, always send the cigarette plummeting to the floor. And she, an avid lover of solitude and silence, rarely allowed herself to call for help.

A cloud of tiny raindrops spread over Osijek that morning, and Nadja stormed out as she widened her giant eyes. She started spinning, bouncing, and even yelling and screaming random words. Then she stopped and looked towards Ilir's wife. Her cigarette was lying on the floor, her head was shaking, and her palms were placed on her lap to ease the horrid image of a dreadful tremor. Nadja tilted her head, feeling Ilir's eyes watching her every move, then stepped on the cigarette and sat in the woman's lap. She embraced her wrinkled neck with her tiny arms, running her right palm through her weary, split hair. She stared directly into her small brown eyes, smiling widely. Nadja started pecking her on the cheeks. But the lady did not smile, nor did she kiss her back. Instead, she just sat there as if she couldn't feel Nadja's touch.

"There, there, child, let's go inside," Ilir took her in his arms. "You'll get all wet."

Unmoved by the old lady's coldness, she sighed through a relentless smile.

"Here, you have to go soon; read something while you're here," he stuffed the picture book in her hands and turned around to attend to a child waiting on his pastries.

Like a small bird flapping its wings around her mind, not wanting to leave her alone, Nadja felt that something wasn't quite right. She jumped off the cupboard and ran towards the storage to her mother. The smile disappeared from her face when she saw a single shiny silver drop rolling down her mother's cheek, and her heart started racing when she noticed her shaking hand holding a small white piece of paper.

Cradle

AUGUST, 1940
OSIJEK

That dark corner of her one-bedroom apartment let her know nothing would ever be the same again. Not one smile, not one zeal of pleasure, not one tear, not one shriek. And henceforth, all of that will leave a strangely dull tone behind. All her senses will be silenced – if she does it. Her young, smooth hand reached out for the black cup of tea. The poignant coldness of the cup sent chills throughout her skin, traveling from the tips of her fingers to her shoulders, finding their way to her anxiety-riddled throat.

The smell of sage tea spread across the whole room. It flowed through the darkness as though cutting it. But, Žanet, don't go. The color of his voice rang in her head. You can stay with me. She closed her eyes and saw him as if he were there. As if he were staring right into her eyes in that wandering twilight. Beside me. She felt his touch on her cheek as if someone had vigorously hit the delicate piano key emitting its sound to the universe. She felt it in a frighteningly precise manner; she felt the way it merged with the softness of her skin while she marveled at the fact that his dark-skinned touch – even in memory – never left a trace on the whiteness of her skin. She wished it weren't so; she wanted the path to remain untouched, visible, and strong. She shut her mouth with her palm to stop her whimper, having seen a lock of his hair in that other dimension woven by memories. And now, as she felt the softness of those big locks, her hands shuddered. At that moment, as if the air was purposely concocting a damnation made just for her, the sage assumed the smell of his skin – that distinctive smell you only feel once but remember forever.

Why don't you think about it, Žanet? What's the problem? I can see that something's wrong. Žanet! Tell me! Were those his last words to her? Was there possibly something her memory was holding back now that she hadn't seen him in nine months? She had no idea the dead could be so close – his image, dark locks, thick eyebrows, and the inexplicable beauty of a chocolate complexion... At that moment, she thought him the Yang to her Yin. She was probably right. But little did she know that she would see all those things once again in her lifetime – those same locks, that same chocolate complexion. A good 47 years later, when a thousand wrinkles will have already marked her hands, neck, and cheeks.

The opposite corner of the room echoed with a child's cry. Žanet flinched and crawled even deeper into the corner she was sitting in. She just stared at the black spot wriggling inside the cradle. She did not like the sound of that voice. It was vigorous, full of dreams, and had a scent of a potential future, but the innate sin cursed it that she committed. She did not like that feeling – it felt like the child called for her help, its tears begging for her love. She stood up and walked up to the cradle. Her face held an expression as though she'd seen something utterly ugly. Something unspeakably nasty.

Trembling from restlessness, she touched the edge of the cradle and looked inside. The only light in the sheer darkness of the room were those giant eyes. It seemed like the creature – that rudely fragile being filled with painful love symbolizing the unity between Yin and Yang – was reaching its hands upwards and silently begging for her embrace, for her to place it on her shoulder and grab its tiny feet in her hands. And one last time, she did exactly that. She picked her daughter up, rested her head gently on her shoulder, and started dancing. When her eyes started stinging and tears finally tickled inside her eyelids, she sang hoarsely.

Three golden jackdaws

Singing louder than me

Three little jackdaws

Playing hungrily

As three silent rivers flowed

And now I have to leave you be.

The little girl fell asleep instantly, loving Žanet so much that her sole touch inexplicably gave her peace. Her chubby cheek was pressed against Žanet's shoulder, her mouth completely open. She was breathing heavily as her exhales produced the sound of a small trumpet. The doctor called it a mild form of asthma, prescribed some medication, and smiled at Žanet, telling her she would be the best mother in the world. Those words stabbed her like a thousand swords. In the depth of her soul, she knew one thing – she would not be the best mother in the world. She would not be a mother at all. But for just a few minutes, as her little girl slept safely and soundly on her shoulder, it seemed as if she had given up on that initial idea.

For that one seemingly eternal moment, it appeared easy to accept this little creature as her whole world, just as it appeared easy to be brave enough to be her entire world in return. She imagined them together ten years later – the little girl crying for her father as she rested her head on Žanet's shoulder. Then fifteen years later – that same head resting on her shoulder, having had her heart broken for the first time. The imaginary likeness of her trapped in Žanet's thoughts was so pretty, even fifteen years later.

The last image that Žanet saw that night was her daughter resting on her shoulder once more, just a few minutes before her wedding. Those big eyes, at times completely gray – just like his were – stared at her, drained the strength out of her – the strength and the courage to step over that threshold and finally head towards the altar. With the last image in her head that night, a tear rolled down Žanet's elongated cheek. She knew that she had to get her dressed and put her in a basket immediately before changing her mind. She had to bring her out like a damn dog, far from her arms and entirely out of sight. And so, she did.

She set her down in a knitted basket, put a gray woolen hat on her small, round head, and ragged black socks on her tiny, chubby feet, placing her hands under the blanket. She put a little scroll next to her little body. A scroll that she sincerely hoped would, strangely and delicately, keep her safe in those moments that Žanet herself decided to give up on. She put on a black hat and a light-yellow jacket, then her black boots, whose high and thick heels echoed across the silence as they hit the creaky wooden flooring.

That summer night was cold, maybe the coldest one in Žanet's life, and the streets were empty. The wind howled powerfully as if it was coming from the other part of this big world. She started walking towards the wind. A long twenty-minute walk was waiting for her, the longest one and the one she would never forget.

The road to creating that new life – the life of the only daughter she'd ever bring to this world – was very short, as though gone with a gentle wind. But the road to conceding that new life to everything else – renouncing the only untainted happiness that Žanet will have ever known and will always remember – was long and painful. She passed by the big post office, through the empty marketplace that smelled like sea water – undoubtedly because of the fish market – and across the square, past the Croatian National Theatre in Osijek, where she got momentarily overwhelmed by the need to perform the burning drama of her life and share her heart-wrenching pain with the world and the people. Then she finally went past the big cathedral whose clock would soon be ticking 2 in the morning. She passed through a few cramped streets, turned right twice, and found herself there.

A dimmed light at the entrance glowed forwardly, mocking her weakness. It plagued her; it penetrated the essence of her bones. Žanet, you'll never be this happy, you know that. Žanet, please. But that was the only thing she knew how to do now. She chose tragedy. Just like tragedy earlier chose her. The orphanage gates creaked open as she approached the entrance and placed the basket outside strangers' doors. She didn't even try to look her in the eyes, lay her lips on that cuddly cheek, or touch her warm hands. She could not claim that right. As she turned her back on the basket, all she could see walking back towards her gloomy home was the brim of her black hat obscuring her view and covering the redness of her thick locks.

***

Her days in that city were spent senselessly; they were ragged and stepped on until the very last breath. She was not one of those girls who healed their sorrow by roaming around the apartment and being filthy, careless, or teary. Her sorrow was different. She would stroll around the city streets dully and brainlessly. She'd watch the flowers in the display windows, roam the shops, buy tasteless vegetables at the marketplace, then go home to cook until the evening, when she'd start cleaning. Then her little apartment would be flawlessly tidy and smell like lavender that she regularly put in a new vase every day, repeatedly trying to find a proper place for it. She did it all faultlessly but aimlessly – out of the sheer banality of her nature.

After that night, when she left a part of her existence in front of the orphanage doors, her every day looked the same, until she decided to go. She emptied her apartment, swept the floors, washed the windows one last time, then left as if she had never lived there. In a way, she never did. Her daughter and Žanet lived there, and that duo did not exist anymore. She gave the keys – the only link between her and that apartment – back to her landlord, paid twice the sum of her rent and disappeared from the streets of Osijek.

Montenegro was her first choice. She didn't have a particular and prominent reason for it, and she traveled on impulse. The city of Budva was a dreamy corner of the world. She often dreamt about its sea foam, the perfect shades of blue and the sky dipping into the clear sea. She'd never been there before, so she opted for the first hotel she saw.

The day she arrived, it was raining as if the sky had a broken heart, which made her feel understood, in a way it felt like the sky was crying with her. She didn't have an umbrella, and her yellow summer jacket got dirty and wet. Her red hair turned brown, her locks transformed from waves to plains, and her nose got covered in tiny raindrops. She approached the receptionist and asked for a room facing the sea. She didn't even unpack before the room service arrived in front of her white door labeled 31.

"A dance party at the hotel restaurant terrace starts at 8pm," the maid informed her casually.

***

She wore a long black dress that was almost touching the ground. She thought she looked like a mermaid. She sat at the edge of her hard bed and put on high-heeled sandals that curled up her young ankles like black snakes. Afterward, she put a thin leather watch on her wrist. She left her scent high and low in the air spraying the perfume all over her neck and bosom. She smelled of cold, sugar, mulberry, and grapes.

The bright light of the hall – a dazzling entrance to a completely different part of life – took her to a place filled with the smell of champagne and marzipan cakes, where the room service was dressed very decently, and the women glistened in black and red night dresses. There was nothing magical or strange about that place. It was simply a place, a different part of the world that allowed her access to everything she had been yearning for. It brought her a world where nothing that she left behind existed anymore. Those big gray eyes, chubby cheeks, and hands – she expelled them all out of existence. For a short while, greed, fervor, and raw lust overtook her spirit. A short time indeed, but long enough to find a man, become his wife, and birth him a son. All of which started unfolding on that very eve.

Mirror

MARCH, 1964
OSIJEK

Her nose gently touched the mirror. The whiffs of her warm breath stuck to it, leaving a trace that looked like spilled flour. She was so close to the glass, gazing so deeply, diving into it so closely that she could see the tiny black spots inside her irises. Then, at the blunt sound of the bathroom door thumping, she moved away from the mirror.

"Mommy!" she heard a child's ringing voice.

Her dusty and flushed black hair covered the golden complexion of her face. Tiny, irregular freckles found their home around her small nose. Plump lips sat under it (the upper one was full and rich), while a short chin sat beneath them. Her forehead was shallow with a couple of black, dry, disobedient locs of hair resting on it. Her hair recalled the ends of a broom and rested at just about half an inch from her broad shoulders that held up her extremely skinny body consisting of small breasts, a narrow waist, and elegant slender legs. Her elongated thin neck was like a confident and slim tree trunk, holding the base to a pretty face. A face that was quite distinctive and irresistible.

"Mommy!" the child uttered again with a somewhat antsy voice.She ran her long fingers over her face as her hair remained standing up, electrified with the anxiety her fingers emanated, unable to decide which direction to go. Inhale. Exhale. She closed her eyes and then opened them.

"Enough! Just wait for a second; I'll be there soon."

The children giggled as they bounced around the door touching the handle. She sat on the bathtub's edge, hunched her shoulders, and gazed into the void. The bathroom door opened, but nobody was there. She heard the children giggling again, even choking a little from all that laughter. A blonde loc of hair appeared behind the door frame, standing only about 3 feet from the floor. The blonde hair was followed by big brown eyes, broad cheeks, and lips that widened in a grin, showing small baby teeth. As soon as she blew her cover, he appeared even more petite than her, with just a lump of blonde hair on his head. He wore a baseball cap, placing it backward so that his blonde locs escaped through the cap's hole on his forehead. He fidgeted his fingers around a yellow toy car.

"Didn't I tell you to wait?" she scratched her cheek nervously.

"We're bored," said the little girl.

"I'm coming," she answered.

"And daddy?" asked the little boy.

"He'll be here in a second."

And as though they'd summoned him with their words, the sound of the entrance door struck the air.

"Daddy!" they screamed in unison.

The cotton socks' thumping on their feet echoed throughout the apartment.

Tabita left the bathroom. A gray cardigan danced on her hips as she moved around like a stork, a mantis, and sometimes like an otter. She was at the same time slow, cold, and dashing. She was bloodcurdling to whoever found themself in her presence, but on the other hand, under a different light, she was as hot as summer, so warm and delicious as if made of chocolate, and chocolate only. She looked into her husband's-tired eyes, teary from all the thinking and the overflowing of sentences in his head, dreamy from writing about the worlds that don't exist. His gaze was trembling from all the cups of coffee he's had; she knew that he drank about four of them during his working hours, and his lips were as dry as the thirst itself. She couldn't look at him for long without thinking of blaming herself for ruining his life, so she bowed her head and walked to their white kitchen. The soup had already started boiling, the potatoes were still soaking inside a water bowl, and the tiny orange kitten they'd bought for the children from a nice man at the marketplace was drinking this morning's lukewarm milk. The children's screams shook her mind uneasily, and her eyes stung from the steam as she hurriedly took the soup off the stove.

***

She sat across from her daughter with her palm on her forehead, watching her chew the last piece of bread. I'm pregnant. That sentence sounded dangerous even in her head. We're pregnant. That also sounded completely wrong – they're pregnant, and it's their fault. We're going to have a baby. Wrong, again. Another baby! A baby that grows and needs food, diapers, clothes, shoes, and socks, which it will outgrow far too quickly. Then it suddenly starts growing up, falling in love, being absent, and spending money. Money that they don't have. Then later, it becomes a person. An expensive person who goes to college and shapes themselves. We're pregnant. We're going to have a baby. So many times had she said those words safely inside her head, but to say them out loud seemed impossible. She sat there, preparing the speech in her close-to-exploding head, waiting for her knees to stop wobbling so she could head towards his study and tell him all about that one more thing that she is going to ruin his life with, one more thing that will sit heavily on his already worn-out shoulders.

"Can I have the caramel now?" her smudgy-faced daughter asked.

"Caramel?"

"Yes, you said we could have some when we eat lunch," she uttered.

"You said you made us caramel sweets," added the son.

Tabita got up and brought the sweets on a small plate.

"Share with your brother," she said while leaving the kitchen.

We're going to have a baby. We're pregnant. I'm pregnant. A baby. Another baby. As she approached the door to his study, her head became louder. It seemed her head was trying to destroy her, eat her alive. Finally, she opened the door and saw him sitting at his desk, immersed in the story he was writing, with his thick-framed glasses leaning softly on his nose. He reached for his cold cup of coffee, slurped loudly, then turned the page and started writing as if fiddling the violin. Tabita leaned on the doorframe and breathed in his scent, smiling lightly with her hands crossed. She watched him run around the world he had created inside his head. One moment he was frowning, the other smiling and pouting. At last, he put his pencil down and looked at her with a warm smile.

"Come," he tapped his knees lightly.

She embraced the softness of his neck with her long fingers, diving into his warm gaze with the grayness of her piercing irises.

"What's the matter, little one?"

She bowed her head. We're pregnant. Her head produced so many versions of his reaction. Whichever way the story went, however, she knew that if he were to have second thoughts, it would be for a reason. His financial contribution to this family was, after all, the only one they had.

"Tabita?" he tilted his head slightly to see her eyes.

"We're pregnant," she uttered silently.

"Pregnant?" he asked with a smile.

"I know what you must be."

He hugged her tightly, squishing her cheeks with his palms and kissing her eyelids. She felt his sweet breath entering her nostrils and his beard pinching the skin of her cheeks.

"What must I be thinking now?" he asked her with a smile.

"Well," she gazed into his widened eyes, "I know how financially limited we are."

"Well, do we have another choice?" he asked, immersing himself in the grayness of her irises once again.

"No," she answered peacefully. "Of course not."

"We should make a toast," he picked up her slender body. "That marvelous brandy for me and tea for you."

He put a smile on her face. Their daughter got the exact smile from her - wide and mystical - a smile that, in a weirdly confident way, revealed a gap tooth.

***

She sat there, with an almost half-empty cup of chamomile tea, her gaze fixed on the faded letters on the paper. So many times had that paper crossed her fingers before, so often did her pupils skim over those letters, so many times had she read it carefully, analyzing every letter, sometimes even crying about it, but never fully understanding it. That letter was like a well-known stranger slowly becoming less transparent and decipherable to her.

She pulled the soft fabric of her shirt up and placed her sweaty palms on her naked belly, her thumbs intertwined above her navel cord. She felt like a lioness taking care of her young. She thought about that little creature growing and maturing inside her. The creature whose life was getting stronger and more real by the moment. Boy or girl? She couldn't foresee what could be or what she'd want more. What will it look like? Will our child finally have his big, dreamy eyes? Their two kids, although blonde-haired like him, did not inherit his eyes. And his eyes were her favorite part of him. Let it be a boy. Yes, it should be a boy. That would make him so happy. She exhaled and then inhaled deeply. Warmth streamed through her fingers. She felt as though the life growing inside of her was greeting her.

"See you soon," she said silently with a smile.

Name! What do we name him? Girls aren't a problem, but a boy? She didn't have ideas for a boy's name. She reached for the paper again. The first page was written in neat italics handwriting, and the other one only half so. She turned the page, skimmed over all those right-leaning letters, and reached the final sentence.

His name was Zair.

Eyes

SEPTEMBER, 1972
OSIJEK

Patrik was sitting at his desk in the living room. A thick book lay before him, waiting for all its secrets to be uncovered. But he was so tired that he, in that foggy moment, hated every book and every man who had ever written something. He had been rubbing his eyes persistently, hoping the fatigue would wear off when he heard the serious tone of his uncle's voice. He knew that his uncle used that tone only when he was nervous and talking about essential business ventures. But, one or the other, it was usually all the same. He left the book on the wooden desk in the corner of the living room, lit up by a long-necked night lamp, then approached the door of his uncle's room silently. Just as he was getting ready to come in, having already touched the elongated thin door handle, his uncle started shouting ferociously.

"Damn it, you moron! He's the best writer we've got! What am I saying? He's the only writer we've got! Everyone else? You're asking me about everyone else? They are just a bunch of journalists and gossipers; they have no story! To hell with all of you. You're making me give up my single high-grade story creator!"

Patrik put his ear against the warm wooden door as his dry red locks, electrified, touched the thick wood. "You think that's any consolation to me? You really think so? The fact that someone else will have my writer! My writer!"

Patrik could swear his uncle was spitting saliva out of his mouth with anger.

"Did you hear me? My writer! I found him, I hired him, and I command him!"

Patrik raised his fist firmly, ready to knock, but his uncle's shriek froze his first in the air.

"Fine! Have it your way! So be it, we'll go down the drain because of you idiots!"

He heard the sharp sound of the phone hitting its base. Encouraged by the phone call's end, Patrik opened the door gently and peeked inside, seeing his uncle's sweaty forehead shining under the touch of the night lamp.

"What is it?" he asked, still visibly upset.

His uncle was a portly man. His hair constantly buzzed short, his chin hiding under neatly distributed thick grayish hairs. His eyes were very small in contrast to his rich beard, so he always looked like he was squinting, and his lips were rich and generally always wet from his enthusiastic talking. That night he wore his favorite outfit – a white shirt and a stiff vest with a pair of horn-rim glasses hanging from it. Whenever he wore something else, he complained about not having a place to put his glasses.

"I'd like to go to sleep," Patrik approached his desk.

"What happened to reading?" he glanced at the watch wrapped around his wrist. "It's only 9:30. Are you feeling sick?"

His uncle reached for his forehead and laid his palm on it.

"Do you have a fever?" he looked up at the ceiling as if he were calculating a complex mathematic operation in his head. "Don't mess with me; there's this bug going around."

Just as Patrik was about to console his uncle and let him know he wasn't sick; his uncle beat him to it.

"There's no fever; nothing's wrong with you," he waved his hand and fixed the watch on his wrist. "Why are you going to bed already? Don't you like the book?"

His uncle gazed into his eyes briefly – a thing he rarely did.

"I'm just tired," Patrik rubbed his eyes.

"Off you go, then," his uncle waved his hand towards the door as he buried himself into the papers on his desk.

Having reached his study door, Patrik stopped and scratched his forehead insecurely. He glanced at his uncle, who was completely detached from their reality, as he ran into his special world.

"Good night," he uttered, even though he felt he had no right to say it.

***

Patrik both loved and hated the moment of lying in his bed and staying alone with a lump of humble thoughts that flowed inside him ever so ferociously. Sometimes, in one of those moments, he would place his head on the unbearable purity of his pillow, watching the wooden ceiling above him descending mutely towards the window, and he would see their eyes. Just their big eyes – glowing in the dark. Hers were gentle, or at least he remembered them so. They had a teary gaze, full of compassion and comfort. His eyes, on the other hand, were crude. But in a completely different way than his uncle's. They emanated pride and strength, keeping warmth in their crudeness. Those two pairs of eyes – big and glowing in the twilight of his memories – were all he had left.

From the bottom of his heart, he loved the moment that pulled him into the fogginess of the dreams, where their gazes would peculiarly touch him. But, on the other hand, he hated that blessed moment because he couldn't see anything else but their gazes in it. From his uncle's stories and the old photographs, he found that he had inherited his dark ginger hair from his mother and the dryness of his locks from his father. He saw so many bits and pieces of himself in those photographs that kept all the secrets of a parent's love hidden inside. Before drifting off to sleep that night, he stared at a black-and-white picture.

They're standing in front of a tall tower in France. He's holding his hands in the pockets of a dark jacket. His lips are full, just like Patrik's. She has her arm locked in his, with a straight line forming a smile on her face.

He came across the fullness of those lips every day when he looked in the mirror. His uncle always claimed that Patrik had inherited the bright green eyes from his mother. But Patrik wasn't all that much bothered by the fact that he couldn't see the color of their eyes with his naked eye or that he couldn't hear the sound of their voices. For him, they always symbolized perfect, untouchable silhouettes. The thing that his heart ached for the most, however, was the sheer perfection of their figures. He didn't get to meet them in all their nuances, human and sinful forms. He didn't get to meet them while they were dirty, ugly, instinctively mean, arrogant, and sometimes even fragile. Yet, in his mind, they were these perfect images. Completely symmetrically painted, without a scratch or a wrinkle. They were like wax figures – beautiful but cold. Patrik never had the chance to ruin his idealized image of them, hate them for their flaws, or ultimately love them without reserve. In that world of extinguished memories, he couldn't love them concretely and unconditionally. He could only imagine what the love towards them would have felt like had the world granted him fate just a tiny bit different. The heaviest part of the pain was the stolen opportunity of feeling their love on his skin.

Clock Hands

OCTOBER, 1972
OSIJEK

She wiped the wet kisses off her face and tightly embraced the brown leather notebook with her small palms sticky from the cream puffs.

"Will you read what I write inside?" she asked Ilir as her eyes glowed.

"Every last bit," he touched the tip of her nose with his index finger.

Her mother approached them slowly, carrying a cake filled with roses on a silver platter, casually singing the well-known birthday song as the seven burning candles lit up the lichen around her lips. Ilir joined in on the singing. Nadja sat on the wooden cupboard, bumping her heels against its small door and clapping her hands with the beat of their voices, her heart overjoyed by the song, the gifts, and the cake.

"Make a wish," her mother uttered softly.

Nadja closed her eyes as if wanting to stop the world's distractions, then squeezed her lips tightly.

"Did you do it?" Ilir asked.

She nodded her head and blew out the seven candles all at once. Nadja loved celebrating birthdays. This was the fifth one that she remembered. She could not find the first two – many ways different – in the chambers of her memories. So she kept them frozen within the photographs. And although they were frozen, Nadja nourished special sympathies precisely towards those two birthdays.

Nadja hid those two photographs underneath her pillow while her mother read her bedtime stories. She'd hide them until her mother went out. Then, if still awake, she would take them out carefully. Those moments seemed more real under the benevolent light of her night lamp. They seemed distinctly more alive. In the calm of the night and with the rhythm of the strange loneliness of a child's heart, Nadja would caress the photograph melancholically with her tiny finger.

She's standing on the table in front of her birthday cake. A bright white light from the kitchen illuminates her toothless smile. Her hair is much shorter and lighter, thinner and flaunting, and she has a green dress. But, of course, she can't stand alone – she's being held by her mother and her father. Nevertheless, everyone is smiling, and the cake looks delicious. Much more appetizing than any cake she's had in her life later on.

***

A well-known Ford Capri stood parked on the gravel in front of their apartment. It was a sophisticated gray color that blindingly reflected the sun, its interior coated with black leather. Yet, that car symbolized eternal abandonment in all its immense ice-cold beauty. But there was one thing in that whole cluster of coldness that exposed a funnily warm and fuzzy tone – a knitted creature dangling from the rear-view mirror like a ticking clock. It was a key chain, a small, yellow elephant that Nadja knitted. She had been knitting it for five hours, tirelessly, without stopping.

"I told you he would come. I told you!" Nadja embraced her mother's car seat and shouted at the top of her lungs.

It was him. He stood next to his car in a gray, neatly ironed suit, with black sunglasses on his head. His black and tidily trimmed hair flickered in sunlight, and his full dark lips – the same fullness that Nadja inherited – stretched into a little smile. The bright sunlight nimbly touched the surface of his wristwatch. Nadja stormed out of her mother's car towards him as he placed his car keys in his pocket in an instant and crouched to pick her up in his arms. Her legs danced in the air.

"Where's my birthday girl?" he rested her weight on his hip.

Nadja could feel his cologne find its way through her nostrils to her throat, making her feel strangely joyful and enchanted.

Her mother got out of the car and, in a swift movement, tried to hide the disgusted and furious look on her face, slammed the door angrily, then approached them, glaring at him, challenging him to feel ashamed. But the challenge didn't work. It seemed that shame could not find a home under his skin.

***

The clock on the wall was ticking, ringing, indicating the passage of time – time that always seemed to take her father away from her at high speed. All three were sitting at the round glass table in the kitchen. Nadja's pink cake stood in the middle of the table, already cut in parts, its candles long extinguished.

"You have to see what Ilir gave me!"

Nadja stormed off to get the notebook and pushed it into her father's hands. Her hungry gaze yearned for what he had to say.

"It's nice," he said.

"Ilir said that I should write my stories in it, that I'll be good at it," she stared at his father's face with a glisten in her eyes.

"You can try," he set the notebook down.

"Nadja," her mother uttered in a muffled voice, "go to your room for a minute."

Nadja grabbed the notebook from the table and bounced off excitedly towards her room, even though some of her quite intensively felt that something was off.

"How long do you plan on doing this?" her mother threw a dish rag onto the table. "You sent me that letter six months ago. Fine, you're going abroad, I understand... But why did it take you a year to come?"

"I couldn't come sooner," he answered uneventfully.

"You couldn't?" the mother shrieked.

Then she calmed herself down and continued in a whisper.

"You couldn't? It's your child we're talking about!"

"That's why I came now," he whispered.

"And you already have to go," she stopped whispering, replying coldly.

"I have no choice," he fixed his wristwatch.

"You could stay; there's plenty of room," the mother continued wiping the dishes.

"No, I can't because of the job. It doesn't leave me much more time than this, and..."

"Of course," she interrupted him, sporting a provocative smile. "I was expecting nothing less."

***

When the air was warm but fresh enough, and the shy fading sunlight squeezed through the tree branches and the leaves that swayed in the early autumn breeze, Nadja's favorite pastime was going to Zrinjevac. Even though she wasn't very fond of hanging out with her peers, she had a few girlfriends that served as a disguise for going there – a disguise for her insatiable appetite for nature. She had so many feelings intensely bubbling up inside her – when the breeze touched her cheek or her wavy eyelash, or when she heard a single rustling of the treetop or noticed a single sun ray making love with the stained glass of the Zrinjevac sports hall. So that day – just like many other days which lacked inspiration – they decided to play the most straightforward game known to kids. It was Nadja's turn to sit on the peculiarly cold wooden bench right up to the path that led to Reisner Street and to close her eyes and start counting.

Ten. She imagines a red sparrow going to Ilir's bakery.

Nine. A blue ship with a sunflower pinned on its turbulent sails.

Eight. Her mother's goulash and the caramel candy cooking inside the pot.

Seven. Caesar is kissing a beautiful black woman whom her mother read to her about.

Six. Cleopatra?

Five. A thousand orange glimmering lanterns.

Four. The ugly, silver shine of her father's expensive wristwatch.

Three. In a big phone factory, phones ring incessantly, and no one picks up. Life is the caller.

Two. A star is dying; it's falling with an imploring shine.

One. Once again, a thousand lanterns flickering as ten years run out in the hourglass.

Zero. She moved her palms away from her face and winced. What is he doing here? Next to her, as if someone had invited him, completely relaxed and utterly unusual, sat a boy with a chocolate complexion. First, she noticed his muddy fingers placed on a soccer ball, with a rotten leaf sticking out from underneath it, and then his sneakers. Very ugly, she thought. His shoelaces weren't tied very tightly. She peered at his wide lips, and it seemed like they took over half of his strangely dark face for a moment. Then she tried to imagine how wide they were when he was smiling. Her lower lip dangled as she gazed into the immense thickness of his neat eyebrows.

"Run," he gestured with his chin towards the green meadow in front of them.

"Why?" she widened her big eyes.

"Because you're bored," he shrugged.

"And how do you know that?" she frowned slightly.

"I know you can have a lot more fun," he cleared his throat. "Come on, run, and I'll catch you."

"Catch me?" she felt the smile on her cheeks squeezing her eye sockets. "Never!" a peculiar sense of joy arose in the depth of her throat.

And truly, she listened to him. She ran onto the meadow, whose greenery was never again as clear as it had been that day. She started running, defying the wind, breathing deeply. She turned around to see how close he was to her and smiled willfully whenever she realized she was getting away from him. The grass creaked under the soles of her shoes, and her heart raced madly because she never ran this much while breathing this clearly. In those sharp turns she took towards him, she saw his thick locks flying through the air as he watched her every move, concentrating on the run. When she finally stopped – in the middle of the meadow – and placed her sticky palms on her stomach, he came running and stopped in front of her.

"I knew I'd catch you," he smiled widely, puffing the locks off his face.

For the first time, a sentence so simple and short coming out of the mouth of her peer seemed warm. Acceptable. Belonging. She squeezed her eyes tightly. You didn't catch me. She was sure he could hear what she was saying with her tightly squeezed gaze.

"You can't run forever," he shrugged.

His eyebrows separated a bit from the sheer widening of his gaze.

"If I hadn't stopped, you wouldn't have caught me," she also shrugged. "It's simple."

She felt her hair start to fall out of her high ponytail.

"I could chase you forever," he straightened up like a gentleman, emanating humble confidence.

"Ha," she laughed creakily, "I've never heard anything more stupid."

He looked straight into her eyes as though astonished by their size and the lighter green color his eyes did not possess. He leaned towards her and scrunched up his face as if looking at something hideous, then crushed a dry leaf with his foot, kicking it towards her. She accepted his challenge, which was very tempting, so she grabbed a bunch of dry leaves and threw them at him. Defeated by the wind, the leaves dispersed in all directions, and the two of them just stood there staring at each other. One moment feistily, with a dash of malice, and the next one dying of laughter.

AUGUST, 1940
BUDVA

Žanet failed to notice how gradually annoyed she was getting by the joyful sound of the accordion. She stared hypnotically into everyone's feet, in awe of their speed and enthusiasm, waiting for someone to magically appear and offer her a drink. But no one was approaching; no one had even noticed the new face on that small, messy dance podium, so she made her way to the bar alone. Leaning her elbows onto the sticky wooden counter, she thought long and hard about what to order.

"Why are you pondering? You know what to drink here!"

A tall young man approached her, somewhat skinny, with thick black hair and two front teeth a bit longer than the rest. He bobbed up and down in the rhythm of the accordion played by a glum obese man. The young man reeked of brandy.

"And what would that be?" she looked at him curiously, questionably even.

At that precise moment, like a godsend, a waitress passed them holding a tray of brandy-filled shots in her hand. The young man turned around gracefully, grabbed a shot of brandy in a twisting movement, and put it in front of Žanet.

"Brandy?"

She tried to appear as nice as possible, like she was afraid of driving him away and staying alone, all by herself once again in a crowd of strangers.

"No, no, thank you."

"You don't refuse brandy here," he winked.

She looked at him softly, powerlessly even, as though she was begging him to give up because she knew she couldn't resist. In fact, she didn't want to resist. Her eyes glimmered; she was hungry for attention and hungry to forget. Nothing else.

"You're very persistent," she poured the brandy down her throat and was left almost breathless from its bitterness.

It was not her last shot of brandy that night. After the second one, all the others weren't as bitter. Her throat wasn't burning, and the feeling of forgetting grew inside her. She didn't remember the exact moment she had stepped on the dance podium, but she remembered his face in front of hers. The feeling she had when she was close to him felt ready-made. Significant, maybe even memorable, but ultimately too ready, too prepared in advance, and not sculpted enough with the hand of the most vital artist of them all – Love.

***

She didn't remember how long she had been dancing for or how many of those shots she had drunk, and thereby she could not figure out how she got there – in a stranger's hotel room. The bathroom wasn't on the left of a short hallway like in her room. The curtains were not white but blue, and the room didn't smell the same as hers when she was last in it. Instead, this room smelled like an awkward mixture of a man's and woman's sweat, fornication, lust, tragedy, and drunken passion. It didn't smell right. Cigarettes? At the bottom of her tongue, on the exact spot where it grows from the throat, she felt parched. Now and then, it felt like she couldn't breathe – from the dryness of her throat and the sight next to her.

He slept with his lips open wide enough for his two elongated front teeth to peek out. The dark thickness of his brows shone under the silver sunlight as he snored deeply in the rhythm of his breaths. She covered her smooth, firm bosom with a thin sheet, then tilted her head and observed him. It was as if an unusual, never seen object had flown in from distant space, and she could not quite figure out whether it was her death or salvation. Every time he exhaled, she would wince lightly at the thought of him waking up. His warm brandy- and cigarette-smelling breath swayed his nose hairs, sending chills down Žanet's spine. Then, wanting to rid herself of disgust, she observed his lips. They were arid, covered in dry white skin, but full and rich. Yes. He must be a good kisser; she consoled herself. Yes, yes. That must be it.

After an hour had passed – which Žanet knew due to her constant staring at the square clock on the wall in front and listening to the latent sound of the ticking – she felt his eyes glued onto her. Still anxious and with her gaze fixated on the clock, her peripheral vision noticed that he was awake and staring at her. With a distraught facial expression, ready to adhere to many things and lose herself in them, she glanced at him out of the corner of her eye. She was not prepared to turn her head, give him more than a peek, and look him dead in the eye. This way, the sight was comfortably blurry. Besides, she'd already carefully examined the subject of her lustful night a little while earlier. She let him speak first, pretending not to realize he was awake. She even wanted to close her eyes and pretend to sleep, but she gave up on that idea.

"Your eyes look green when you give me that thieving look," he laughed muffled.

She noticed his voice had a strange accent. It sounded like the voice of the ice cream man she ran after about ten years ago to buy another scoop of ice cream.

"But I know they're brown," he added.

Finally, she turned and looked at him with her almond-shaped brown eyes.

"There, what did I say?"

His gaze touched her shivering palms that clutched the sheet tightly over her bosom.

"You have lovely breasts. I don't know why you're hiding them."

She pulled the sheet up towards her neck like a terrified child.

"And a lovely voice. I don't know why you're tongue-tied suddenly," he leaned on his elbow.

"You say all that like you know me," she uttered silently.

"I'd like to."

She was silent once again.

"Come on, put your clothes on," he got out of bed and made his way toward the bathroom. "I don't want you to feel uneasy," he added.

***

She rolled the chunks of meat all over her giant white plate as she felt the cold touch of the fork on her fingertips. The coldness was not a stranger to her. It lurked from the shadows of her life like a peculiar curse. Just like it did that night – the night she closed the creaky gates of the orphanage behind her. Her gaze was locked on the rays of the nippy sunlight humbly squeezing through the white clouds that day. The sun reflected onto her cup of black tea, pouring itself into messy yellow circles on the tea's surface. His annoying munching distracted her. He was breathing too loudly, inadvertently chewing the food he filled his plate with a few minutes earlier when they mingled around the buffet. She stared at his partly chewed-off pickle sunbathing on his white plate and his left hand frozen in the air, tense from all the energy he poured into his eating. Whether his nose hairs were still there looped through her mind. The sunlight must be obscuring them, she thought. Then, after feeling momentarily disgusted, she started observing his lips again, the way they widened and loosened with the rhythm of his chewing. That was the only thing she found sweet about that strange creature sitting before her.

"Oh, such a pretty girl!"

An obese woman wrapped in an apron with her hair tied up in a measly bun approached Žanet and opened her eyes widely in delight. The man nodded because his mouth was full of fried squid and burnt potato, his lips bathing in grease.

"What's your name, dear?"

She placed her chubby hand on her shoulder and glared significantly at him.

"And why are you so rude? You could at least introduce us!"

"My name is Žanet," she stretched out her neck so that she could see her.

"What a lovely name!"

Her eyes never really seemed to close.

Žanet just stared blankly into his dark eyes, trying desperately to find an explanation of the whole situation to the obese woman but to herself as well.

"You didn't even touch this food! Don't you like it?"

Just as Žanet inhaled deeply, getting ready to answer her sudden question, he interrupted her. He gestured with his fork towards the strangely curious woman whose grand appearance threw a wide shade on Žanet.

"Watch what you say; she's the one cooking here!" he uncovered a long-lost bit of salad between his teeth as he smiled.

"Of course I like it," she smiled squirrelly, "I'm just not that hungry."

The woman pinched Žanet's cheeks tightly with her big hands, showering her with the scent of garlic.

"You lost your appetite watching this one eating, surely! He's revolting!"

Žanet flashed her the sincerest smile she had had these last two swirling days.

"Mom, why are you here?" he asked through a napkin, wiping his greasy lips.

"I had to see who this pretty little lady keeping you company was," she winked at Žanet, "since you didn't show her off yourself."

"I thought we should have breakfast first," he cleaned his teeth with his tongue.

"Your father will be overjoyed when he sees her," she said, picking up the dirty dishes from the table. "Go on, piglet, get ready, then bring her to us!"

She grinned and smiled at Žanet, who was burning up from the horrendous sickness that overtook the essence of her being.

"We'll take good care of her," she uttered, strolling back to the kitchen.

Žanet had no idea how she found herself here, so far from her hometown and her consciousness, entirely out of reach of her memories.

***

Žanet noticed a thick, high wall rising around her, feeling that stubborn smell of the moist air of the hotel's hallways filling her nostrils while she walked right next to him – him who was calm and strangely particular. It was a wall that separated her from everything she ever was and could have been – had she done one thing differently that night. It was truly magical how that one simple thread from the giant bundle of our decisions could make a difference and ultimately overturn the pattern of our life.

Everything would have been entirely different had she stayed there, holding a gray-eyed little girl in her arms. But now she was cursed with the silence boiling inside of her, cursed to walk the streets of that unknown city, only a couple of minutes away from the doorstep of two people who would, just nine months later, become the grandparents of her son.

The Boy

OCTOBER, 1972
OSIJEK

Nadja's bag was a pound or two heavier because of the notebook she got from Ilir for her birthday. It was still unopened; all the pages were glued to one another and smelled like fresh, untouched new paper. The sun was shining unusually that day like it was the first day of summer. But it was autumn and the most ordinary day for her. In a dark corner of the school, while the bell still rang and the students' footsteps echoed throughout, Nadja pretended to look for something in her bag. She waited for her friends to leave without her, then zipped her bag up and headed home alone, just as she had planned. The glow in her eyes betrayed her. It was evident that she was awaiting something, looking forward to something.

Her palms grinded against the shoulder straps of her backpack as her knees weakened from excitement, and her lips formed a reluctant, almost despicable smile with only two dimples on her cheeks revealing its presence. She was sitting on the edge of a giant concrete bench – the one that was forbidden – and bending her knees under her long white dress. She took the notebook from her backpack, and her gaze revealed a visible but strange hunger. She sniffed its covers with her snub nose. They smelled exactly like the little rooms of all the most famous writers smelled, or so she imagined. As her fingertips touched the notebook leather, she felt she was being called into that mysterious world of creation. She flung her heavy braid backward so it touched the end of her back, then started writing her first story ever.

I met a boy with very ugly fingernails. When I first saw his gray eyes, he was holding a soccer ball in his lap. He made me run. And he was the first one ever to realize how bored I was. He couldn't catch me. We threw dry leaves into the air. I remember the colors green, brown, yellow, and orange. I would love to watch and catch the first snow of the ye-

A heavy soccer ball flew into her head, hitting one of her big eyes. The boy, as mentioned earlier, was standing about 30 feet from her. She must have summoned him when her pen touched the paper. He was smiling so much that the corners of his lips almost touched his ears. She stared at him as if he were merely a character, a part of her story brought to life. Her mother used to tell her that every writer has that one special thing that he ends up pursuing his whole life. Sometimes it is a city, a specific type of flower, a season, a certain kind of injustice, or a window that recalls memories. But sometimes, and most often, that specific mortal person touches the writer's life and highlights his story.

The writer then – rarely conscious of his actions – vivifies that person as a character in every story. First, he gifts the character with that person's facial lines, gaze, dreaminess of their eyes, the soft touch of their fingertips, or the scent of their body which is, in most cases, pleasant only to the writer himself because it is destined just for him. Then, to that character, he assigns that person's walk, their movements, maybe the dryness of their lips or the uniqueness of their accent, their final goodbyes, tears, and even laughter. Sometimes, the writer cuts that person into pieces, magically morphing them into a few different characters, giving every one of them a cut-off part of that mortal person, hoping warily that those bits will that way live forever, hidden from the transience of the mortal world.

Her mother told her that every writer is cursed with that one thing, or that one person he can't run away from and whom he hopelessly tries to describe without fault, pushing hard for his simple words to be enough. And that day, Nadja looked at him exactly like that. That day, and years later as well.

She observed the corners of his eyes that comically tried to hide under his curls and stared carefully at his arrogant and untamed shoulders. His palms gave her the energy to describe the stiff and solid but skimming impression she had of him, and in his gaze, she found the meaning of her sentences that served as proof that everything had a more profound sense. His funny sneakers allowed her to recall the innocence of those days when she had observed his younger self. But, as with most writers, that magical fact hid in the chambers of her subconscious, far away from her reach. He seemed like a fine, expensive, and highly paid material to her.

"It wasn't an accident," he shouted at her.

"Really?"

"Yes," he approached her with a smile. "It was completely on purpose."

He stopped in front of her, his eyes wide open, his lips droopy as if looking at something ugly once again.

"You're familiar to me," he tilted his head.

"Really?" her lips formed a slight smile.

"Yes. Have we met before?"

"Have we?" she asked, hiding the letters on the paper with her fingers.

"Yes!" he ruffled his curls with his dirty palms. "We played tag," he said, gesturing at the meadow behind him. "And you ran pretty slowly," he added.

"No, I didn't," she waved her head. "You didn't even catch me; I had to stop!"

She pressed the notebook closer to her chest, fearing that he would take away the parts of her that she'd neatly hidden in the chambers of her clandestine world if he were ever to recognize himself in the substance of her dreams.

"Alright, well, whatever. I completely forgot about you anyway."

"Yes, of course, and I about you," she put the notebook in her backpack. "I barely remembered who you were right now."

"Where are you going?" he asked.

"I have to go home," she threw the heavy backpack onto her back.

"Chocolate," he shouted readily.

"Sorry?"

Her gaze ran off to his one curl swaying in the wind.

"I like the chocolate one."

"What?" she shrugged. "You're so weird!"

"Chocolate ice cream," he gestured towards the skinny ice cream man passing them by.

"You want ice cream?" she asked him.

They both gazed at the ice cream man momentarily, listening to the creaking of the ice cream trailer's wheels he was pulling, probably for the last time that season.

"I do," he answered. "But I don't have any money."

"Fine," she uttered with a detective-like tone. "I'll buy you ice cream, but first, you must come to help me steal six dimes from my mom."

"Six?" he waved his head joyfully. "But ice cream is only three dimes."

"Strawberry," she said with a smile.

"Sorry?" he flinched as if an unknown coldness flew through his body.

"I like the strawberry one."

***

That day marked a change in Nadja's life – a change that felt like a peculiar falling comet that soared through the sky. She'd run straight home from school, throw the schoolbag in the corner of her room next to the dolls she rarely played with, eat her lunch to please her mother, then storm off to Zrinjevac. For the first couple of days of their acquaintanceship, she would bring the curly boy home, sit with him on the high windowsill in her room and read him her favorite stories. She loved the peacefulness and the devotion with which he listened, as if she were a portal to a magical world, even though she'd often stutter reading some long words aloud. She felt her mother's gaze on her from the door and the sheer disbelief in her eyes as she stared at the purple bruise around Nadja's eye; the bruise that was the curly boy's fault – the same boy sitting right across the table from her. Her mother's inability to understand the nature of Nadja's affection towards the boy that hit her head with a soccer ball filled her with inexplicable joy and enthusiasm because deep inside her, it created a piercing feeling of belonging to a hidden world that only the two of them knew; a secret world that was made the moment they stepped onto the green meadow.

Before leaving for Zrinjevac, Nadja would secretly fill her bag. – the one in which she'd also put the leather-covered notebook in – with gingerbread cookies every time her mother made them. She would be grumpy until he agreed to eat them, and when he did, she'd laugh out loud watching him eat. She would watch him completely up close, which annoyed him the most, and she knew it.

After they finished eating, they'd run around that same meadow just like they did the first day, and not once in those two weeks of their sparkling acquaintance did she get tired of running away from him, nor he of chasing her, screaming her name angrily, being unable to catch her. After their running session, she would sit on the soft black picnic blanket he brought. At the same time, he dribbled the ball around the meadow, kicking it or grumpily but devotedly trying to pass it from one knee to the other, thoroughly annoying himself in the process. It was strictly between him and the ball, but a game that Nadja would notice now and then when she glanced his way from the corner of her eye, trying to think of the right thing to write.

It rained a few times during those two weeks they spent together. When it did, they hid in front of the sports hall entrance, concentrating on counting the raindrops like they were essential scientists working on a big experiment, one step closer to a grand discovery.

Her girlfriends joined them twice she counted. She noticed a subtle difference between how he looked at them and how he looked at her. He paid close attention to their hair and how they dressed, talked, or smiled. He even admitted that he liked one of the girl's eyes. Nadja didn't love her, neither before nor after that. When he talked about them – how those princes in fairytales talk about their infallibly beautiful princesses – Nadja felt bitter heat in the back of her head. She completely ignored that feeling, not knowing what it represented, while her essence continued to imperceptibly merge with his as if he were the beat of her heart.

In those two weeks, he became Nadja's tradition. She never asked him where he lived, if he had brothers or sisters, or if he was coming tomorrow. She was sure he would. All that she knew about him was his name – Zair. She knew that he smiled widely only when he was delighted. And when he wasn't, his lips would form a slightly twisted smile. She knew that he hated winter and the cold that tickled his palms. She knew that he had a tendency to run his dirty fingers through his curls while trying to perform a complicated move with the ball and that his palms would start shaking peculiarly every time he ran for too long or bounced in circles around her. She knew that he always nodded softly while she read to him and that he walked awkwardly, not limberly, but nimbly.

She could recognize the rhythm of his breath when she'd close her eyes and start counting down while he tried to find a place to hide, even though, in the end, he never really hid. He would sit there next to her, watching her count down. She knew that he had a small scar on the sole tip of his chin that reminded her of a broken branch and that his laugh was substantial. She thought it sounded like a voice of an immortal song. She knew his upper lip's position when it leaned on his lower lip; his lips met in the middle very precisely, creating harmonious wavy lines. She knew he smelled like chocolate cooked for too long.

She knew only that, and nothing else. Every morning on her way to school, she would pass by that park and see their silhouettes running across the meadow or sitting in the grass. She would always be entirely convinced that they would meet up there in the afternoon, filling in the spaces of the dark silhouettes etched in her mind. Finally, after two weeks of that precious tradition, she approached an empty meadow.

AUGUST, 1973
ZAGREB

Tabita was trying to figure out what exactly was the thing tearing her insides apart. Marko's reckless driving, the high C of Karla's pubertal voice, or the sheer excitement before his first soccer game ever. The one he had been waiting for so long, practicing tricks in their two-bedroom apartment, crossing his heart every night for luck. She turned around and saw his eyes glued to the car window, staring at the road ahead as his pupils fixated on a specific spot and moved forwards, synchronized with the fluidity of the car. One curl of his hair was stuck firmly on his forehead, but it didn't bother him. He was sitting there, watching the road closely. She extended her arm to move the curl off his forehead, grazing him with the warmth of a mother's touch. He smiled and closed his eyes. Upon arrival, the car stopped with a sharp creaking of the worn-out brakes. Tabita went outside first and crouched right next to the back seat.

"Zair," she reached for his tiny hands. "Listen to me; you'll do great."

A slight smile unfolded on his face as if he enjoyed the hoarseness of her voice or the curliness of her hair escaping her messy ponytail.

"Alright?" she smiled back at him.

"You promise?" his eyes squeezed as the stubborn sunlight caressed them.

"I promise you everything in the whole wide world."

She removed the rebellious curl off his face and kissed the tip of his nose.

***

Tabita watched him run towards the dressing rooms carrying a small black backpack as the sun's rays reflected on his curls. His clumsy gestures always made her smile. It seemed like he wanted to stay a five-year-old forever, even though he was already a bit older than that. She could see a dash of obedience and naiveté in his movements. Characteristics which were indeed a part of his unfading personality. She often wondered if he'd gotten it from him – the man that Zair would never get to meet, jump into his lap, clasp his thigh, or lean his head on his chest and hear the beat of his heart. But the man Zair was named after has already been gone for far too long.

The unsightly blue doors of the dressing room opened as a horde of seven and eight-year-olds ran out, Zair being the last one in the field. Sporting a blue jersey with his leg warmers pulled almost up the top of his legs, he looked like every other boy on his team. But his rebellious curls gave him away and distinguished him from the rest of the blue-jersey squad. He ran up to Marko, who picked him up in his arms and gazed into his eyes carefully, trying to notice any anxiety in them. She observed the two of them serenely and proudly while she tied her dry hair into a wavy ponytail.

"He'll do great," she smiled, "There's no doubt about it."

Marko set him down on the ground. She placed her palm on his shoulder, feeling his body wince under it with a genuine child's fear burning through his bloodstream at immense speed. Prone to humble bravery even at that young age, he tried to hide his excitement with a smile, but to no avail. Wordless, she took his warm hand and led him toward the field entrance.

It stood there, immersed in the dusty ground, almost growing into the dirt below, while the sun reflected off of it like a boomerang. Zair noticed it first, so he let go of her hand and wriggled toward it to pick it up. So many women would run after their children in fear, smack their fingers commanding them to put the thing back where they found it, and then mumble to them about not knowing who had held it before. But she didn't do that.

Deep inside her golden skin, she kept the memory of her childhood filled with an infinite number of objects just like that one; dusty, old, and accidentally found. Even Marko was one of them. She knew very well that coincidences were the best joy-bringers and that life was, above all, in the end, woven only out of coincidences. Nobody ever told her (nor the other kids living in the same cold institution she lived in) that she had to give up the lost things found somewhere along the way. And that was why she – enlightened by the peculiarity of the remarkable coincidences that ever so fluidly touch our life – never took that spark away from her children either.

A camera stood between Zair's tiny fingers. He blew the dust off and started rotating it in his hands, observing how it worked.

"Honey, it's ancient. Maybe it doesn't even work anymore," she finally said.

Just as she uttered those words that sounded like the usual parental skepticism that lacked a child's dreaminess, Zair pushed the black oblong button at the top of the camera, to which the camera responded with a creaky tone. Nevertheless, the photograph emerged out of it as if chased by some magic. It was a pretty photograph, faithfully representing that moment, that Saturday, August 1973. That first soccer field.

A sun ray in its infinite line of blinding light touches the soccer net turned sideways to the dressing rooms, the tips of the destitute field grass, and the baseball cap of their team's coach that's crossing the field with an unfiltered cigarette between his teeth, holding his hand against his slouched back. A short fence, serving as the only barrier dividing the fans from the players covers the complete scene of the field.

The photograph reflected Zair's frog's-eye view and the moment of his first soccer match ever.

"It's pretty, isn't it?" She immersed her lips into the softness of his cheek.

"You think?" the photograph trembled in his fingers.

"I do. Keep it. It'll be a nice memory someday."

She bent down and lightly touched the tip of his nose with her index finger.

"When you become a world-famous soccer player," she added.

She had no idea at that time how right she was.

***

Marko and Karla argued loudly on whether or not Karla should get a Cockta now or wait until the game finished, while David, on the other hand, watched the game silently. Tabita sat on an uncomfortable blue chair attached to the concrete of the bleachers. She paid full attention to a soccer game for the first time in her life. She observed his every move, smiled at every bounce of his thick curl falling on top of his forehead, and felt warmth in her throat when she caught his gaze over the field filled with sun rays and stuffy air. As he followed the ball closely with his eyes, she recognized a spark of a primordial purpose in him. The true sense of life as if nothing else existed for him in this world except the ball and the silhouettes of his teammates whom he formed a minor unwritten pact of trust with the moment they entered the field.

The opposing team leads 1-0. Zair is agitated. His heartbeat is making the blue jersey bounce right off his chest. A couple of boys from his team glance toward him like they are expecting something. He glances towards the coach, who is lighting another cigarette.

The opposing team leads 2-0. Zair grabs his thick curls, flicks them off his forehead, and frowns, glancing towards the bleachers. He was mad because she was watching his defeat. A chubbier boy from his team was hollering at him. But Tabita could only hear the final words: "...throw it in!"

The chubby kid from Zair's team scores a goal for 2-1. It seems like a coincidence. She's happy, filled with hope. Karla and Marko are clapping, and David puts his hands up in the air, shouting at Zair to keep going.

The opposing team scores another goal for 3-1 in the very next minute. It seemed like a joke or some magic – the ball passing through their skinny goalkeeper's legs and entering the net. Zair was silently watching his teammates, tongue-tied.

The opposing team scores their own goal, and the result is 3-2. Zair's team gets a golden chance for a draw. She found a small, extremely short boy from the opposing team reasonably attractive. But, unfortunately, he didn't understand what he was doing there.

It's a draw, 3-3. Zair's face lights up. He glances towards her with a smile, then turns his head as his eyes start following the ball rolling slowly beneath his feet.

The result is 3-4, and it's the last minute. She wasn't sure when it happened or how he did it. The sun's warm rays stroke the joyful faces of Zair's teammates, that jump and bounce around him, pinching his cheeks, hugging him, and calling out his name. Finally, he scored the final, winning goal.

MARCH, 1948
BUDVA

The red soup started foaming up and traveling up the edge of the pot, crawling out of it. Finally, the smell of burnt tomato reached the bathroom. The stove started hissing like a cat, and Žanet never particularly liked cats. She set Petar's homework down and ran to the kitchen. Grabbing the first dish rag she saw, she removed the big green pot from the burning stove and started waving the rag around the small, smoke-filled kitchen to clear up the air.

"My mom's a true chef," Petar entered the kitchen with a notebook in his arms, pretending to write an essay about Žanet.

"Knock it off," she smiled, wiping the edge of the pot with a napkin. "And write that essay already."

"Alright, then," he hid his nose behind the notebook, pretending to read. "Today, we slurped the soup off the stove."

"You little tart!"

She pulled his long nose – the one he inherited from his father – as he spread his full lips into a smile – which he also inherited from his father. The only thing that Žanet loved about his father was his lips morphing into a smile.

Petar was the main reason for her seven years of joy. He was her penance prayer that unconditionally provided forgiveness for her past sins and a replacement for the pretty gray eyes and chubby cheeks that she squared away deep into her subconscious. In addition, she was an impeccable mother and a loyal wife. Every day she cooked their favorite meals, walked with her husband around their garden, thought up puppet shows with Petar, took an interest in every ship in a bottle he'd make, and brought a cake to her in-laws every Sunday – even though her ambitions and dreams used to look very different once upon a time. She completes her daily routine by ironing Petar's school outfit for tomorrow before bedtime.

She'd feel both miserable and joyful during the visits to her in-laws. The misery hid behind a sad truth; she never loved their son like a woman should love a man. To her, he was simply a thin straw of salvation that rarely dipped into the drink of love. That day, she stacked the cakes on a tray while her mother-in-law made coffee and tried to tie an apron around her large waist. Žanet was singing a song she'd learned long ago in elementary school when her mother-in-law suddenly interrupted her.

"Do you think my Liri is happy?" she asked.

"What do you mean?" Žanet cleared her throat.

"I just think he is blind."

She poured coffee into a cup.

"Why would he be blind?" Žanet smiled anxiously.

"If he believes his wife loves him, he is surely blind."

That sentence felt like a blade cutting Žanet slowly from her throat to the end of her stomach. It was like a horrendous revelation – she felt completely naked, like standing in a forest on a winter night while the whole world revolved around her. Yet, he was also so distant and beautiful there, holding an abandoned gray-eyed girl in his arms.

"No one would do anything like this for your son."

She placed the final cake on the tray angrily and took the tray out into the backyard that reeked of pig feces and hens. In that turbulent world of surrender and oblivion, Žanet did much for her husband. She gave him everything that people give to their loved ones, but she lacked the main ingredient. Love. In her eyes, it was a bit like making apple pie without having the apples and, for that reason, being condemned to roam an endless forest in search of an apple tree repeatedly, every day.

***

Žanet's favorite thing was watching Petar make his ships in bottles. She never completely understood how he did it, even though he explained it to her a million times, but the whole process seemed like a miracle, like magic. They built a small room in their home that looked like a tightly cramped hallway, exclusively for Petar's inventions. Even though he already had about two hundred of them by then, not one ship ever resembled the other. Some of them he placed in bigger bottles, some in smaller, always aiming for different shapes. He'd spend hours there. Sometimes just staring at his crafts and sometimes working tirelessly on a single ship. His favorite was a yellow ship in a small bottle with an irremovable stain on its neck. He called it L'eternità. He was barely six when he made it, and she never forgot what he said on that occasion.

Mom, I know we have to die someday. That's not nice. He reached towards her with his fragile hands, holding the little ship bravely. That's why I made this ship that will take us to eternity. She took the ship in her shivering hands as his words gently started evoking the feelings of awe coming alive inside of her. I know it's always lovely in Heaven, so we'll always sail on this ship.

At night we'll count the stars and sleep, and during the day... we can go swimming. I'm sure it's always sunny in Heaven.

Žanet never really doubted the existence of Heaven. She saw all the nooks and crannies of that Promised Land. They were shimmering there, like a reflection, neatly distributed in Petar's eyes. But, what worried her the most was her questionable belonging to the goodness of that place.

***

Just before Petar fell asleep at night, she would sit on the edge of his bed. Very briefly, however, because he fell asleep fast. He had only expressed his wish for a lullaby a couple of times, but whenever the words reached the tip of her tongue, something would detain her voice, and she'd stay silent.

"I can't sing, son," she'd tell him.

Then she'd kiss his scalp, pull the covers up to his nose and tiptoe out of the room. The path to the bedroom always seemed too short, even though she tried her best to stroll. Something strange would hide in those ghastly, slow movements of her limbs. Sometimes she would pretend that she had some things left to do in the kitchen or couldn't sleep, so she'd stay and read a book in the living room. Those kinds of dreams, crammed into an armchair and a whole story away from the nest of a love never born, were her most serene ones.

Žanet disliked lying. Her husband knew the whole story. He knew how much she loved, how much she lost, how much she decided to yield, and how deep her scar was. That was why she hoped he would always understand just how little the love she had for him was; for the only husband she'll ever have.

FEBRUARY, 1975
OSIJEK

He was crouching in the dark hallway, trying to tie the shoelaces of his shiny polished shoes as neatly as possible. He was wondering if he had secured his tie right, if he was too ginger, and if his uncle would like the way he did his hair. Then, he heard confident and sharp steps coming from the living room. Patrik's heart was pounding tremendously under his freshly ironed clothes, just like it did every time they went somewhere immensely important for his uncle's reputation. With a swift movement, he fixed his tie and glanced at his shoes. Everything seemed alright.

"Ready?" his uncle smiled faintly.

The air was filled with his cologne. Patrik didn't like that smell. It reminded him of his uncle's business partners and half-naked women who came and kept them company late at night, then left a mere couple of hours later.

"Yes," Patrik nodded his head insecurely.

"Well, what are you waiting for then?"

He swung his black leather backpack behind him as the inside notebook chafed his back. He opened the door very clumsily.

“Let’s go then; the car is waiting,” his uncle nudged him over the threshold.

***

Every Tuesday and Thursday, on his uncle’s initiative, Patrik took classes in creative writing. One writer taught the course on Tuesdays and a different one on Thursdays. The uncle knew both of them personally. The one who taught the class on Thursdays was Patrik’s favorite. Even though his uncle used to say that he was constantly beating a dead horse, which made Patrik laugh inside because that same writer claimed that worn-out phrases such as ‘to beat a dead horse’ were not the preferred vocabulary of a serious writer. But regardless of his occasional use of clichéd expressions to slander his acquaintance, Franjo Bošnjak was an exceptional writer. If you were to ask all the literary critics who had a chance to read his published books and many other people who played poker in their homes and filled their living rooms with cigar smoke, Patrik slept safely and soundly in the other room.

Franjo Bošnjak was also the creator and editor of Strike Hunt, a trendy magazine that published famous writers' works and sometimes even up-and-coming ones. All those works, naturally, had to be approved by Franjo Bošnjak before being published. All the articles, including the reviews and critiques of the works published in that particular issue and interviews with various writers, were made by writers picked personally by Bošnjak with the help of Oto Gamulin, the co-owner of the magazine, who worked in Zagreb. Led by his vices, the uncle decided to make a writer out of Patrik, and that decision was, above all, something worth every penny. Even if it meant that Patrik would one day live someone else’s dreams.

Patrik loved to read and admire the prowess of literacy, but the urge rarely pulled him in to create his own words; very rarely pulled in by the scent of the fresh, blank paper, and his heart never skipped a beat at the arrival of various typewriters his uncle had been ordering from Germany. Patrik was one of those people that loved someone else's written word but never found their own creative expression in it. Divided between his nature and the wish to please his uncle, he decided to become a writer. At twelve, he already had three written-out notebooks of stories. Written so neatly, with firm and straightforward sentences, that every bohemian soul would shake like a leaf before the tidiness of his creative world. Patrik's works emanated an exceptional amount of willpower – but nothing other or more profound than that.

***

His uncle's car always smelled like a mixture of disinfectant and cologne. A golden fountain pen key chain dangled from the rear-view mirror, where Patrik could always see the reflection of his frightened eyes. His uncle claimed it was hundreds of years old and came from the world's oldest library. Still, Patrik knew that it was just another one of his harmless lies in an effort to convince him that a writer is the most sublime being in this world and that books are – having been produced by that sublime being – the most significant treasure given to the world. Patrik believed that books were a treasure, but he was also convinced that they were not the only form of it.

As they approached the tall brick building where the creative writing course was being held, his uncle cleared his throat a couple of times and Patrik already knew what he was about to say.

"Be polite, don't embarrass me."

"Alright," he placed his hand on the handle, waiting for a car to pass by so he could open the door.

"Be a gentleman."

He saw his uncle wink at him in the rear-view mirror.

***

Other than writing, his uncle was also obsessed with fishing. So every weekend, if the weather served them, they'd get dressed, pack their things, and hit the road for two hours to get to his uncle's favorite lake. Patrik always observed his uncle's sideburns peeking under his green hat, above his big hairy ears that looked like a weird set of horns. The maid who took care of their home on the weekends would always pack four apples, two thin sandwiches with barely a taste of dry ham, and two glass bottles of water in their picnic basket.

Upon arriving, his uncle would set two wooden chairs next to the lake, sit on the one closer to the big tree, and keep quiet for the next couple of hours. It was strange how a man that lived off the abundance of words distributed in meaningful units could be so loudly silent. Yet, deep inside, Patrik knew that his uncle cared about him. Above all, he cared for him when he could have left him at the mercy of the orphanage. But sometimes, he wasn't sure if he cared about him because he was his nephew and the only son figure he'd ever known or because of the image of his brother that Patrik resembled.

"All that I have to say, I say in my stories," the uncle would state.

That sentence often echoed in Patrik's mind, especially when sitting in the classroom during the creative writing course. There was something very wondrous in that sentence that made Patrik think that he could do it as well – he could write. So he decided to reach that level of consciousness – the level of his uncle – where he'd be able to dissolve all of his thoughts and merge them into stories. The idea of reincarnating those two sets of eyes that watch him before he goes to sleep was more blissful than anything sacred he'd ever known. But back then, Patrik didn't realize that one important thing, one of the most significant truths of a writer's world – the writer doesn't choose his own stories. The stories choose him.

Olympia

DECEMBER, 1978
OSIJEK

She stood in front of a giant Christmas tree in the mall. The red Christmas lights and golden decorations gently and messily twisted around the sharp branches, coating the needles with gold as the round Christmas ornaments revealed her reflection. Her long blonde hair, her apple-shaped cheeks with a dimple on the right side, her big green eyes and a pronounced jaw which served as proof that she wasn't as little anymore as she was the last time she stood here, in this same mall, in front of the Christmas tree – in 1969. Then, in the multitude of voices, she heard her stepmother's.

"We said we won't spend that much money, so what happened?"

She knew her words were meant for her and her father's intention to buy her something. She rolled her eyes and swallowed a few curses that came to her mind as she heard her stepmother's tone of voice.

"Nadja, come here," her father called out to her.

One last time she glanced at the redness of the Christmas lights and then turned around and headed towards them, her hands stuffed deep in the pockets of her red coat. Breaking through the crowd, she grazed a middle-aged woman carrying a big rag doll in a plastic bag. The same rag doll she had seen earlier while they wandered around the shops looking for a gift for her half-sister Lorna, who was two years old already. She spent the next few hours thinking about that woman she grazed. She served as a symbol of the mall and its crowds of people who hopelessly wander around the shops, tired and uncertain as to what they're even looking for, but with the intention of making their loved ones smile.

The last shop they entered was a clothing store. Nadja rarely went shopping because she paid little attention to her appearance and avoided making friends, especially with girls. Her stepmother bounced beside her, gluing her eyes on the price of almost every piece of clothing Nadja would even glance at. After a while, out of sheer fun, Nadja started glancing at some more expensive things, reveling in her stepmother's insanity. In the end, she chose a denim backpack, placed it in her father's hands, smiled at him lightly, and exited the store leaving her father with a choice: buy it, or get off easy by using the ace up his sleeve that he was great at – making up an excuse. While she waited in front of the store in the foggy crowd of people, she couldn't help but solve a simple equation – the rag doll was about five dollars, while her backpack was only three.

***

She was sitting across from her mother, listening to the old clock ticking and drinking a cup of hot coffee as the taste of the first cigarette she tried the night before still rifled through the back of her mind. She wanted to know what lay behind the fogginess of the cigarette smoke. The taste wasn't as bad as she thought it would be. For quite a while, she managed to put off indulging in a bohemian lifestyle that many well-known writers could not resist. At that time, her favorite was Ivo Andrić. She read all his works that she borrowed from the library, feeling a whiff of sadness in every letter read, given that he had passed away a few years earlier. She had a strangely great desire to meet the man who, with his words and longings, managed to represent the parts of her nature so particularly – the parts she alone couldn't explain so intensely.

Her mother cleared her throat and closed the newspaper she held between her soft, gentle palms.

"How was it?" she squinted over her reading glasses.

"Great," Nadja looked to the side. "Eleonora and I had a blast."

"What did she do this time?" she took the thin glasses off her nose.

"Only had a mini heart attack every time she saw the price of anything I even remotely glanced at," she sat and folded her legs on the chair. "Nothing special."

"You have to get used to those kinds of situations." She got up to draw the curtains. "What did she say? When will you see each other again?"

"What do you think?" Nadja put the cup down on the wooden table in front of her. "She didn't say anything."

***

Bedtime stories and all the articles of her mother's taste turned into Shakespeare's plays or classics of Ilir's suggestion. Then, finally, her mother came in, kissed her forehead softly, then went out, leaving Nadja in a room that had started rapidly filling with sharp, deep dreams in a mere minute's time.

"Are you coming with me tomorrow?" she asked as she exited.

"Yes."

***

The mornings were now unfolding more silently than ever. The two of them would have their own rules for waking up; they would comb their hair and wake up to the sound of the alarm. Her mother still reached for her black coffee while Nadja reached for hot cocoa. Then their hungry bellies would find their way to Ilir's bakery and have breakfast there.

"There's my princess," he said.

Ilir's belly was getting strangely but sweetly chubbier by the year. Then, as usual, she placed her head on his shoulder and uttered a word describing her problem on that particular day.

"Math."

"Come on, Bella, just one more week until the holidays."

He caressed the softness of her cheek.

"Are you staying here for the holidays?" she reached for a salted pastry. "Or are you going traveling again?"

"We're staying," he nodded his head calmly, his gaze fixed on the back of his wife's head as she sat in front of the bakery.

"You know," she talked as she chewed the pastry, "I wrote a new story."

"If you didn't bring it, you're walking home to get it," he smiled.

She laughed out loud from the bottom of her stomach.

"It's my Christmas gift to you," she softly pecked him on the cheek.

***

School was one of the most hated institutions in Nadja's world. She disliked its smell, the way her eyes stung every time she walked in, and she despised nearly every one of her schoolmates. It seemed as if they didn't understand the meaning of many things. So during the breaks, she often walked the halls of the school alone, staring at the freedom of the landscape around the school through the stained glass of the high windows, and while all the other students ate their lunch boxes brought from home, she dreamt about the day she would set foot into her college building. She wasn't exactly sure about her major or what she wanted to do in life at that, but she was convinced that her life would, whether she liked it or not, always be defined by writing, one way or the other.

Every time she heard the bell indicating the end of the short break and the commotion of the students in the halls, she'd calmly step aside, holding her books and notebooks against her chest, at a safe distance from those who rushed to get inside first. The only thing she truly loved in that school was the music classroom. The sunlight was always dancing in that room – sunlight from both ends of the classroom, clashing in the middle as if it belonged to a different dimension. Despite the sheer hatred towards the school, Nadja was an excellent student. The teachers liked her, and in a way, even approved of her tendencies towards the untouchable, but only as much as she let them. She tried to stay unnoticed. No one in that school had direct contact with her literary works. No one in the world except her mother and Ilir.

***

One of Nadja's loudest classroom colleagues held a white piece of paper in her hand and waved it around as she searched for Nadja, who was right in the middle of reading Strike Hunt and who, by accident, managed to hear the vowels and the consonants that made up her first and last name as the girl called her out.

"Nadja Silvia! Nadja Silvia!"

The girl fluttered right by her and handed her the bundle of paper – inside it, touched by the light falling across her shoulder on the school desk, stood an invitation.

You are invited to my New Year's Eve party, beginning at 9pm.

Bring lots of joy with you and a couple of 'juice' bottles!

Yours,
Ana

Nadja knew she was invited to those parties because of her looks. She had overheard that her long golden locks, defined breasts, and the length of her puberty-stricken legs, all the things that made her seem older, were the main bullseye for the boys' eyes. If she had it her way, she'd spend New Year's Eve with her mother and Ilir at the bakery, but Nadja rarely had it her way, and her mother wanted her to make some friends.

***

So she stepped into 1979 next to a boy. He was tall, his black hair thick, and his shoulders wide. He wore a blue suit that reeked of cigarettes and was the type of guy that turned the girls' giggly heads like some magnet field. To the sound of the countdown and the rambling sounds of rock music in the background, Nadja felt his coarse tongue make its way into her mouth as though searching for something. Something that she didn't seem to have – at least not for him. With the last tones of the countdown and the white wine in her system, Nadja stepped into 1979, a moment closer to being fourteen.

***

January was frigid. Nadja could almost feel the chill biting her hands with its touch. She was trying to put the leather glove on her left hand while her mother set up the sleigh – trying to set it to a right angle so they'd bounce off in the middle of the slope, then continue gliding smoothly until the end.

"Ready?" she asked, inhaling the cold air as her red scarf swayed in the wind.

"Born ready," Nadja answered, stuffing the ends of her scarf under her thick collar.

"Come on, Hanuma, sit down," her mother tapped the sleigh with her hand.

Even though their life had become much more serious, and their mornings came about much more silently without the enthusiasm and the exciting mutual hair combing, they never forgot to laugh together.

They sat on the sleigh in complete silence and inhaled deeply as if getting ready to break a Guinness record. Nadja stretched her legs as her mother pushed them off firmly towards the slope. The snow creaked loudly, and the icy wind pierced Nadja's cheeks, reddening them like royal blood. As the sleigh slid down, the lines of their lips formed a smile. They laughed loudly in unison when they bounced off the top of a small hill in the middle of the slope. As they reached the end of the slope, they rushed back up and did it all over again. A dozen times. Those moments, as light as a feather and as therapeutic as nature, kept Nadja's stories sharp. Something dotting the i's and crossing the t's. They were an ornament, fulfillment, completeness, sense, and strength. Just a little while later, all those moments of beauty and courage, albeit rarely, started merging arrogantly with her weak spots.

At that time, Nadja was writing about her mother, her thick eyebrows and the prettiness of her smile, and the lichen around her lips. So deftly that the lichen meant beauty in her words. She wrote about the crushed snow, the coldness of the wind, the sound of the river Drava calling to her as she walked the promenade, Baranja on the other side of the forceful river, and finally, about her father whose image was slowly fading in her mind. Sometimes, she wrote about Ilir and his wife, whom she knew nothing about other than the fact that she was in a wheelchair, that she smoked one cigarette after another, and that she shook her head when upset. Ilir was, on the other hand, sort of a savior in her story, the one who believed in her, especially in the moments when she was not capable of believing in herself. Or the world in general. Although, those two little spots – she and the world in general – very often seemed unbreakably similar. That is why the prettiest detail on Ilir was his eyes, where she could see herself as a notable, successful writer.

Sometimes, blown away by Shakespeare's Romeo and Juliet, she'd close her eyes and imagine her soul mate. The image was immensely foggy but soft, like a pillow or silk. She wrote about her soul mate instinctively – evoking him, flying somewhere between the past, the present, and the future, and making her home in the hidden world of the infinite. For Nadja and her stories, love was just a logical and sublime act, not relative. Not even one bit. Reading her stories, Ilir and her mother did not object to that. On the contrary, bearing witness to many unhappy loves, they hoped she'd never have to walk that line.

APRIL, 1979
OSIJEK

The winter of 1979 flew by Nadja's eyes. The greenery of young leaves had decorated the naked branches of the trees in a blink of an eye. The spring sun rays lighted up Osijek's paths, Zrinjevac started gaining its golden strength, and the promenade was once again full of people walking up and down with their heads held high.

For a school assignment, Nadja's class was tasked with writing a report on the game that the soccer team Olympia played at the Spring Cup. Their job was to visit the soccer field, watch the game, support the players, and write a report on the whole thing. All in all, it was their choice; run twice the length of about four miles for P.E., or write this report. Girls, on the one hand, weren't fans of either the sport or running, while boys were big fans of soccer. It was a simple equation; everyone was going to write a report.

Being used to writing to make the world around her prettier and recognize all the wondrous and magical things in it, Nadja believed that this assignment wasn't within her area of expertise. The soccer match limited the freedom of her mind – the freedom to depict reality with the words of the unreal and the unreal with parts of reality. She believed the writer had to know his motives in detail to play with them.

"How should I know if they're good at soccer?"

She asked her mother as she added sugar to her cup of coffee. "I don't know anything about that sport," Nadja repeated relentlessly.

"You're a writer, Nadja; think of something," she stirred her coffee, then set the spoon down on a small plate.

"It's meaningless," Nadja shook her head. "A writer should have his freedom."

"Why do you think this report takes your freedom away?"

Nadja put her brown notebook into her denim backpack as her pale blue pajama danced around her calves.

"I don't know; it's just the fact that it has a topic," a flash of bitterness emanated from her voice.

"I still think that the real freedom is the one the writer makes for himself," her mother sipped a cup of coffee. "Even in the narrowest of subjects."

"Then maybe I'm not a very good writer after all," Nadja set the empty cup in the sink.

"You're not coming with me today?"

"I can't make it," Nadja kissed her forehead. "I have to shower."

She stared at the tiny holes in the shower with her giant eyes. Then, for the first time, she noticed rust accumulating around them and asked herself when it happened, digging around the writer's vortex in her head. The vortex is where big, magical things are born out of the smallest details. Then, as if trying to punish herself for her inability to comprehend the importance of that one soccer match, she let the ice-cold water hit her forehead, eyes, shoulders, back, and finally, her calves. She felt her skin crawl with every touch of the heavy drops of water.

"Nadja, I'm leaving; good luck!" her mother shouted from the depths of the hall.

"Thanks!" she yelled back.

She opened and closed her lips, swallowing the cold water that tasted like iron. Losing herself in the timeless existence of the immortal heavy drops of water, she wasn't sure as to how long she'd been there or when exactly she had applied the rose-scented soap on her pearly body, but the touch of the wet tips of her hair woke her up from her daydreams. She stepped on the coldness of the white, dewy bathroom tiles, digging her face into a thick towel whose white fabric hairs tickled her nose gently. She waited for her rebellious hair to dry, then tied it in a high ponytail while dipping her body into a fluttering white tulle dress that reached down to her strangely dented knees. On her way out, she flicked a denim jacket - paired with her denim backpack - over her shoulder, locking the door very clumsily as she put on her black leather ankle boots, her thoughts already rushing towards the soccer match.

The sun revealed itself shyly. One half hidden behind an ashen cloud, the other seemingly greeting her. Her paths crossed with an old lady carrying two bags of cabbage, leaning on a worn-out wooden walking stick and smelling like a freshly washed cat. She spent the next ten minutes pondering whether or not she should have helped her. Then she passed by a skinny man with a mustache who held a pipe between his teeth, nimbly puffing smoke in three almost regularly shaped circles. Adequately shaped, just like the ones she saw on the train, her father left in. When she approached Olympia and passed through a wavy street, her heart was beating like a fast rhythm on a rock concert.

The bleachers had no chairs. They consisted just of massive blocks of cement that formed giant steps. Many people were there for Nadja, truth be told, way too many. Her peers generally sat on the massive concrete steps while the older population gathered around the fence like passionate fans. The game hadn't started yet, and everyone was talking to each other, creating a big clump of noise in the air, mainly about the things that weren't strictly connected to the game or soccer. She pressed her notebook against her chest, embracing it tightly with her hands, blocking her fingers' bloodstream, and then proceeded towards the other side of the bleachers – the side positioned far away from the entrance and far away from all the people that were yet to arrive.

Passing through, she grazed a couple of shoulders, passed between two older ladies amid their talking, then sat beside a little boy who was there with his father. Or maybe his grandfather; she was trying to assess. The boy was, by her estimate, around five or six years old. The gentleman was over fifty, according to his droopy eyelids.

"When will it start?" the boy asked.

The boy's agitated voice made it seem like he was afraid of his shadow.

"In a minute," the father-grandfather replied in a deep voice.

Only when she'd heard the restlessness of the people around her – their agitation, seat-adjusting, whispering, and silencing – did Nadja look up and see the greenness of the field. The first scene won her over – the impeccable green color of the soccer field. It looked like a carpet, like home, like a piece of the universe calling out to her. She opened her notebook – which felt like opening her heart widely and touching the point where its light is the brightest – and started writing. In her world, everything revolved around writing – she didn't make up stories; stories came to her like they were coming home, and she, in turn, gifted them with immortality, converting their every atom into lively letters.

The result is 1-0. Ball here, ball there. Ball rolling, ball flying, ball touching the sky, falling, then bouncing off. An Olympia player leaps for it, touches it in the air boldly, and scores.

She was supposed to be happy, to jump up like the rest of the people, but she was there in the story. She laughed at herself. That was probably the first soccer match she'd watched.

The sun is obscuring her view. The ball is flying through the air, rolling around in its density, cutting the sun's rays. It touches the grass and, like a tamed animal, rolls beneath the feet of an opposing team's player.

The little boy standing beside her on his scrawny legs, watching their every move, held his breath while his father-grandfather smoked a cigarette.

The opposing team seems very dangerous and gloomy but playful. Their every move seems unpredictable, threatening, and fatal.

After a couple of seconds of the game, or so it felt to Nadja, who got lost in the world of writing – the judge signaled the end of Half-Time. She dove out and gazed at all the people around her, who seemed so far away from her, then glanced at the small leather watch wrapped around her wrist – she had been writing for 46 minutes.

***

The result is 1-1. The opposing team's player rushes toward the goal that a plump young boy guards. The plump boy loses control of his arms; he starts flailing them everywhere without aimlessly. The opposing team's player touches the ball with his foot as it loyally finds its way through between the plump boy's legs, entering the net.

An opposing team's player falls, rolls around the inexplicably green field then leaves the game limping.

Nadja got on her tiptoes, surprising herself with the depth of her curiosity. Enamored by the world in which a moment could last an eternity, her eyes expected a slow entrance to the field, but instead, a young boy came in running. While the people around her observed other players, she caught sight of some intensely familiar curls. Five pages of her notebook were written out. As the adrenaline in the players' blood grew, her mind harmoniously merged with them. She could almost feel the strength and the beating of their hearts as her sentences materialized on the paper with ease.

The result is 2-1. An Olympia player approaches the opposing team's goal and sends the ball up in the air, to which it responds by flying obediently. Then, his teammate hits it with his head as it gymnastically enters the goal over the shoulder of a tall goalkeeper, touching the dirtiness of the white net.

Although the childish part of Nadja knew very well that game equaled joy, the scene where people of all ages enjoyed the game was astounding in her eyes. Their voices intertwined in a big vocal braid, dancing their victory dance in the air as if a mere goal was enough to save them from the monotony of the adult world.

***

The ground didn't seem so green anymore, and the sun looked like it had suddenly lost its briskness as if something was despicably diminishing its shine – like the magic had never been there. The excitement deep inside her subsided, and hunger overwhelmed her stomach like a snake that finally found a hole to crawl out of. The sweet flavor of hunger consumed her throat as her rebellious baby hairs escaped the tightly tied ponytail and her dress wrinkled.

She got up holding the edges of her dress, feeling a sharp pain in her knees, like a slight atrophy of her muscles from those ninety minutes of sitting down. A few groups of players still hung around by the fence as the air around them echoed with curses, complaints, and sighs. She came down the irregular massive stairs, squinting tightly to protect herself from the sun's brightness that had already started setting. Nadja got interrupted by a familiar sight just as she began to wish she'd brought that big linen hat that her father gave her two years ago – the bouncing of the ball from one knee to the other and a set of frowning but intimate eyes. She approached the puny fence and directed her eyes toward a boy standing between the rusty wires. The last rays of sunset their sights upon the field, revealing a scar on the boy's chin. It looks like a crack. Or…? It seems like a twig. A broken twig. A frantic gaze fussed under his thick eyebrows. Men never want to pluck them, she thought. His thick curls danced in the air, seemingly cracking the determination of the sun's rays. Gingerbread cookies. The fabric hairs of a black blanket touched the soft grass. Leaves, a lot of them. Dirty fingernails. A soccer ball.

She glued herself to the fence like a magnetic field was pulling her body towards it. She could feel her belly merging with the cold wire. Her mind started spinning in its own direction, her heart following the rhythm of a strong sentiment, and her throat – getting ready to utter words – completely constricted. She didn't know what her mouth would utter, but she felt her sheer essence longing to talk to him.

"When I last saw you do this, you weren't as skilled as you are now!" she shouted, her voice trembling from excitement.

He turned his head, still frowning, as his eyebrows wrinkled his forehead. She pressed the notebook firmly against her chest, sporting a vibrant smile on her face. One second. Two seconds. Three seconds. Nothing. There was no answer, and the ball again stole his attention. I was wrong. It was a long time ago. She stepped over the puddle of spilled juice and finally reached the meandering street. She deeply breathed in the fresh air flowing through the street like she had just escaped from a dungeon and longed to breathe. Two men – who looked like coaches of the Olympia team – passed her by, holding big bags.

"...in defense," the skinnier one said.

Then she heard the muffled beginning of the other one's sentence – he was a lot shorter but wide-shouldered, with a coarse voice.

"But I didn't know...."

They crossed the road warily as a big truck interrupted Nadja's view. In that silent moment, when peace and quiet were finally filling the air, she heard a thick cluster of voices behind her. Someone grazed her shoulder. She replied with a startled jump and a peculiar sense of hope. She felt a touch on her forearm.

"Sorry."

A long-nosed, short-haired boy dove into her eyes with his weary gaze, waiting impatiently for her to accept his apology.

"It's alright," she shook her head.

Nadja rushed her step so the crowd wouldn't eat her alive. As she kept walking, she allowed herself one final turn to make sure: No, that wasn't him. It was a long time ago.

"I know!" she heard a panting exclamation behind her.

She stopped walking as her feet hesitated curiously, and her body turned around silently. He was standing there with his arms in the pockets of his washed-out jeans, one dark curl touching the tip of his nose. His teammates stood behind him like they were his subjects, smiling at him provocatively.

"It's you," he stepped towards her, his gaze diving into her face curiously. "You're that kid with the notebook."

A smile started breaking out on her face, ready to show itself.

"You bought me ice cream," he smiled.

"I thought you were going back to Zagreb," with her notebook, she gestured toward the scraggy bus parked next to them.

"We're staying here for a couple more hours," he answered with a shy and trembling gesture toward the bus.

A few powerful moments took hold of them, separating them from reality, gifting them with bits and pieces of the eternal. Their gazes touched as if they could clearly understand each other and gave each other strength that danced joyfully on some strange layers of livelihood.

"That means I have some time left," he tilted his head, and his curls followed.

***

They were sitting in the middle of the pedestrian bridge in Osijek, their eyes following the river flowing through the giant metal bars as the soft moonlight kept blinking on the surface of the restless water. She could feel the breeze greeting the tip of her scalp.

"You never said goodbye."

"I didn't," he answered.

He brushed her softly rounded cheek with his gaze, then her big eyes that stared up at the starry cloak that spread above them.

"How's Zagreb?" she leaned on her palms.

"Ordinary."

"Ordinary?"

Now she, in return, grazed his pronounced jaw with her gaze.

"Nothing special."

"Do you miss it?" she tilted her head, staring at his messy curls with a smile.

"Osijek?"

She nodded her head sharply, squeezing her lips.

"Sometimes," he nodded. "But it was such a long time ago."

She remembered how she had uttered that same sentence in her head about an hour earlier. Even then, her mind was painted with a strange idea: the two of them were, in an ever so gentle way, oddly synchronized.

"Yes," she laughed silently. "It was."

Silence took over, split in half only by an occasional whiff of wind.

"What does it feel like?"

Reclining on her palms, she leaned her head back and closed her eyes, letting the wind caress her face.

"What does what feel like?"

"Playing soccer."

The wrinkles on his forehead and the soft trembling of his head revealed that he didn't know the answer. He didn't know how to put it in words nimbly enough. That small gap, that small torn-off part of his skills; it was as if it passed from him to her a long time ago in the hope that, in a certain moment of light, that torn-off part of him would find its way home.

"Uncertain," he answered finally.

She just nodded her head, now staring at her legs situated between the bars of the bridge.

"You're still writing," he smiled. "I didn't think you'd keep at it for so long."

"Many people didn't."

"I can't believe it."

"What?"

She leaned towards him and opened her eyes wide as the tip of her nose almost touched the tip of his. She was entirely close to him – precisely in the way she knew annoyed him the most. His throat let out a harsh laugh, like a wind that hadn't had a chance to blow in a while. She didn't recall that kind of roughness and force in him. He seemed happier. Or he simply liked her more.

"I can't," he cleared his throat from all that laughter, "believe I'm seeing you again."

With a swift movement, she distanced herself, flinching at the fact that he even remembered her and that he marveled at their reunion.

"I mean," he looked away, "I had completely forgotten about you."

"Have you ever kissed a girl?" she turned her gaze towards the river.

He cleared his throat again, visibly uneasy.

"Well?" she gazed at him shyly. "Have you?"

"Yes," he nodded.

"And have you ever seen a girl naked?" her voice shyly got quieter.

"Nadja Silvia," he nimbly evaded her gaze, leaning towards his feet. "I thought you were a decent girl."

“I’m just wondering,” she leaned on her palms again. “Women are beautiful when they’re exposed.”

“I believe you,” he replied.

***

Half an hour later, she stood beside the road, holding her notebook and watching him pull away. She couldn’t see his scar – that broken twig on his chin – nor his thick curls through the blurry window of the bus. She only saw his big, dreamy eyes glued to the glass and his wide smile, almost touching the tips of his ears, addressed to her. She didn’t wave at him. She said goodbye with a simple, honest smile, and a couple of moments later, his figure was merely a silhouette merging itself with the road.

Again, she knew nothing about him. She knew that his name was Zair, that he shared an extraordinary passion with a soccer ball, that his lips became infinitely wide when he smiled genuinely, and that they’d turn into a weakly curve when he was sad. She knew that he thought Zagreb was a very ordinary city, and so was his life there. She knew the air beside him was warm, even when the wind breezed and touched her scalp. She knew that he had an urge to stare at her cheek, the one where her dimple is deeper, and that he understood the sordidness of her decent nature. She knew only that. And nothing else.

The Lost Compass

AUGUST, 1958
BUDVA

Her ear touched his shoulder bone, and his wide palm absorbed her sweat. They watched the vehicle move away, leaving a thick swarm of dust behind it. She didn't know how to fall asleep with Petar over there – in the hands of strangers ripping his heart out and trying to fit him a new one.

That night, Žanet had no wish to fall asleep in the shell of her armchair. Instead, she lay beside him, leaning her head on his soft chest. His breath warmed her scalp with the heat of a husband who had spent an eternity preparing to receive her affection finally. In the depth of her soul, like a needle that had been stuck there forever but has, in this particular instant, moved inappropriately to the side, Žanet felt guilty. It was a selfish act. She didn't love him; she merely extracted strength from his love while knowing deep inside how incapable she was. She knew very well that the blessing was never in accepting the love but in the fervor we feel within ourselves when we're driven by the phenomenon within a soul other than our own. The biggest prize always hid behind the concept of giving. Providing. Creating. Emitting.

Žanet did not provide. She simply consumed. She consumed everything and was never thankful for it. A man could have the whole world in the palm of his hand, but how rich could he truly be if he wasn't grateful for that same world? Yet again, she reached for the thing that unconditionally and unduly belonged to her. She still had to break her sorrow in two – one part for herself and one part for him. She had to share with him her trepidation as she waited for the phone call. In the fogginess of all the hypothetical outcomes of the phone call, she finally fell asleep counting black, rotten sheep.

***

The sun shone brightly that morning, and the burnt grass in their garden gleamed at the touch of the stubborn sun rays. Žanet stirred the cold tea in her cup and stared at the living room windows. The sunlight exposed the stains on them as much as it exposed her sorrow. The phone hadn't rung yet. Hours and hours of silence had passed, leaving behind the apparition of a vehicle taking her son away. Far from the safety of their home, far from health, far from love, far from her. In those moments of silent waiting, she felt like he had traveled to a world filled with sickness.

After a couple of strolls around the living room to break the monotony of her sadness, he sat down and hid his face behind the newspaper. Although her line of sight couldn't reach his face, she clearly felt the density of his worry in the air around them. She assumed it was the magic of unhappy marriages – to familiarize oneself with the essence of one's sorrow telepathically. However, she felt no need to drive the heavy clouds of his sadness away. Even though she knew she could.

***

The ruthlessly descending night, unwilling and unobligated to wait for that phone call with them, was the perfect representation of Žanet's feelings – of the gnawing darkness she had ever so ably reigned over.

"Please, Žanet," he leaned on the doorframe. "Come to bed."

She did what she had always been best at – stayed silent.

"I'm sure everything is fine," he added.

The window glass separated her from the darkness of the evening, but she could still feel it like she and darkness were sisters.

"Why is the phone not ringing?" she asked.

"They still have no news for us," he sat on the small sofa in the corner of the living room. "But that's not so bad."

Her piercing gaze shifted towards him as the heartbeat inside her chest pounded through her amber-colored fabric.

"It means there is no bad news either," he nodded calmly.

She felt the heat accumulating in the corners of her eyes, and then that same heat flowed down her pearly white cheeks.

"I'm not leaving you alone."

He took a small blanket from the edge of the sofa, covered his long body with it, and gently tapped the place beside him with his hand. For the first time, it didn't bother her. It didn't bother her seeing her husband under the blanket of her solitude. The same blanket she hid under all those nights in the living room, with a book resting on her chest. Instead, she crawled into the shell of his embrace as though pulled into a truce, into a corner feeling some unknown but soft love. Her ginger curls, covered in the light of the night lamp sitting in the corner, diffused all over the edge of the sofa, and his voice found its way to her mind as she drifted off to sleep.

"Do you want me to read you something?" he asked.

She heard the ringing of his coarse voice somewhere on the fields of no man's world, in the space forever hidden from the human eye. It was like a lullaby caressing her eyes, dipping her into a world where her pain was reduced. On a slope where reality ends and dreams begin, she heard his voice and one salty tear traveled gently down her cheek.

"The lanterns will go out."

***

Sometimes, our reality is as bitter as our dreams are sweet. She was woken up by the sound of the phone ringing. For the first couple of moments, she wasn't sure whether her dreams had been sheltering her biggest trepidation or if they had treacherously and abruptly opened the door to reality after the lightness of her dreams.

"Are you sure?"

She heard her husband's voice and felt a blunt pain in her stomach. Suddenly she realized: that the dreams had ended. This is reality.

"How is that possible?"

She approached the door in her wrinkled dress, her wavy hair touching the middle of her beautiful but utterly convulsed back. The floor creaked under her steps. She didn't want her steps to be heard, but she wasn't sure whom she was hiding from. Him? Herself? Or the truth?

"...tell my wife," his voice trembled.

She squeezed the edge of the door strongly enough to keep her on her feet and to chase the blood out of her fingertips. She could feel pain in the depth of her essence. It was the kind of pain that one couldn't put into words. The type of pain that, with an invisible written law, separated a child from its mother.

"Thank you."

He hung up the phone forcefully. The palm of her hand squeezed the door harder as her big eye peeked at him, gazing at his sorrowful presence. Her bright curls fell down her forehead. The question remained somewhere in the void, in the depth of her being, too scared to come out in the shape of letters and words. Still, she realized that if the world gives you something, and you reject it, it finds a way to come back to you so that it can be taken away again – once you acknowledge the value of the thing you rejected earlier. For a moment, it seemed to her that nothing in this world was worth asking the question anymore. She stayed silent, waiting for him to utter a word first, even though she knew very well that nothing would be the same ever again.

JULY, 1982
ZAGREB

"What if she dies before you make up your mind?" he caressed her palm.

Her head repeated that question, basking in its variations: what if? If she dies. What if... if. After all those years, she still felt the atoms of restless rage flowing through her. But she felt joy in some kind of an inter-world between anger and reality. Joy that felt like one of those moments right before her wedding – which she almost missed – or that significant moment when she gazed at a pair of eyes for the first time – the pair of eyes that the two of them had created with their love. The part of her that belonged to that foggy inter-world kept pulling her by the sleeve, calling for her: Go before it's too late. There was, however, always a question standing in the way: but where?

"What if," she exhaled and lowered her gaze towards their intertwined hands, "she already is dead?"

"That fear is reasonable."

His irises moved from left to right as he tried looking at both of her eyes simultaneously.

"No," she pulled her hand out of his. "I didn't know until now. So I don't have to know now, either."

"Tabita," he tilted his head as though trying to reach her carefully hidden world with his gaze, "you deserve to know."

She opened the letter, not even sure herself about the number of times she had been over these same decrepit words.

Miraculous girl,

As much as my soul wants to call you my daughter, I cannot do it. I lost the right to it the moment I decided to concede you to your fate. You made me realize that I am a weak woman of simple principles, lost in this tragedy that struck me. Your life next to me would never have made sense. Mostly, it never would have been beautiful. I wish you all the luck in this world. Let the anger you will likely taste every time you read this letter accompany you in every moment of your life. You ought to deal with life ferociously, especially when it toys with you. If you ever muster the strength to forgive me, it would be a gift I am not worthy of.

P. S. I shan't leave my name between these lines. It's best for you if I stayed dead. Your father... he truly is dead. He lives now only in my memories. His name was Zair.

"How would that even be possible?" she dropped the letter from her hands as it landed on the table. "Where should I look for her?"

"Anywhere," he shrugged. "She's got to be somewhere."

"We've had this conversation a thousand times," she placed her chin in her palm. "And I made inquiries."

Marko grabbed the letter, hoping he would find some new information in it this time.

"It's hopeless," she added.

Karla entered the kitchen and opened the fridge, followed by the clacking sound of high heels.

“I’m late,” she stood on her toes to reach for a glass from the shelf.

“How many times have I told you not to drink cold milk?” Tabita asked.

Karla’s loud swallows became fraught with silence.

“I’m sorry, mommy,” she kissed her, leaving the traces of her milk mustache on her forehead.

“See you,” Karla left the kitchen hurriedly, flaunting the scent of lavender perfume behind her.

She watched her figure disappear at the door. There was something strange in the love towards one’s children. In a roguish way, a parent sees himself through his child. In his scars, he can see the reflection of his mistakes. In his smile, the image of his successes, and parts of their beauty, he starts to love himself. That was precisely what Tabita saw in Karla’s figure. Slenderness, determination, warmth, and bravery. But if she’d seen all those parts in the mirror, she wouldn’t be able to love them so flawlessly. This way, looking at her virtues from a distance, she loved them indestructibly.

Karla was one of Tabita’s biggest loves, and precisely she triggered her hesitation. The thought of never being loved the way she loved Karla, of Karla never being her mother’s mirror, was tough to accept. But the thing that pulled at her other sleeve was a different question: what if my nameless mother doesn’t see anything of hers in me?

“Franjo called me,” he said, chasing away the fog of her thoughts.

She got up and put the coffee pot on.

“What does he want?” she dropped in a teaspoon of sugar into the pot. “That man is manipulating our lives.”

"He's calling me back," he paused. "To Osijek."

Tabita inhaled deeply.

"They need me," he added.

"No," she shook her head and leaned on the thin wood of the kitchen cupboard. "No way."

"I understand," he sighed gently. "But you know very well that's my home."

"Yes," she threw a dirty white dish rag over her shoulder. "I know."

The water started boiling louder, like it desperately wanted to be a part of their argument. She removed the pot from the stove, added two teaspoons of black coffee then put it back on the stove again. They listened to the coffee whispering, crawling toward the edges of the pot.

"Sometimes I wonder if you think you live alone," she watched the darkness of the coffee touch the inside of the white cup. "Are you aware of the fact that we're a family?"

He sighed again, loudly this time.

"Yes," she turned towards him, leaning on the kitchen cupboard. "That is your home, but this is our home."

Just as he prepared to utter a word, she interrupted him.

"And it's not a home we chose for ourselves," she talked through her teeth. "It's a home we created here because of you."

"And we'll do it again," he waved his hands as if searching for answers in the air. "The important thing is that we're okay."

They kept quiet again, diving into each other's eyes – her gaze angry, and his fearful.

“And it’s important,” he got up and approached her, “that you and I stick together.”

“You have children too, you know,” she turned around and started piling up the plates on the tray and the cups on the plates. “We’re not alone.”

“The children will go their own way,” she felt his warm breath on her neck, “because that’s the way it should be. And the best we can do for them is to always,” he placed his lips on her ear, “stick together.”

The rhythm of her heart slowed as her veins welcomed the feeling that only he could fully provoke – peace.

“So, what’s the plan?” she turned to face him.

“Karla will stay here and continue her studies,” he wrapped his arms around her waist.

She nodded.

“It’s better for a student to live alone anyway,” he smiled lightly. “There’s no point in her sharing the apartment with her parents.”

“There’s no point in her living with her brother, either,” she returned the smile.

“That’s between them,” he ran his fingers through her dry and short curls. “For now, they’ll share this apartment.”

She stared into the void, trying to figure things out in her head.

“Zair should come with us,” he stared at her straying eyes. “He can play for Olympia,” he turned her head gently towards him. “You know as well as I do how highly he thinks of them.”

A tear appeared in the corner of her eye.

"Tabita," a wholehearted smile widened his lips, "it's our hometown."

"What about Oto?" she asked.

"Oto will be just fine."

SEPTEMBER, 1980
OSIJEK

He crumpled the paper as it ceased to exist in the pit of his palm. He breathed loudly, heavily, like a buffalo. He didn't recognize an ounce of humanity inside himself. He was like an animal, his instincts barren, destructible even. About twenty crumpled papers lay beside his desk discarded and unacceptable: simply incorrect. The night had started devouring the window glass in front of him like it was hurrying him. A large quantity of work was waiting for him in between the covers of his school notebooks, but not a thing of that work had to do with what he wanted to become – a writer. The night was descending, ruthless towards his tendencies, as he crumpled one paper after another, his mind a vortex trying to think of an ideal man for Dorothy.

Dorothy was the main character of his debut novel. The novel should have already been done by now, according to Patrik's liking. His uncle had already arranged its publication. But the end was not yet near. Dorothy was somewhat of a femme fatale. Her big eyes sucked everyone inside her peculiar world, and her golden hair lured everyone's attention unconditionally. Much of her feminine beauty hid in her hair which housed an almost wicked nature in its threads. Even though Dorothy was a woman that mathematically attracted the male population like a magnet, Patrik could not find an ideal man for her. He wasn't sure whether that inspiration block happened because no man of his imagination would be a good enough yang for her yin or if, somewhere deep inside, he was furious at the fact that he was not a man suitable enough to dive into her world.

***

Patrik's peers were almost always walking in groups towards school, mellowing in mutual exclamations, cigarette smoke, and the smell of colognes stolen from their fathers' shelves, but Patrik walked alone. He believed that was how things were with writers because writers were already too busy with the company of the characters born from the tint of their letters.

That day, as he was being touched by the coldness of the autumn air and the shy sun rays, he thought about Dorothy. Do I know her enough? Who is she, really? Dorothy. The letters of her name. A girl. A woman. A princess. Or a queen? He shook his head. Why is she so evasive? It's like she doesn't want to be described. It's as if she doesn't want to be placed in a frame of my small letters. He watched as his black leather shoes touched the rotten leaves. She's so... distant. Private. I have to see her. Truly see her. She has to reveal herself to me. He shuddered lightly at the thought. His words seemed to have a life of their own. I must see her naked, hear her moan, and meet her essence. He inhaled deeply as lust started filling his body. I have to feel the smell of her breath in the morning and the scent of her body after making love.

Dorothy was the first real character in his stories. His uncle told him about the fact that every writer, at a particular moment in his creation, has this tendency to make his characters truly alive. For the writer, they become tangible, permanent, just like any other known reality. And then chaos starts to reign. The writer begins living for his characters, just like he does for every other physical person. He hears them calling to him, begging him to continue the story, breathe life into them, and give them tragedy, love, and death. A limit can never exist between a true character and a true writer – they tangle with each other, unite, and merge.

For a long time, Patrik didn't realize what his uncle was talking about. For years he thought up some layered stories and made-up loyal characters. But when he met Dorothy, he realized those characters before her weren't true. Those were simply ordinary figures subjecting themselves to the story's circumstances and needs. Nothing more.

Dorothy sometimes subjected herself to the story's circumstances as well, but above all, the circumstances subjected themselves to her. Every moment that Patrik experienced had already in advance belonged to her, driven by some invisible law. All of his reality – gathered in an immensely small lump of life – he gifted to Dorothy. Sometimes, that would drain his youth and eat away at his livelihood, but at the same time, it would fill him with the powers of immortality. The powers that he so grudgingly and silently reigned over.

***

The unpleasant odor of the rooms after the lunch break, that mixture of food and sweat, and the giant birthmark on their teacher's chin would be the only thing Patrik remembered from the whole school day upon returning home. Feeling weary, he'd sit across the table from his uncle in their spacious kitchen at one of the two heads of the heavy, wooden table. Sometimes he would be surprised as to how they even heard each other, given the fact that the table was more than 13 feet long. Then, every evening anew, he'd listen to his uncle's stories about the writers of the Strike Hunt magazine. How mentally weak and submissive they were and much too soulless in their writing. Then he would slowly get up from the table, trying hard not to offend his uncle with the interruption of his same old story, and take a seat in his corner of the living room.

Dorothy was his biggest curse for the next few years. He could hardly fathom how many of her character traits belonged to a girl that had been striding through his school hallways.

Metamorphoses

AUGUST, 1958
BUDVA

She couldn't hear nor understand the priest's words over her wails. They were constant wails that took over everyone's presence at the funeral like a powerful vortex. He held her in his arms, squeezing his fingertips into her sullen shoulders, barely keeping her decrepit soul alive, while all she felt was a squeeze of some unknown palms. It felt like her spirit and Petar's abandoned body was traveling underground. Angel. Angel. He's an Angel. My Angel. He is. My son... She tried to restrain the bitterness in her throat, but the touch was so pungent, and the vigorous outflow of sorrow had to find its way out somehow.

"No!" she tore herself away from his arms and kneeled on the wet ground.

His warmth heeded over her, embracing her convulsed body, trapping her in the world of life.

"Get him out," she talked through the foam accumulating between her two weary lips. "Get him out," her hands started trembling. "Get him out."

They threw dark, moist dirt on Petar's hardly two decades-old dead body, neatly placed in a brown casket that was the shape of the biggest sorrow that would ever mark her life. They headed back, together with the buglers' sounds and the lingering rattle of the raindrops that cried with them. Where? No. Her legs tread, but her mind seemed to control her body for her. They were heading back, but she didn't know where. The life that continued for her, that senselessness that she stepped into that day, had become illiterate, unsaid. All the days that passed by had no basis, and all the hatred that she felt toward her fate seemed to pour right into him. Her husband became the nucleus of her rage, her unstoppable despair, and her lead-heavy sorrow. The sorrow that would never heal. And somewhere in the depths of her soul, the depths that stood there like mere ruins of a castle that once stood high above the ground, she knew he understood that.

***

She stopped talking for a couple of months after Petar died. At that time, the only thing she did was cook. The same meal, over and over. Petar's favorite, polenta. She made polenta for breakfast, lunch, and dinner. Her husband, in turn, ate polenta for breakfast, lunch, and dinner. Every night before reclining in the armchair and falling asleep while staring at an empty wall stained with moisture, she'd spend time in the room where Petar once made his ships in bottles.

"My son is just in a deep sleep," those were the only words she knew how to utter.

Every night he would diligently sit next to her, embracing her somber dead-like body, kissing her sullen cheeks, combing through her ginger hair with his fingers, trying to breathe life into her being. But like all the years before, the love was not returned. After a few painstaking months, he gave up on that, too.

In the morning, he'd peck her on the cheek to thank her for breakfast, eat his portion of polenta and leave for the garden that was now prettier than ever before. Unlike the one that reigned over his wife, his sorrow always found a way to blossom. Every person in a particular moment in their life falls into one of those two groups. The first group is made of people who leave their sorrow as it is, in that dark form that it first appeared in, watering its black roots so that its tentacles can enclose the walls of their life. The people from the other group are the ones who submit their sorrow to metamorphosis. Their sorrow, over time, turns from an unsightly caterpillar into a colorful butterfly flying around the room. Those kinds of people, imprisoned in the insurmountable thirst for the sun, weave the smiles of others out of their sorrow.

Then, when the friendship between him and his greenery ceased for the day, he'd leave for his workshop at the end of the garden. That workshop was the summit on the slope of their sorrow, with a view of the valleys of some other worlds. When the clock in the corner of the workshop ticked noon, he'd return home and eat his second portion of polenta, which was only a few hours later than the last one, classified as lunch. Then he'd put Žanet in Petar's bed for her afternoon nap and return to the workshop.

When the night started descending, and when he caught sight of the initial thin outline of the moon on the clear sky stretched above his glass workshop, he would return inside, lock the door, and eat his third portion of polenta that under the starry night's touch, classified as dinner. After the last morsels of his food, he would close himself in the bathroom for ten minutes, then make his way to the room painfully filled with ships in bottles. He'd carry her fragile body to the armchair, kiss her forehead good night, and after passing the Stations of the Cross that marked the way to the upper floor, he'd lie in their bedroom's cold bed.

SEPTEMBER, 1982
OSIJEK

"That's how you do it," his uncle laid his bear-like hand on his shoulder. "You'll finally make a name for our small family."

He shook his shoulders, not wiping the smile off his face; his gaze locked on everyone in front of them waiting for Patrik's promotion. He knew his uncle was proud of him – the sole rhythm of his breathing and the strength of the touch on Patrik's trembling shoulder revealed it to him. For a long time, he feared he'd never become a good enough writer, that a story worth telling would never cross his mind, and that he'd never create a chain of letters worth reading. However, his fear had come to an end. They were standing there, side by side, strangely united, getting ready to promote his collection of eleven prose works.

However, he still hadn't finished his debut novel. He couldn't find the right man for Dorothy. In those two heavy years of sheer devotion, there had been but one change, her long blonde hair he adored so intensely was now cut off. Killed. But, to his amazement, Dorothy remained as impeccable as ever. It seemed there was no way for her to lose her significance, instead, she poured her charms from one thing to another: from one palm to the other, from her bosom to her hips, from her eyes to her teeth, from her hair to her lips, and so on into infinity. Strange magic hid behind her value. She was almost like the first real perpetuum mobile.

He observed the abundance of people in front of him that restlessly stared. One moment at him, the next one at the book in front of them. Then a grand silence came upon them; a silence that opened an invisible door to the applause. The applause's piercing and brilliant sound would remain echoing in Patrik's mind for the next few years. The sound of the thrill, the approval, the acceptance. The sound of silent belonging. Patrik might not possess all the qualities of a writer, but he had a writer's eye. Instead of looking at the crowds and the size of it all, his pupil was always aimed at the details. At his promotion, a woman caught his eye in that massive cluster of people. Pregnant, curly hair, big green eyes. Her snub nose gave her beauty a dash of oddity. He'll always remember her smile that gave way to her uneven teeth and the warmth of support she emanated as a symbol of his first book promotion. It must have been that motherly smile that his mind kept conjuring up. He realized that the shadows of motherhood could be recognized even in strangers.

***

The sickness that ruled over him whenever he'd leave for class in high school stopped the moment he stepped into his college building. He studied literature. After that, his favorite subject, Croatian language, broke into interesting pieces, and all the other obnoxious high school subjects disappeared. Even though for years he had been waiting for the time he'd no longer have to set foot into his high school's building, he'd always pass by the high school's backyard. Sometimes, the end of his classes would coincide with the school lunch break.

Then he'd see her there chewing the apple, skimming through some papers, leaning on the black iron fence. Her lips were always moist, and her soft fingertips with aggressively clipped nails were always sensually touching the apple's redness. The ends of her short hair danced defiantly above her round shoulders, and the messy fringe on her forehead awakened the lust in his body and mind. It seemed she had that subtle power to unite those two lusts in him. That erotic desire at its peak ended with the urge to lay his lips on that bright forehead. He was sure of one thing, no one in this world was smarter than that woman.

One ordinary, sunny Wednesday, not knowing how he even managed to muster up the courage, he approached the iron fence.

“Hi,” he grabbed onto the iron bend of the fence. “Sorry if I’m bothering you.”

Her eye caught a glimpse of his, making its way through the gate's iron bars.

“I’ve been watching you for quite some time and,” the excitement made his voice tremble. “I’d like to give you a book.”

A frown arose on her face.

“You’ve been watching me for quite some time,” she placed the half-eaten apple in her backpack and wiped her lips with her palm.

“Well,” he waved his hand. “My college is hereabouts, and you’re always eating in the same place,” he gestured at the air where a couple of seconds earlier she held her apple, “so it wasn’t all that hard to notice you.”

Quietly, her lips widened into a gentle smile.

“Uh-huh,” she locked her gaze on the book he held under his armpit, still chewing on that bit of apple. “And what kind of a book is that?”

“It’s my book,” he grabbed it in his hands. “I published it recently, and,” he tilted his head lightly, “you look like someone who could understand it.”

For the first time in the history of his existence, he felt the warmth of his own smile.

"Well, alright then," she reached through the gate, picking through her teeth with her tongue, "I'll read it."

DECEMBER, 1982
OSIJEK

A glum expression was painted on her face the whole day. She was trying to solve a single mathematical equation in her head repeatedly. The cold breeze touched her cheeks, her nose seemed to have frozen completely, and the fingers in her pockets weren't far from the same fate. It was starting to get dark outside, bringing peace to her body. Unlike the darkness, the light didn't suit her those days because it tirelessly reminded her of all her daily chores and obligations that she had never been good at. Her mind kept choosing letters and words, while the other subjects like math, physics, and chemistry were all related to numbers, one way or the other – and numbers were, at the very least, the other side of the coin of the world she was so extremely and particularly immersed in. Luckily, it was the last day of the first semester, and the classes were over.

Two kids ran past her. A girl with long, brown hair hidden underneath a white woolly hat with the ends of her hair folded up from the cold, and the boy, a bit taller than her, blonde, without his two front teeth. They sang Christmas songs. She smiled at them slightly and pushed the bakery door, then started taking off all the layers of her clothes as she stepped in.

"Sorry, the traffic was really heavy," she tied the apron around her waist.

"It's fine," he placed the raw dough on the counter and started taking his apron off. "The important thing is that you're here."

She fixed her ponytail, staring at his agitated reflection in the mirror.

"Thank you for stepping in," he stuffed his body in an old, worn-out coat.

"How is she?"

"They say she'll be fine," he grabbed his black hat from the coat hanger in the corner. "She had a difficult day."

He went out without a goodbye. But she couldn't hold it against him – his wife was, after all, the most valuable thing in his life. He couldn't find the time to spend with her from all the work, but in his heart, he felt the kind of love for her that made even Nadja feel goosebumps.

***

She didn't like how the pastries looked in the display window, so she rearranged them. Doughnuts always brought back memories - of mornings, of Ilir's hugs, of her mother, of the cupboard and her legs dancing above it, of the first stories and the purity of childhood. Then, a sudden touch of coldness brought an abrupt stop to her thoughts. The room where her mother baked pastries every morning was freezing, and the window was open. Ilir probably forgot to close it before he went home; his mind had already wandered off into his wife's embrace. She closed the window, cursed the cold, and heard the bell that indicated someone was entering.

It was a young man in a gray coat with a woolly hat on his head. She reckoned he was about her age, but she was in no mood for that sort of company, not in the least.

"Good evening," she grabbed a rag from the counter, "How can I help you, sir?"

She started wiping the bread slicer, wondering if she seemed too rude for not looking into her client's eyes. There was no response. She looked up and saw him standing mutely holding a worn-out leather wallet, observing all the pastries – braided bagels, kifli, small kifli, pretzels, and doughnuts. The doughnuts were the main attraction of their offer.

"What will it be, Sir?"

She felt strange referring to him as "Sir," given the fact that they seemed to be peers. She continued polishing the bread slicer leaving the young man alone with his thoughts.

"Chocolate."

"Sorry?" she was now brushing the bread slicer with a dry rag.

"Chocolate. I love the chocolate ones."

Chocolate. Chocolate. Leaves. Ball. Bruise on her eye. Soccer field. Gate. Curly hair. Chocolate. A tingling sensation danced through her body, and her hand stopped moving without her control as it rested on the dirty rag.

"Strawberry," she muttered, still gazing at the rag under her hand. "I love the strawberry ones."

She heard a muffled laugh and the sound of the tiny wallet pocket opening.

"Ah, strawberry doughnut," he placed the coins on the display window. "Nadja, you love the impossible."

She watched him close his wallet while a stray curl of hair curiously crawled from underneath his hat.

"Maybe you're right," she crossed her arms on her chest.

"We're not talking about ice cream here anymore," a faint smile crept up on one side of his lips.

She dove into his gaze with a peculiar desire to cut into the sole essence of his pupils and leave him with an indelible memory of her eyes.

"One chocolate doughnut, please."

He stuffed his hands in his coat pockets and observed her the way people observe something they know belongs to them.

"You always just appear out of nowhere," she put the doughnut in a paper bag.

"It just seems that way."

"Maybe you're right," she handed him the bag.

His index finger was sticking out of his glove.

"You know," he uttered, having already placed his hand on the door handle, "I live here now."

She placed her hand on the rag again without any particular reason.

"So I thought, if you have time...."

A colorful silence reigned among them.

"It's winter break," she smiled.

***

Nadja's mother was a pretty woman. She had an elongated face, a slightly tapered chin, blue cat-like eyes, a snub nose, and hair that always neatly fell to the middle of her back. Nadja observed her as she drank her morning coffee and skimmed through the newspaper.

"You're so pretty," she rested her head on her palm.

"Goodness, Nadja," she smiled shyly. "What came over you?"

"Nothing," she wrapped a lock of hair around her finger. "You're just pretty."

"You, my dear," she licked her finger and turned the page, "are blind."

"Says the woman with glasses on her nose."

"Hanuma," she raised her eyebrows. "Don't mess with me." She took a sip of coffee. "So – how did you sleep?"

"Alright," she circled the edge of the cup with her fingers. "I didn't read myself to sleep last night, and my brain is oddly rested."

"You liked it better when your mother used to read to you. I know it."

The sound of the doorbell interrupted their dialogue. Nadja got up to stir the semolina they decided to have for breakfast, and her mother went to open the door. As the semolina bounced around the pot, all bubbly, she perked her ears to try to hear who was at the door. But alas, unsuccessfully. She could only hear her mother's mumbling. Then, she heard steps – her mother's morning ones, but also a set of another, louder ones which sounded much more shrewd. She thought she heard the clacking of heels – and truly, she wasn't wrong – but they were man's shoes.

"Nadja," her mother tightened her bathrobe shyly, "this gentleman's asking for you."

She stood there, exposed in her white spotted pajamas and the ragged slippers that her mother knitted for her two years earlier. Her hair a complete mess, and her fringe almost electrified.

"Good day, Nadja."

"Good day," she tried to fix her hair as best she could.

Her mother widened her gaze, gesturing at the gentleman's hand with her eyes, to which Nadja – as baffled as she was – flinched and shook the stranger's hand.

"Would you like some coffee?" her mother took the burnt semolina off the stove. "Maybe a brandy?"

"Coffee is fine," the gentleman sat at the table and answered, smiling at Nadja. "To energize us."

Although Nadja estimated his age was around fifty, his appearance was rich with something youthful and presentable. He wore a white shirt, completely skin-tight to his colossal body, and around it, a gray vest made from a stiff material, with round-framed glasses hanging off the small pocket on the vest.

"Let us not delay this anxiety-riddled moment of your lack of understanding as to why I'm here," he reached for his cup of coffee. "I came here because I'm interested in Nadja."

Nadja and her mother shared a questionable look: Because he's what?

"Interested?" her mother cleared her throat.

"Certainly," the gentleman took a sip of coffee and placed the cup back on its plate. "I've heard that Nadja writes."

Her mother exhaled in relief, but Nadja grew frightened and exposed.

"You heard what?" she asked.

"What is more," the gentleman turned towards Nadja, "I read some of your works."

She felt all her works slipping through her fingers, like parts of her soul that she couldn't hold anymore. She felt like she couldn't hide from this hungry world.

"That's not possible," she shook her head. "Nothing that I wrote was ever published."

"No, nobody read your works," he placed his palms in front of him, cupping the plate, "except your mother," he looked at her and nodded as if he were elegantly bowing down to her, "and Mr. Ilir."

"Ilir," she laid her hands in her lap, "that's right."

"I like your writing style."

"Thank you," she replied formally.

She felt exposed. Betrayed. Sold out.

"Well, it's time to introduce myself finally, isn't it?" he flattened his vest. "Franjo Bošnjak," he got up and shook her mother's hand, then Nadja's, "a pleasure."

His surname seemed familiar to Nadja.

"I'm the editor of the magazine Strike Hunt," he sat down again.

Nadja opened her big eyes widely. She knew about that magazine. In fact, she read their issues regularly.

"Have you had any chance to skim over an issue or two?"

Her mother fidgeted in her chair.

"Yes," Nadja cleared her throat. "I read it often."

“Then, I believe,” he crossed his legs, “that you would like very much to write something for us.”

A short silence reigned over them. Nadja could almost feel her mother’s lit-up gaze touching her.

“M-me?” she felt short of breath.

“Surely,” he carefully pushed the cup away from him, letting them know how he’d soon be ready to leave.

Although she’d never discussed business before with anyone, especially having to do with writing, a part of her soul whispered to her: authority emits strength.

“Could I have some time,” she cleared her throat again, “to think about it?”

“As much as you need.”

***

She went out onto the freshness of the December air, inhaling its prudence as it grazed the irregular circles of her ears. Writing for a magazine. A magazine. Our dreams always tend to be brave when they’re sitting protected in the depths of our minds, under the cover of the unreal, but their bravery subsides the moment they touch the light of day. No matter how many times Nadja asked herself why – why was it that the dreams often wanted to remain just dreams – she had no better answer but a simple fact in our minds when they’re the most protected and the most powerful, our dreams can be whatever we wish them to be. When they come out and finally reveal themselves, they become a strange mixture of us and the rest of the world. But those dreams exist precisely because of their tendency towards blending with the world, which seemed to be the essence of their true magic. I have to. There’s no other choice.

At that precise moment, when she didn’t know where she was headed off to other than to her mind, her heartbeat hastened.

He was standing there, blended with the ramshackle façade of her house, with his hands in his pockets.

"You again," a shy smile quivered on her lips.

"Me again."

"And right in front of my house," she looked at the ground, boldly hiding her smile.

"I know where you live," he stood in front of her. "I guess you've forgotten that."

"I thought you'd forgotten," she dove into him with her gaze.

"You don't forget things like that," he shook his head.

"Like what?"

"Childhood things," he smiled and nodded his head.

She tilted her head gently, staring at him – how people stare at something they know belongs to them.

"Cherry."

"Cherry?" he chuckled quizzically.

"I like cherry tea," she bit on her lower lip.

And suddenly, there was silence, soft silence.

"I don't like tea."

Her breath caught. The door leading them to the next moment had suddenly disappeared.

"But we have to stop with these games," he created a new door, which seemed an inch more infinite than the last one. "Shall we?"

"Let's."

***

They were sitting on the flat roof of the skyscraper he lived in. She snuck out for the first time, knowing that her mother wouldn't wake up and thus wouldn't worry or get mad. The essence of human feelings always had that one loophole where ignorance nullified the pain.

"Why did you do it?"

"Why did I do what?" she tucked her knees under her long coat.

"Your hair," he stared at the foggy winter sky above them.

"Why did I cut it?" she glanced at the tips of her blonde locks that barely reached her shoulders. "I don't know, I felt like it."

"I like your fringe," he glanced at it, all wavy from the cold.

She stared into his eyes and peacefully admitted to herself: there was something magical in staring into the eyes that are staring back at us.

"It's so ugly," he smiled softly.

Then she realized the ugliest words could hide the prettiest of meanings. Her laugh sailed through the sky, synchronizing with the sound of the wind. He absorbed her laugh with his whole being as if he wanted to bite out and swallow a chunk of it –to keep it there forever, in the essence of his soul.

Her leather boots creaked as she got up to kneel while her orange leg warmers relieved the coldness of the roof. He didn't turn around as curiosity coursed through her veins: is he scared? Or does he genuinely know my presence so instinctively that he feels it's not the right time to turn around?

"Are they ugly?" she asked with a muffled, self-contained voice.

He turned around as the partial grayness of his eyes gazed towards her naked moonlit breasts that magically peeked out of her black woolly dress. The two halves of her rich lips separated, and her big eyes found their way to his figure through the darkness. He had a hunger in his eyes that she never forgot as his trembling hands remained on the coldness of the roof. She knew very well that those hands wanted to touch her; the pit of his stomach was filled with a burning sensation from the desire to do so. She could hear his ragged exhale, which she loved the sound of. Even though she'd never heard it before, she knew she had loved it since the beginning of time. It's funny how prone some people are to turning our whole world upside down, shattering even the smallest part of our previous reality, and creating a timeless world without rules, regulations, or questions. Justified precisely by that newly created world, she felt the essence of his being inside her. Even though there was some blank space between them.

"Yes," he replied.

"They must be two of the ugliest things you've ever seen."

"Everything that you know, I know, too" he answered.

***

She was once again, after three long years, sitting on the same bleachers, holding the brown (now almost fully written out) leather notebook that Ilir got her for her birthday in her lap. It survived, truth be told, just because she decided to write only her favorite and most important stories. She watched his movements follow the ball, how he juggled it from one knee to the other, jumping in the air, touching it with the softness of his curls, then looking at her, breathless. She thought of herself as the ball of his life, the one whom his gaze would always wander off to and the one who would always somehow – following the simple rules of physics – roll under his feet.

She could hardly believe the thick heads of those soccer players who, along with him, honed their abilities in the coldest of winters. She was a writer. Her field was the warmth of her home, an autumn or summer night, tea, cocoa, and, maybe sometimes, the touch of the record player needle.

Upon the end of his practice, they'd usually go to Trica, a small café close to the river Drava. She would sip her tea, and his cappuccino, and her words would keep piling up. She would tell him about the novels she was working on, the collaboration with Franjo Bošnjak and his mellifluous praises, her inspiration, the things she was at that moment, and the things she was hoping to become. Had she said any of those things to someone else, someone who wasn't Zair – whose eyebrows weren't so funnily united in the middle of his forehead, whose smile wasn't so wide, and whose hands weren't so desirable – she'd think that her stories were far too tiresome. But when she felt his gaze glued to her face humbly, she even loved talking about herself.

***

Four months of their tradition passed instantly. A tradition where not a day passed without their trajectories intertwining, at least for a short while. She knew every most profound detail of his being.

She knew that his mother was an orphan, never having met her mother, and that he was named after her mother's father, who died before she was even born. At least, that's what his grandmother said in a letter to his mother. She knew the hoarseness of her voice and the distinctiveness of the gray eyes that Zair inherited from her.

She knew he had a sister named Karla, who was studying medicine in Zagreb, and a brother named David, who remained in Zagreb because of his girlfriend. She knew that his father was a writer for the magazine she had been writing for. She knew that

Zair had unveiled the secrets of sex for the first time when he was sixteen and with a girl six years older than him.

She knew he didn't like coffee, and when he did drink it, he did so without milk, bottoms up, and closed eyes. She knew that he was never particularly fond of school, having been dragged out by the ears on the last day of it – which was also the last day of his high school in Zagreb – and that in those three years of high school, it always took a makeup exam for him to pass math. She also knew that math was his strongest suit, but he rarely skimmed through his notebook, which he didn't write much in during class anyway.

She knew that his brother and sister would almost always eat all of his dinner because he had a habit of practicing his soccer moves in the living room and therefore sitting at the table much later than everyone else. She knew that his cheek was truly soft to the touch and that he had this unbelievably nimble tendency to caress the back of her head as her hair squeaked under his touch. She knew just that, and nothing else. And in those four months of tradition, she hadn't laid her lips on his, not once.

Zair

APRIL, 1983
OSIJEK

They were gaining distance from Olympia down the wavy street.

“Nadja, you don’t understand,” his hands danced through the air. “I’m not good enough.”

“But you only just got here,” she was sure that she had already said that out loud a good couple of times by now, “give them time to get to know you.”

“I didn’t only just get here,” he scratched his lips nervously. “I’ve been on their team for half a year already and still haven’t made first line.”

“What about the others?” she stepped out in front of him, blocking his path. “They’ve been playing for this team for years.”

Silence crawled in between them, broken up only by his agitated sighs. She approached him and tilted her head so she could see both of his eyes.

“Your half a year doesn’t seem so bad compared to their years.”

“But I’m not a beginner,” he bowed his head. “I’m not.”

"Hey," she gently touched the edge of his chin with her fingers.

His lips anxiously squeezed against one another. Hers. Hers. Hers. It was all hers. The depths of her insides whispered to her as if translating the hidden codes of his soul, exposing the secrets of his body language: every last bit. Every bit of his being belonged to her – his wide smile, ever so often caused by her, and that fitful warp of his lips. The universe spared no expense. It placed a whole being in the pit of her palm. Zair came with a set of happiness that they multiplied and the sadness they cut in half.

Her eyes, as if torn away from the rest of her body, ran towards his lips which also seemed like a torn part of her, waiting to merge with her again. But she was convinced that he'd push her away. He'd run away once their two kindred bodies connected, scared by the light that would arise from it. Just as the fear once again almost overpowered the feeling of belonging, that inner flashing light of her soul whispered to her: every last bit.

Ten. Heated needles dance inside her body.

Nine. Especially around her waist that the palm of his hand is placed on.

Eight. Her nose dips into the softness of his cheeks.

Seven. He lets out a muffled groan.

Six. Enormous tenderness prances up to her eyelids.

Five. His lips are slowing their rhythm as though putting magic itself to sleep.

Four. His fingertips firmly dive into the skin of her waist.

Three. The pain he inflicts doesn't hurt.

Two. With a final gentle touch, he separates his lips from hers.

One. He kisses the tip of her nose.

***

The night was shimmery. One of those nights that announce the summer with its smell. The smell of the grass slowly burns, the tarmac warming up, and clean clothes drying in the backyard of almost everyone in Osijek.

Across the big Ante Starčević Square, they descended towards the promenade that bloomed with life. The children ran around loudly, personifying the heralds of spring and summer, and the adults tread gently toward beauty. A boy with his hair reaching the tips of his shoulders grazed Nadja's hip while running. She turned around and realized he was running into an embrace of an older gentleman. Grandfather – that's his grandfather. Running had this impenetrable beauty to it, especially if we run toward the safety of someone's arms.

They sat on the sole edge of the promenade. The almost inaudible murmuring of the river that ever so magnificently crawled in its undisturbed direction reminded her of the fire crackling. The crackling, on the other hand – penetrating the veil of memories – reminded her of that time she went camping with her father. The camping happened only once. Even though she was promised they would do it every six months. Zair's slurping placed the memory cluster back in its place, in that foggy inter-world, and she glued her eyes on his figure. As usual, he elicited a smile from her face. He sucked the ice cream from its tip as the melted chocolate painted his mustache and beard.

With a swift whistling movement, he threw half his ice cream into the river and started looking around. She knew very well of his provocation. He'd hold a bite of something in his mouth, usually something sweet, and start looking around, all confused, waiting for her to take that last bite. With her lips. With her teeth, screaming from all the fun she was having. Because she never had nearly as much fun as she had while next to him. And so she accepted his challenge. She pinched his lip with hers, claiming that lost piece of the chocolate ice cream and with it claiming a piece of him as well.

She loved the ordinary nights spent with him. Ordinary people sometimes had this extraordinary tendency to reshape our moments into something marvelous and unforgettable out of only a few worn-out mundane pieces. That way, all those colorfully assembled moments of our life stay engraved in the line of our fate, like mute childhood scars. And just like that, ordinary people become magical. The two of them sat on the riverbank - a highlight of her childhood. They were under some sort of eternal code as the river wrote down her dreams and the traits of her piercing nature in the nooks and crannies of its magnificent flowing. She tucked her hands under her legs, feeling the sharp concrete jab into them. That unfaltering feeling of enlightenment struck her: Never again – this exact moment. Never again – the same feeling. And then a funny truth quivered in the air before her: shades, hues, and tones of this life are one hell of a powerful thing.

She glanced to the left. His profile. He had tiny nostrils; she often wondered how he managed to breathe, and his forehead housed a small dent that only she could notice. It would be a truly unattractive detail if anyone else were in question. But this way, in their comfortable reality, it was him she was talking about, and every time he lay his head in her lap, as he often did, that small dent made her want to touch his forehead, kiss it, lean her round cheek on it.

"I'll give it to you someday."

He gazed at the starry sky that was so full of stars that night. It looked like the moon died, and billions of stars burst out of it. She gazed at him – at the billions of stars hidden in the pocket of his being.

"Give me what?"

"A star," she joined his gaze towards the sky. "One star." He smiled. It was not a half-assed or a sour smile but an honest and fluid line on his face. "Heh, that's easy," he pressed his lips to her ear, "when they're free."

She bit her lower lip ferociously, trying to prevent the smile wanting to arise to the touch of his soft breath.

"Free things tend to be the most expensive," she touched the tip of his nose with hers.

***

The hands of the living room clock concluded yet another circle, and it was midnight. The night embraced their windows as the streetlights remained the only wake figure in a usually very crowded street. Zair and Nadja were still concentrating on making her mother's birthday cake.

They burned the first cake, which ended up in the trash, while the second one – somewhat more successful – slipped out of Zair's hands, blew up all over the sticky kitchen floor, and ended up in that same trash. The third cake was promising, but Zair was banned from participating. Nadja baked it herself while he sat guiltily at the table and watched her hair sway left and right above her shoulders as she stirred the cream. Nadja wondered how exhausted her mother had to be to not hear all those fishy sounds of midnight baking coming from the kitchen.

"There," she placed the tray with the cake on the table, "What do you think?"

The cake was as white as snow, with clumsily cut strawberries placed on the edges of it. In the middle stood Nadja's chocolate-filled handwriting inside a circle made out of small candles.

Happy birthday, girl!

"I think it's..." he smiled widely, hoping that her anger about the cake that he ruined had subsided by now, "perfect!"

"You better," she took the cake off the table and put it in the fridge.

"I never wanted to...."

"Enough!" she turned towards him, yelling in a whisper. "We could have been done with this ages ago if it weren't for your...."

"I'm sorry," his lips formed a diagonal line as his puppy eyes stared at her.

"You're so clumsy!"

"I know," he approached her from the back as she wiped the kitchen cupboard clean.

She dove into his embrace with the back of her head and exhaled. As she bowed her head, she noticed how dirty and flour-stained her jeans were.

"You're so," his breath caressed her ear, "dirty." He emphasized the letter *r*.

***

Her mother didn't suspect a thing. Nadja gave her a gift over breakfast: flamingly red slippers that she knitted herself, and her mother, pleased as she was, thought it was the last of her celebrations. When they came to the bakery, after she'd already put her white apron on and humbly decided to forget that it was her day, Ilir and Nadja welcomed her with cake and song. Nadja noticed a tear rolling down her face, lit up by the light of the candles, humbly fused with the beauty of the moment. Sometimes only a handful of those right people are the ones who make an actual crowd. As her mother cut the cake, Nadja noticed Zair's figure approaching the bakery rapidly.

"I didn't miss much, did I?" he asked, breathless.

"Not at all," she embraced his neck with her arms. "Let's go inside and eat cake."

Ilir's wife was, just like every other day in Nadja's memory, sitting in front of the bakery in a wheelchair. Her weak knees covered with a blanket and her dry lips squeezing a cigarette. Although silence and instability were part of her nature, she uttered an indistinguishable sound. Her body started shaking, her forehead dampened, the cigarette fell from her lips to the ground, and her eyes filled with thick tears.

"Goodness," Nadja crouched beside her and placed her palms on her trembling knees. "What's wrong?"

Her tremor grew into resistance, and Nadja wasn't sure whether her presence was more helpful or harmful.

"Don't," Ilir approached, cupping her face with his chubby hands. "Don't, everything is fine."

With a handkerchief, he wiped the saliva that started dripping down the edges of her lips and caressed her dry hairs that loosened out of control. She continued speaking indistinguishably, and Ilir moved his ear closer to her lips to understand her better.

"Everything is fine," he spoke, looking at Nadja serenely. "Don't..."

His gaze, always so placid and unshakably steady, now assumed a shade that Nadja couldn't recognize. He seemed stunned.

"No," he said quietly, still listening to what she was saying. "My love, you know that's not possible."

The stunned look in his eyes turned into something more specific. Something delicate. What did she tell him? Then, with a gentle sigh, he broke eye contact with Nadja and pointed his gaze toward Zair.

"He's gone, my darling," he kissed her forehead. "You imagined it."

She leaned her head on Ilir's wide shoulder as the tremor in her body faded.

"It's all in your head, darling," he started gently rocking her head on his shoulder, "it's all in your head."

Chameleons

OCTOBER, 1960
BUDVA

"...without the wheelchair," she heard her husband's muffled voice coming from the doctor's office, "I'd help her."

She couldn't decipher the doctor's words; his voice was far too gentle.

"If you give us time..." she heard her husband's hacking words once again. "...would help her."

She was unsure why she couldn't discern what they were talking about. Was it because of the thick wall separating them, the door not being ajar enough, or because her mind was slowly retreating from the grasp of her control?

"Alright, ... will that be?" her husband's enthusiastic tone faded briefly. "...that I'll currently be able to."

She brought a cigarette to her lips and lit a match with her trembling fingers. She loved that first piercing huff of smoke, which gave the dark corners of her mind a blissful feeling, provoking the thought: let it kill me slowly.

"Certainly," her husband's voice was approaching the door. "Thank you, doctor."

His eyes widened in a stupefied gaze.

"Žanet, not here!" he leaped towards her, kissed her forehead, and pulled the cigarette out of her mouth. "When we get home," he stepped on it, then picked up the butt, placing it in the pocket of his brown jacket, "you can do it as much as you like."

She smiled brokenly, ridiculing every inch of his existence.

***

She did not make polenta anymore. She did not cook at all anymore. He did all the housework while she sat, sometimes holding a book on her knees without reading it, and smoked cigarettes. Sometimes she emerged from the darkness of her soul for just a moment – as he washed the dishes or swept the floor – and she would hear his sobs. But it was all the same to her whether the dishes would be washed, the floors swept, or ultimately, how he felt.

When the morning dawned, he gently persuaded her to sit on the veranda and catch a glimpse of the sun. She caught a chance to see her husband through a different set of eyes. Every morning the same woman approached their gate. She was plump, her hair distinctly black and long, her eyebrows dark, and her eyes big. So big that Žanet herself – a few feet away and besotted by her psyche – could discern that they were dark brown. She'd stand there, her hands pressed against the short wooden fence, her eyes filled with joy. Žanet's husband, on the other hand, had only one pair of eyes that he looked at with genuine joy, as loyalty locked his heart away for all the other women of the world. Sometimes, our unhappiness lies precisely in trying to please the hearts that save no place for us.

Had her sanity served her more faithfully, maybe she would have driven him away into the arms of that woman who would bring about a new world – a better one. However, so many sensations were missing in her essence that she couldn't paint a clear picture of the happiness and unhappiness of others.

Everything was an incomprehensible straight line for her – an overmuch colorless one.

JUNE, 1983
OSIJEK

Nadja's plans preoccupied her mind as she wondered what would happen to her writing once she started university. So many nights she'd spent beside the warm orange light of the night lamp, her nose stuffed in a book.

Sometimes, Zair would sit on her bedroom window, leaning on the window frame, watching her repeat what she had already read. She could feel his gaze – touching the roundness of her cheeks, the tips of her long blonde eyelashes, her lips in movement, her pale fingertips dancing through the air, the light baby hairs emerging from her high, long ponytail, and the dimple in her right cheek. She tried to familiarize him with the possibility of attending college, but she soon realized that it would not be a part of his world. So she settled for a mighty sight: Zair, a successful soccer player. Living his dream and feeding off of it.

Nadja's mother was losing her mind, even more so than Nadja herself. She loved her writing and encouraged her reading, but by no means did she want it to be the thing Nadja did for a living. She did not deem real the possibility of a writer bringing food on the table. Nadja saw it in her mother's gaze and her hands, which now tended to hold Nadja's works clammily and impatiently. Her mother found it easy to hate Nadja's writing, for it threatened the quality of her life.On the other hand, Ilir found it easy to take a step back from her work because by doing so, he did her mother a favor. But for Nadja it was impossible. She could move the notebook out of her sight or use a pen for a different purpose, but she could not turn off the voices in her head that whispered; Write us. Turn us into a story.

Just as the decision regarding Nadja's choice of university started seeming like a race lost before it even began, and as her writing started taking on a much more agitated tone seeing as her father now started dropping a line ever so rarely, Franjo Bošnjak showed up at their doorstep. Nadja's relationship with Mr. Bošnjak was strictly professional, even though he had full access to her thoughts. The essence of Nadja's writing was like a creek flowing from her soul; she inserted her whole and imperfect self in every text she wrote. But she didn't know anything about him. Does he have a wife? Kids? Where does he live? For her, Mr. Bošnjak was made out of question marks and suppositions. Does he live meagerly or luxuriously?

She believed in the meagerness of his life. After all, with everything said and done, he was a mere writer. And writing was a hackneyed craft in the eyes of the world. Regardless, he was – in a way – a memory of the world. But she was completely wrong. Franjo Bošnjak loved luxury. And luxury, in turn, loved him.

That Tuesday, when the small clock hand was nearing twelve, and the cathedral was getting ready to chime, Nadja heard the doorbell. She was convinced it was Zair, but she was wrong. Once again, she listened to the penetrating sound of the steps and the clacking of men's heels on the floor of their home. Mr. Bošnjak had only stepped foot in their home twice, both times turning Nadja's world upside down without question.

They were sitting at the same table, concocting some mind-bending offers.

"Paris," Mr. Bošnjak turned his head elegantly. "The city of love," he opened his arms widely, "the center of culture and writing."

For the first time in her existence, Nadja could not assemble letters into words and words into meaningful sentences. She stirred her coffee silently as if the cup was a sign of the end. The end of her chapter and the opening of another one that she was expected to start living.

"Of course, Mr. Bošnjak," her mother replied, "but we have a life here."

"Let's be reasonable," Mr. Bošnjak widened a confident smile on his face. "What do you have here that Paris could not replace?"

Zair. We have Zair. Her mother stayed silent.

"Paris can give you a lot more," he added.

Not more than Ilir.

"And the accommodation?" her mother asked.

"Everything's been taken care of," Mr. Bošnjak nodded softly.

Everything's been taken care of? We haven't even accepted the offer yet.

"Nadja doesn't know the language," her mother uttered insecurely.

"Ah, us writers, we are chameleons," Mr. Bošnjak glanced at Nadja, lit up by his own words; "we blend in with our surroundings and then reign over them."

I don't want to reign there.

"Look," Mr. Bošnjak dove into her mother's eyes with his gaze as if trying to buy her mind, "the magazine is falling apart, and Nadja will not have a secured job anymore, and in Paris, you'll have everything that you need."

"And even more than that," he added after a pause. "I guarantee."

DECEMBER, 1982
OSIJEK

Patrik's mornings started turning corrosively gray. He wasn't sure whether it was the fact that he nearly stopped talking to people – or at least the ones who weren't located in the depths of his imagination – or because, from time to time, a few conversations crept in, but with people that didn't belong in his hidden world. All those conversations that took place on the other side of the walls of his imagination were far too meaningless. What to eat for lunch, when to eat lunch, when is he coming home, and how long will he be gone? Most of those talks were held with their maid, who now resided with them on a daily basis.

To chase away the shade of gray, he'd pour a few drops of rum into his coffee every morning. That was partly enough to survive the day. Now that he already had two decades on his shoulders, he did not possess that old power anymore – that sharp old sight that remembered those two pairs of eyes. It was a foggy combination of a blessing and a curse – two in one. Sometimes, we cannot be entirely sure what brings bigger pain – forgetting or remembering. To fill the void those two pairs of eyes left behind, he let Dorothy even further into his being.

He felt her presence tremble under his thighs, her invisible fingers sliding down his spine and her voice whispering: Be brave, and I will be yours. When he felt even the slightest indication of her potential death, he'd go out into the night – into the vastness of the city streets. That way, he breathed life into Dorothy again – recognizing her in the sound of the stiff snow under his feet, on the tips of the naked branches of the lonely trees, in the whistle of the wind, or the brakes of a vehicle. Sometimes, he'd find her in the library. Even though it reeked of rotten wood and cigarettes, it was spacious and silent enough. Devoid of any external stimuli that would push Dorothy into the stifling fog. Dorothy and a few drops of rum in his morning coffee became his two inherent vices. But magical stories had a habit of entering our ordinary days uninvited. Precisely in that treacherous way, magic snuck into Patrik's life, stepping into his ordinary day uninvited.

***

He was standing on the crosswalk across the high school building that he tirelessly kept returning to. Vehicles slid down the road without even noticing him standing there on one side and a red-headed girl on the other side. Thick red curls slid from underneath her navy-blue hat. With only the crosswalk separating him and that strange figure, Patrik dove into his well-known inter-world that had the power to turn the foreign into the known, the distant into the near. And it was precisely there, in that space, that she became his sister. Her giant curls became a part of their mutual inheritance, and their pain for their long-lost parents was now cut in half. But the illusion of the inter-world was that the world of the accepted reality isn't standing still after we escape it, and all the rules of the inter-world stop applying the moment we dive out of the world that people call 'imagination.' With a blink of an eye, he found himself back in reality, and once again, only two of them existed like two souls merged into one: him and Dorothy.

He stood in front of the big high school entrance. He could feel his cramped toes wanting to run far away from his black leather boots. The students flocked towards the exit, each stepping towards their own world, and his gaze narrowed: Dorothy. Once again, his two urges – human and divine, animal and sacred, Yin and Yang – merged into one. She wore a burgundy coat that reached down to her knees and her black wooly hat pulled back to the nape of her head, revealing the tips of her golden fringe. He could feel his lips forming a wide smile. A smile invoked by her big, piercing, green gaze.

"I read it," she stood beside him.

She pulled a cigarette out of her pocket and lit it, bouncing in one place, her gaze fixed on the cars passing by.

"You're very specific," she added as she blew out the smoke. "Did you take classes?"

"Yes," his gaze started narrowing from her astuteness. "How did you know?"

"Your writing seems learned."

"Do you read a lot?"

"You could say that."

She smiled lightly, then let out a ring of smoke.

"Your characters are faithfully described," she tapped the cigarette with her index finger, "but I have a feeling they're a bit too distant."

They are. Because they're not Dorothy. They're not... You.

"A little bit," he replied.

"That's unusual," she glanced at him, then fixated her gaze on the road once again.

"What is?"

"It's unusual that I hadn't run into that character in any of your stories," she shook the ashes off again. "That one character that steals the show from all your other characters."

Dorothy.

"There must be that one character that you fully succumb to," she inhaled the smoke, "that sometimes even drives you crazy," she looked at him again, this time keeping her gaze fixated straight on him, "that makes every other character seem like a shadow."

She took her last drag, threw the cigarette to the moist ground filled with melted snow, stepped on it with her black boot then placed her hands in her coat pockets.

"They're good," she added, "but they're shadows."

"You're a writer," he dove into the greenness of her eyes as if he wanted to find his answer in advance in them. "Am I right?"

"God forbid," she glanced back at the road. "I'm just assuming."

She blended in with the long County Street with her hands tucked in her burgundy pockets and the hardly decipherable smile that turned her cheeks into two apples. Suddenly the world became unbearably loud. The cars growled monstrously, the people stomped, and the cathedral rang two hours and fifteen minutes in the afternoon.

Dorothy. Her name started assuming an even more layered meaning. Dorothy is a writer. She became reachable. Dorothy sits in the darkness of the room. She outgrows dimensions. She sits at the table without description. In front of her is an unforgivable white sheet of paper. She leaves traces of her mind on that unforgivable white sheet of paper. She creates a language unknown to him. Yes… Dorothy – a writer.

Suitcase

MAY, 1961
BUDVA

She was sitting in the living room. Her loving armchair now took the form of a wheelchair, not permitting her to ever make a step again in her life. She heard the doorbell, recognizing the postman by the clinking of his boots. He wore strapped boots that always let out the same sound behind as they clashed together when he walked.

"It's hot outside, isn't it?" her husband's cheery voice asked the postman.

"You have no idea, sir."

She imagined the postman wiping his forehead with his hand.

"Come on in," the husband said, "I have lemonade."

"That's alright," the postman replied, "I must go on."

"Another time, then."

The sound of the wooden chair legs scraping on the tiles let her know that he had sat down in the kitchen. She heard the envelope ripping, and she asked herself whether she might have recognized the careful lick of his finger he always did before grabbing the paper inside it. She despised the depth of how they knew each other now that she had no chance to know her son the same way. She heard him clearing his throat, knowing well enough that he only did it out of sheer habit. She lit another cigarette. The new and fresh smoke stroked her throat and caressed her lungs. Sometimes the cigarette smoke had the power to make her feel alive better than anything else in the world because it just burned at her throat so intensely, and she wanted to suffer. She had to suffer. She had to pay.

The chair's creaking was once again heard from the kitchen, and his gentle steps started nearing. She knew that he was happy. She could smell it off of him for miles. He always held his breath when he was pleased, as if he were restraining himself as if he didn't want to laugh too loudly in front of her, as if he felt guilty because of a sentiment that had been long gone from her body. Or did she chase it away herself?

"Žanet," he approached her from behind and rested her head gently against his stomach, caressing her dry hair with his fingers, "everything is settled."

Her palm trembled as though trying to prevent her from taking another drag, but her desire for destruction was, in a sort of melancholic way, always stronger.

"Look," he crouched next to her wheelchair and showed her the white envelope.

She stared at the envelope, completely indifferent to ever finding out what was in it.

"I handled everything," he opened the envelope, pulling a paper filled with dark letters out of it. "We leave in two days."

Other than losing her talking and writing skills, reading didn't go smoothly for her anymore, either. Her vision became foggy, and letters became a hieroglyphic puzzle. She could discern only one thing from it all, and it felt like seeing the more unsightly profile of her face in a crowd after a long time – Osijek.

“You’re going home, darling!” he stared at her face as his eyes glimmered. “And you don’t have to worry.”

She didn’t worry.

“I’m opening a bakery,” his lips widened into a humble smile, “close to the school. That means it will always be busy.”

Her head shivered.

“You won’t have to do a thing,” he kissed her head as he stood up, “I’ll handle everything."

He pressed her head tight to his stomach once again, touching her chin with his palms.

“You’ll be happier,” he exhaled, seemingly full of hope, “and peaceful, I promise you.”

AUGUST, 1983
OSIJEK

She watched his distorted face, misty from the tears.

"I'll write to you," she pressed his cheeks tightly with her palms.

Did she really say those words out loud? She reduced their world, that special world that few understood, to a sheet of paper with letters written on it. Is she supposed to believe that a piece of paper with letters will be able to replace the true physical, irreplaceable presence? He stayed silent like a distraught kid that understood nothing but felt everything. She knew very well that we understood our feelings best.

"I'll come back," she caressed his upper lip with her thumb, "I'll come back soon."

She caught herself in a lie. She knew very well that her mother was still controlling her life, and her control greatly disregarded young love. But, more than any other truth at that moment, there was one that hurt her the most: he knew she was lying, too.

"Tell me," she whispered, gluing her nose to his.

She heard her mother's voice in the background, hurrying her. The voice that seemed to bring the walls around their world crashing down. Her mother's mind didn't care about her inter-world, universes, and deepest dreams. But every young heart has one flaw: the fear of meeting a parent's dark, imperfect, and sometimes deadly face. That fear was precisely what parents kept tucked away in the pit of their palms, allowing them to break a young heart that might never be whole again.

"Always," he uttered powerlessly, brokenly, as a large teardrop rolled down his lips.

Always. Just always. The word always held a special promise, but promises existed in the mundane, human world which often tended to break them. The word always was infinite, unlimited, and instinctual. It simply was. Hence, they chose to simply always be wherever they found themselves.

"Always," she repeated after him.

"Everything that you know, I know too," he let go of her hand, but she was the one who had to let go and leave.

***

The night crept in. Sometimes, all those apocalypses that happen do so in the quietest and the gentlest of surroundings – as if nothing ever happened. She stared at the stained window glass and noticed a spot that looked like a withered pansy.

For Nadja, the world that raced around them as they calmly sat in the train that reeked of old iron and sweat was just a sloppy mix of colors on a wooden palette belonging to a painter shamelessly making an abstract of the future. This future saved no space for him. With his abrupt and surreal movements, the painter pulverized the eroticism of their innocent love. Three stains on the window glass, just a couple of inches below the withered pansy, became three golden stars sleeping in the sky. And that sky served as the only remaining evidence of them living in the same world, dreaming under the same sky, walking the same ground – albeit thousands of miles away.

She felt her forehead hitting the hard window frame every time the train car bounced. Her sorrow was much stronger and more decisive in its desire to hide from the real world and disappear into the one far more protected – the dream world. She sailed into the realm of dreams with a single feeling in her chest – a deep black hole.

***

Her mother's voice penetrated her dreams.

"Nadja," she uttered as she took the suitcases off the shelf above her. "Get up. We're almost there."

Sometimes even the dream world has its faults: it mesmerizes us so that we forget, and then it catapults us back into the real world, where we again end up disappointed, like unprepared children.

She grabbed the navy-blue suitcase and thought, "that's it." Everything inside the suitcase was the only remaining piece of her life. A single suitcase represented her life, while a single person seemed to represent what she truly was. And that genuine part of her stayed there, lost in the streets of Osijek. Then she realized how funny the amount of difference between our inner self and our outside life truly is.

She put on a black hat and hung the denim backpack – now too empty as she ate all the food – over her shoulder. Finally, after pushing through the narrow hallway of the train car where everyone reeked of traveling, hunger, thirst, lack of sleep, onions, and expensive perfumes – they got off the train and stepped on the ground of the famous Paris – the city of love for the whole world. Still, for Nadja, it was the sheer opposite.

AUGUST, 1983
PARIS

Even though the spark between him and the croissants seemed to be love at first taste, they did not sit well with him that morning. He felt sick and was sure it was the flu. At least he hoped it was the flu and not one of his thousand hidden faces of anxiety. He knew that his uncle didn't take kindly to weaklings.

He tried not to stare at his uncle eating one croissant after another, soaking them in a glass of hot milk. He glanced around the room. There were no diners within train stations in Croatia. Croatian train stations usually reeked of emptiness and goodbyes, but that was, in a way, their charm: they were typically unsightly, cursed with a sense of overwhelming pain of departures and goodbyes. There, in that unfamiliar city, surrounded by a million unknown words, he felt like an orphan stepping into his biological father's castle where, unbeknownst to him, lay hidden a treasure that, as far as circumstances go, belonged to him. That's what Paris was for him, a giant castle, carved in gold and left for him to use.

"I have to go to the toilet," he got up.

"You're a weakling," the uncle didn't even try to keep the croissant inside his mouth.

He noticed a drop of milk on his mustache. A revolting man. Completely unaware of how revolting he is.

"I'm glad you find it tasty," he tried his best to drag a smile onto his face, but it was unnecessary as his uncle didn't even bat an eye.

***

He approached the bar. A tiny waitress in a red plaid dress touching the tip of her knees stood behind it. Her weakly black hair was tied in a long, high ponytail. The fluency of her French accent was stunningly attractive, and her smile chased Patrik's grumpiness away. He tried talking to her in as clear and articulate English as possible.

"Could I have a cup of chamomile tea, please?"

"Excusez-moi?"

Don't tell me you can't speak a word of English.

"Could I have a cup of chamomile tea?" he asked once again, slowly this time.

"Oh," she replied in fluent English. "Of course."

***

His uncle was now bored, having eaten all the croissants, including Patrik's. He was getting annoyed as he stared through the window, sporting a strange look on his face like he was ready to birth a story for a new novel.

"Tell me one more time," Patrik took a sip of his tea, "why you had to drag that kid over here?"

"She's a good writer," he glanced at him absently. "Why do you ask?"

"A lot of people are good writers," he couldn't hide his animosity.

"She's very good," the uncle nodded as though talking to a child, "you'll see."

"A good thing you didn't force them to live with us."

"You're annoying," he rolled his eyes. "And what if I had done that?"

"I just don't see the point in wasting your money like that."

"It's not wasting my money," his uncle got up. "Shut up, and let's go get them."

***

They pushed through the crowd that dragged children, suitcases, and small high-pitched barking dogs with them. His uncle leaned towards him when he caught sight of the train. The passengers had already started hoarding the exits like ants.

"Once again, be polite. Don't embarrass me."

His uncle's gaze touched every passenger, still not finding what it came here for. Patrik dove into his inter-world, feeling trapped in the density of the reality that tore the Yin away from his Yang. He wanted to escape. To keep alive the image he would never see clearly again, the hard forehead, the golden locks, the short fingers, and the big eyes. As he fixated on the last thought in his head, dotting that 'i', his inter-world merged with reality. She was standing there. Dorothy.

Dorothy got off the train wearing a black hat and a denim backpack. How did he not see this before? Her hat partly covered her eyes as she dragged the navy-blue suitcase behind her.

"Why are you gawking?" he heard his uncle's voice. "There they are. Let's go."

No. He could not allow this. He could not spread his wings and fly away toward some strangers while she stood there. The girl from the high school. The girl with the apple in her hand. The girl that embodied Dorothy. And the girl that Dorothy embodied.

"Patrik," his uncle pulled at his sleeve, "what in the hell are you waiting for?"

No. He had to stay there. She was coming towards him.

"We're going to lose them!"

His uncle waved his hand and then left.

"Sorry," he heard his uncle's voice in the crowd. "It's my nephew," he said with a rarely used kindness in his voice, "he's a little confused."

She was standing only a few feet away from his uncle, fiddling her fingers, appearing much sadder than the last time he'd seen her.

"Patrik," his uncle turned towards him, hissing through his teeth, "God damn it!"

He moved his gaze away from Dorothy, again choosing the world his uncle had picked for him.

"I want you to meet Nadja," his uncle pointed his finger at her.

His heart stopped beating, separating him and his body as though they were two different halves. Dorothy.

"And her mother," the uncle gestured towards the black-haired woman beside her.

Finally, his body willingly returned to the safety of his control. He shook hands with her mother, then with her.

"We actually," she uttered shyly, trying her hardest to keep the sorrow hidden from her eyes, "know each other."

"You know each other?" his uncle asked joyously. "Well then, you know, Nadja, what a yahoo I have at home!"

Clamor echoed throughout the train station, but silence reigned over their newly created world.

"Well," his uncle gestures towards the exit with a soft bow, "my ladies...."

Fairy Godmothers

DECEMBER, 1962
OSIJEK

Thin snowflakes merged one by one with the glass of the entrance doors of the bakery as though moving in an arranged rhythm. The smell of yeast and heat kept thickening the air in their room – a room safe from the winter cold. Her nose could barely discern all the different scents. It seemed as though her body followed the lapsing of her mind.

People came and went. Mostly leaving with bread in their hands. In all that clamor of voices, she could only discern her husband's unpleasantly, but the only one clearly recognizable for some reason. He indeed seemed to be a piece of her, in a way. A piece that exuded a certain kind of beauty but that in no way belonged to the rest of her being, and that was slowly distracting her from everything that the rest of her tried so fiercely to become. Was it working? She couldn't say so. He slowed down the collapsing process that was bound to happen anyway, what with her devoted commitment to the darkness. Sometimes, the collapsing of our being has an insidious habit of unfolding ever so slowly, bit by bit. Almost unnoticeable.

A girl, hidden underneath her jacket a few sizes too big, laid foot into the bakery while her cat-like eyes squinted under a green wooly hat, her black hair crawling from under it like a pile of worms. She held a couple of paintings in her hands as her fingers, all red from the cold, peeked out of her gloves.

"Good day," the husband extended a smile.

The girl nodded.

"Are we hungry?" the husband asked, glancing at the holes in her gloves.

The girl glanced at the neatly arranged pastries, then looked at the husband and shook her head.

"These are my paintings," she turned one towards him.

The painting depicted the Osijek cathedral, blending in with the blue sky.

"Are you perhaps interested?" she asked.

The husband gazed at the painting, taking his time as if running away from a predicament, and then he looked at Žanet. Žanet, as indifferent as always, left him a simple choice: take it or don't take it. I don't care.

"How much is it?" he asked with an insecure smile.

The girl shrugged.

"As much as you give me," she approached the small counter.

"You have to appreciate your work," he glanced at her ripped gloves again and then at her jacket, a couple of sizes too big. "Or no one else will, either."

The girl shrugged again.

"You appreciate it, don't you?" she placed the painting on the counter.

He dove into her eyes, seemingly taking a moment to arrange letters in his head into a coherent sentence.

"Sure I do," he grabbed the painting, "but I can't possibly presume how much you thought you'd get for it."

The girl was silent.

"You know," he placed the painting on the counter again, "not every individual appreciates things the same way."

"As much as you give me," the girl shook her head.

The husband glanced at Žanet again as if begging her to help. Even though he knew that he would never receive it.

"Do you have a job?" he glanced at the girl's torn gloves again.

The girl nodded her head.

"Other than selling paintings?" he asked.

The girl gazed into his eyes as though fighting with herself, then shook her head slowly. The husband looked towards Žanet again, then at the painting and the girl.

"Come here a minute," he went towards the back end of the bakery.

The girl followed him silently.

When the room emptied, and Žanet stayed alone, some serenity grew inside her – a serenity that opened up the possibility of drowning in her misery. However, that peace would always have a grain of fear in it that the somewhat pretty but still unacceptable part of her had torn off for a short while and wandered off. After all, her husband was the only meaningful mirror of her existence. She heard his voice, veiled with the blur of distance.

"... while I'm busy."

There was silence in the room, and Žanet thought of two possibilities: the girl was nodding her head and accepting to take over the burden of taking care of her, or she was shaking her head and refusing that burden which seemingly only her husband deemed essential.

"Money is always welcome, and..." a customer entering the bakery interrupted her eavesdropping, "...such high expectations."

They returned to the front of the bakery, and her husband immediately greeted the plump man waiting to be served.

"Welcome," he smiled, "what will it be?"

The girl stood next to Žanet, tightly pressing her paintings to her chest. Her eyes were filled with complacency, doubt, and rigidity. But also a tiny drop of light – hope.

"This braided pastry," the customer pointed his finger, "please."

The girl got on her toes, trying to see something outside the bakery, but the plump man blocked her view as he went out.

"Then we have a deal?" he asked.

"Yes," the girl answered, standing still.

"Do you have anyone?" he asked. "Family?"

She nodded her head.

"Who?"

For a few seconds, she gazed at him as though weighing a choice, to trust or not to trust? Then she left the bakery, placed her paintings next to the entrance door, and disappeared. Žanet watched the paintings she left there to guarantee her return while her husband stood there astonished, with question marks dancing around his head.

Not long after that, the girl returned with a small, four-legged figure beside her.

"Oh, lord," the husband's lips widened sympathetically.

The girl opened the door holding a dog on a leash. He was white with a couple of brown spots, reaching up to her knees, with one ear torn off. He seemed dirty, just like she was. But both of them exuded a strange kind of beauty.

"We'll find him a place to be," the husband said, "while you work."

SEPTEMBER, 1983
PARIS

What she loved most about Paris was her morning coffee on the small balcony of their one-bedroom apartment. The balcony had a thin iron fence that housed three small flowerpots so the balcony wouldn't look too dull. Flowers are always able to breathe life into the emptiness of any space. There was a short wooden table in the middle of the balcony, and around it stood two wooden chairs where they would always sit for their morning coffee. There was also a small easel crammed into a corner for her mother's occasional whims and remembrances of some other times.

Franjo Bošnjak took the question of Nadja's education into his own hands, as well as a lot of other things. Having already been introduced to the essence of her soul that he so neatly got to know through her works, he decided that the Faculty of Teacher Education, along with the Academy of Dramatic Arts, was the choice for her. Nadja and her mother were taken aback by fear rather than happiness upon facing the challenges and obligations that those two colleges would bring. Up until Nadja, carried away by her dreams, started enjoying both of them.

***

Tuesdays were scheduled for evening walks through the streets of Paris. It was neither a Monday when the body returns to its state of shock caused by the start of the workweek, nor a Saturday, which is intended for rest anyway. A mere Tuesday – so the beginning of the week gets some soft wind in its sails. They never walked the same streets for two Tuesdays in a row. Franjo Bošnjak would choose a different path every Tuesday and follow it decidedly. There was always a funny truth hiding behind the beauty of walking through a new city. You can't get lost because you never really know where you're headed anyway. Problems start appearing when we choose a destination. Only then can we get lost – and only then can we be found.

Nadja fell in love with the streets of Paris quickly. They seemed strong and independent, separated from the world, but still sweet. Friendly. Frenchwomen sent out an irresistible energy, just like the streets themselves. They weren't like any other women she'd met in her parts of the world. They emanated divine energy but, at the same time, seemed to tread across some devilish paths that, like opium, attracted gazes from both men and women.

They would walk for about two hours, all thanks to Mr. Bošnjak's stories. During every walk of theirs, he'd dig up a new story to tell from the depths of his mind. Thought up at the spot, or a story from his life, or most often, a fishing story. One story of his remained especially engraved into Nadja's mind, like a forever-reminding scar. He thought it up at the spot. The Seventh Hill.

Look, Mr. Bošnjak spread his palms as if opening the doors of the story; there was once a world. There is no point in losing words and time explaining what kind of a world that was and when exactly it was, seeing as it does not condition this story in any way. The important thing to know is that it was a world.

This world had seven hills. On the seventh hill, once upon a time – long before the time of this story we're diving into – there was a kingdom. In that kingdom lived a large royal family, every bit as prominent as the other. The whole family was born with an innate prominence surging through their veins – impenetrable, persistent, and determined. Never could a human mind understand: what brought the kingdom to ruins?

It was not the castle crumbling nor its golden beauty. It was the people. The people had started to fade, to fall down a black hole, together with all their glory. Mr. Bošnjak stopped briefly, allowing them to paint this picture in their minds. And so the kingdom, where even the smallest objects were made out of the finest gold and jewels, was left desolate. Only a slight draft caressed its curtains and swayed the petals of the gleaming flowers on the spacious balconies. Everybody disappeared, gone with a gentle breeze. Everybody; except her.

Only the princess remained. Trapped in the richness of a family forever lost. Mr. Bošnjak smiled and gave Nadja a long and most trustful gaze. It was said that she would be freed on a crystal-clear starry night, free from her and her long-lost family's shackles. On that starry night, she was promised the other half of her frightened soul would come. "The prince," Mr. Bošnjak stopped for a second, tastefully uttering the word 'prince.' The princess was not bound with shackles, imprisoned in a dungeon, or as it usually is, enchanted by some evil magic. No, she was simply trapped. She never wondered why it was so, how it happened, or why she even had to wait for the prince. She just waited patiently. And she was trapped because the fairy godmothers told her so.

One night, a beggar knocked on her door, interrupting her waiting. He seemed to be just a simple and hungry young man. But what does one even know about rare and unique people? Honestly, nothing except that they start as ordinary people who, extraordinarily, reach our hearts. The young man had come to ask for refuge from the princess, to rest a bit on his travels. Namely, it had been said that a better world existed behind the seventh hill. And that's where he was headed. The princess, kind-hearted as she was, sent him to the golden guest room. She fed him and treated him with the most pristine fruits.

Mr. Bošnjak raised his palms in the air. And what do you know? He lowered his palms and smiled. That night, the princess fell irrevocably in love with the beggar. And the beggar in her. Until sunrise, they sat on the side of the balcony, gazing into each other's eyes as if they could recognize each other in their eyes while the crystal-clear sky lay spread out above them.

He cleared his throat – a sound that awakened a memory in Nadja's mind – the cough of Ilir's wife and Ilir himself. Her best friend. Then she realized – sometimes the prettiest of things can lead us into the worst of the worlds, just like an awful thing has the power to lead us into the warmest corners of our souls. The next morning, Mr. Bošnjak continued, the young man asked for the princess's hand in marriage, inviting her to come with him to the new world. Having placed her trust in the fairy godmothers, the princess refused. She believed wholeheartedly that the fairy godmothers could not be wrong.

Although Mr. Bošnjak glanced at them, fairy godmothers are mothers. They are parents, and a parent always instinctively believes in one thing: that his child's life belongs to him. What does the child believe then? He glanced at them again as if challenging them to answer that question themselves. The same thing, naturally. She did not shed a tear as he left. After all, she held on to a certain precious sophistication. Our soul sometimes cries, but our body hides it skillfully.

A few months later, a prince showed up on her doorstep. The promised prince. He did not wait a moment to ask for her hand and to invite her to come with him to the new world. Mr. Bošnjak paused momentarily, looked at the ground he was stepping on, and then continued. But how does one reach the new world if it is destined for a different ending? She did not go. That night she opened the door for the prince, noticing in the corner of her eye that not one star shone in the sky.

They were standing in front of their building. Mr. Bošnjak held a simple smile on his face as if he had told her just a simple good night story. But Nadja knew that the story was anything but simple. She knew that no stories are truly ever just told.

Writing out the pages of her mind, one question overcame Nadja's soul, do her mother and Mr. Bošnjak know that they are her fairy godmothers?

***

There was a package for Nadja, creeping into the dark corner of the ground floor of their apartment building, hidden in the coldness of their mailbox. She smiled genuinely, warmly, and wearily. Happiness sometimes has a certain way of wearing us out if we hold on to it too weakly. It was Zair's first letter. A small envelope, its corner slightly bent, and in it photographs of soccer fields.

One. A big field. The lower left side of the photo shows a few plastic blue chairs on the bleachers, and the upper left corner is very pale, almost white. It's where the sun nests. Right in the middle of the photo is the beautiful greenery of the field.

Two. A bird's eye view. The upper right corner of the photo shows a river. The fence that separates the field from the mortal world is very short, dividing the photograph into two halves. The field's greenery shows its face again in the lower part of the photo under weaker sunlight.

On the back of the photograph, she noticed his thin and messy handwriting: Slavonski Brod. The river you see is Sava.

Three. Evening. The redness of the sky represents the death of the day and the birth of the night, and the soccer field takes second place in the photograph. A woman with a black hat is positioned in the upper right corner of the photograph. She's sitting high up on the bleachers.

On the back of the photograph: The red sky reminds me of you. It's different and nice, and it's always too damn easy to stare at anything and everything that looks like you.

Four. A small and messy field. The grass in the sole center of the photo gleams under the sunlight. There are only two thick rods serving as a fence.

Five. The edge of the clear green field in the upper part of the photo touches the crystal blue sky. Next to it is a small white house with the coach and three reserve players sitting inside.

Iris

DECEMBER, 1983
PARIS

Saturdays were always designated for dinner in the Bouillon Chartier, one of Paris's oldest and most famous restaurants. It was, naturally, Mr. Bošnjak's choice. Round lights on the seemingly thin threads descended from the glass ceiling in an almost supernatural manner. Indeed, there was not a part of Paris that a writer could ignore.

Nadja did not like the sophistication that was getting under her and her mother's skin. Her mother, on the other hand, seemed to feel like home. Everything up until this point had been a mask of poverty that nattily hid her royal heart underneath a dozen layers. The company of Mr. Bošnjak and his nephew had an ethereal power to reshape Nadja and her mother's presence, their chewing, smiles, and words into a form they had not known before.

The French version of the magazine *Strike Hunt* was called *Lettres Magiques.* It was not easy pushing a magazine into the market, but Mr. Bošnjak never jumped into the water before ensuring it was pleasant enough for a swim. *Lettres Magiques* was placed on the French market in advance when they all sat comfortably in their Croatian homes. A specific routine had been adopted upon their arrival in Paris. The Croatian writers continued to write for the magazine while the translators translated them into French. It was, in a way, like opening a

Croatian restaurant outside of Croatia. Bošnjak served the food, and the Frenchmen chewed it. When has it even happened, that a person refused to eat the food someone else had served? Franjo Bošnjak knew the truth: someone else's food was tastier to most people than their own was. No matter the taste.

That evening, cold drops of rain washed the streets, pouring down the big restaurant windows. They ate bourride with brioche on the side. Saturdays were not meant to satisfy their hunger but merely for their metamorphosis from humble people into other more demanding ones. For the next hour, Nadja felt an unpleasant bitter taste of the fish in her mouth, which reminded her that a hefty price does not guarantee a good taste. For dessert, they had a Tarte Tatin that she hoped would remove the bitterness from the roof of her mouth, but it did not.

***

She opened the mailbox as her mother climbed the gigantic stairs of their apartment building. Once again, a small envelope containing five photographs.

Six. A big, green field under the sun. Judging by the jersey colors, two boys from Zair's team, standing next to a big white fence, not far from the goal. They are looking into the eye of the camera, laughing.

Seven. One half of a field. The photo's upper right corner shows a fence separating the field from the mortal world, while a dark stormy cloud prey over it in the upper left corner.

On the back of the photograph: We were soaking wet.

Eight. The whole right side of the photo shows an edge of the wet concrete bleachers, while a muddy soccer net and one-half of the green field fill the left side of the photo.

On the back of the photograph, "I got soaked, plus I'm as dirty as a pig."

Nine. The lower part of the photo shows Zair's cleats lying on a beam separating the audience from the field, and the upper part shows a clear sky with two small clouds.

Ten. The lower half of the photo shows the clear greenness of the field framed with a white fence as birds carved into the cloudless sky fill the upper part of the photo.

On the back of the photograph: Wish you were here. You would have written one hell of a story. We won!

Nadja replied with a letter and one photograph.

Zair Lončar,

Writing your African name next to a typical Croatian surname is genuinely hilarious. You're unique, Zair Lončar! There's no one like you. I love your photographs (did you maybe miss your true calling?), and I expect to see more. I'm sending you a photo of me in front of the oldest restaurant in Paris.

I want to let you know that I'm good at French, for now. It would not be decent to presume what you would do to me if you heard how I pronounce my r's, so I'm leaving that out. Everything that I know, you know too.

Both of my colleges are great, but they leave me only a little bit of time. Mother and I often wish that we could skip sleep for a night or two and stretch the day to last at least 48 hours. Regarding the balcony I mentioned earlier on the phone, I'm falling increasingly in love with it by the minute. (Maybe more than I do with you. You never know.)

Half an hour ago, as I was sitting on that same balcony, I saw a star. One of the shiniest ones I'd ever seen. I think it's part of Orion's belt. I named it Iris. And I'm giving it to you, just like I promised I would someday.

Always,
N.

P. S.

French has an interesting version of the phrase 'I miss you.' In a literal way, it means that someone is missing from you as if they were an essential part of you. So, I decided to be as sincere as possible for you: Tu me manques.

***

Sundays were reserved primarily for their Croatian tummies. Nadja and her mother were making lunch in their apartment as all kinds of smells penetrated its walls, including juicy baked chicken, homemade chicken soup, and apple and cheese pie.

She loved Croatian cuisine but didn't particularly like the people they were preparing it for. On the other hand, her mother happily chirped the songs from Ilir's playlist, expecting their guests with pleasure. To Nadja, it seemed she was evoking painfully beautiful memories of Ilir, whom they talked to very rarely. More rarely than she'd liked, merely once every two weeks when both sides managed to find sufficient time for it.

Their kitchen was fairly tiny, just like their apartment as a whole. So tiny that they could hardly fit inside simultaneously. It was open and separated by a small counter facing the living room. The living room led to the balcony as if yearning for any light. A green sofa with two brown cushions pressed against the wall is next to the balcony door. On the rare occasion when her university or the Bošnjak family refrained from stealing Nadja's time, she and her mother would cuddle together on the sofa and watch one of the many French movies, as per Mr. Bošnjak's suggestion. An unwritten and settled law stated: what Franjo Bošnjak suggests, one does not refuse.

Mr. Bošnjak and his nephew usually rang the doorbell at noon. They were always as punctual as a Swiss watch which was truly ironic for Croats that were stealing the show on French streets. Nadja would open the door, already dressed up, smiling fiercely and bravely, hiding all the holes that had only recently ruptured her soul. Bošnjak would give them whatever he had bought that day in the bakery or the small store on the ground floor of their building and then let himself in as if he owned every corner of the place. This was ultimately true because he financed much of their life in Paris.

A bottle of wine on the dining table was obligatory. One of Mr. Bošnjak's choosing, and Nadja's favorite part of their meals was precisely the wine. It brought her dizziness, but it made her forget. Although forgetting things while drunk has one flaw, it only works until the morning. And then, like a boomerang, the morning brings exactly what we wanted to rid ourselves of. When the time for wine came, Mr. Bošnjak would play a song, and her mother would – like a perfectly trained marionette of a glamorous show – put a record on and satisfy his spoiled ear. That Sunday, while her mother and Mr. Bošnjak were chirping around the table, Nadja dove into the shell of the armchair as Bošnjak's nephew sat next to her for the first time.

"You're a good liar," he took a sip.

She could feel his gaze glued onto her profile, his eyes sliding up and down nervously.

"We all are," she stared at the turned-off TV in front of her.

"Actually, you're a great writer."

For a moment, she hesitated, debating with herself: to accept or not to accept? However, a hint of warmth snuck into the pores of their conversation.

"Thank you," she nodded her head. "I'm glad you think that."

“I’d like to read something that isn’t an article,” he tilted his head. “Something more personal.”

“I don’t give that out to just anyone.”

“I’m not just anyone,” his gaze yearned for a response. “Am I?”

Everyone except Zair and Ilir is just anyone. But it’s not your fault you’re just anyone.

“It’s too early to judge,” she uttered rapidly.

“You’re right,” he nodded his head. “Have you seen Les parapluies de Cherbourg?”

“No,” she cleared her throat. “Not yet.”

“I’d like to do that someday.”

“Do what?”

“A movie,” he gestured towards the turned-off TV with his glass. “Make a movie.”

“A French movie?”

“I don’t mind,” he replied with an unusual zeal in his eyes.

I do mind.

***

Zair’s third letter.

Eleven. A raindrop sat on the lens, forever marking its short existence. The lower part of the photo shows a black fence with three rods, while the upper part of the photo is just gray.

On the back of the photograph: We lost 5-0. The coach is furious.

Twelve. The grayness of the sky occupies the upper part of the photo, this time touching the edge of the dressing rooms from which a giant brown fence spreads like a net, closing off the field that is all shoveled from the thin layer of snow.

On the back of the photograph: I saw how you play in the leaves, but I'd like to know how you play in the snow, too.

Thirteen. Evening. A blurry photo. The middle of it shows the center of the field as a thick fog spreads across the vastness behind the short fence that clasps it.

Fourteen. Two of Zair's teammates are smoking cigarettes wrapped in baggy jackets. Their bodies pressed against the fence. They're looking toward the soccer net that has a giant hole in it.

On the back of the photograph: Cigarettes reminded me of you.

Fifteen. The fence separates the photo in two. On the upper part of the photo, there's a train that goes past their field, and the lower part is, once again, the greenness of the field – bathed in shy sunshine.

APRIL, 1964
OSIJEK

She was sitting across from her – the girl with the cat-like eyes with now tidily combed long hair. They stared at each other like two cats – struggling with two choices repeatedly: to love or not to love?

"He ordered me to feed you," she held the spoon in front of her mouth. "Please, don't resist again."

Žanet was quiet.

"Three," she looked at her boldly, "two," she moved the spoon just a little bit closer, "one."

To love.

"There we go," the girl pulled the spoon out of Žanet's mouth, "thank you very much."

She heard her husband's footsteps, recognizing their tenderness. But he was not the only mirror of her existence anymore. The girl with the cat-like eyes had crept into the abstraction of her life like an uninvited ally.

"Lea, the shipment has arrived," he placed his hand on Žanet's shoulder. "I'll take it from here."

***

Lea became an integral part of their bakery. Few things happened in the bakery that directly concerned her but that she hadn't been a part of, from planning, to executing, to cleaning. Even though in the beginning, they employed her solely to serve as Žanet's arms and legs when her husband was too busy for it. In time, she nestled into their job and then their life like a pearl that fit perfectly in that one shell. They protected her, and she brought them beauty.

At 5:30 AM, when Žanet was still fast asleep, Lea started preparing everything with her husband. They would knead the dough, heat the furnace, wash the floors, and wipe the shelves. When morning arrived, and the floors gleamed blindingly, the girl would wake Žanet – who did not like to be woken up. There were always two types of people – the ones whose dreams reek of life and those whose dreams reek of death. Žanet belonged to the second type. Dreams were, however, most often a simple image of the reality we yearned for or sometimes, the embodiment of our elementary fears.

When Žanet finally agreed to wake up, it was time for basic hygiene. In that entrapment between life and death, Žanet could not recognize the cleanliness in things clean or the health in things healthy. For her, there was only perdition. Slow, gentle perdition no matter the path she took in her mind. But it was freeing, in a way. She did not like touching. She did not accept the connection. She did not want to be tied to life or anything else that was part of that package. But Lea was something else. Lea did not summon her to the land of the living. Curiously, she took Žanet's darkness by the hand and eased her path toward death. She was her partner in crime, helping her build a mask to protect her from all the life lovers around her. Žanet realized then and there: in darkness, there is always a pinch of light we cannot push away, no matter how hard we try.

By the time Lea finished Žanet's hygiene, they'd climb down to the bakery, where Žanet's husband was already working full force.

"You're here," he'd smile, "just in time for breakfast."

There would be a breakfast waiting for them in the back. Polenta for Žanet and donuts for Lea. They would eat their breakfast in silence, looking through the back window of the bakery. They could only see a few tips and edges of some buildings. Sometimes, Žanet would eat alone, holding her spoon without the tremor in her hands, but other days she'd shut her lips tightly, refusing to eat. It all came down to the dreams she'd had the previous night. Her mind was always struggling between two loud voices. Give in? Or growl?

The rest of the day would play out according to Žanet's wishes. Lea would work, and Žanet would sit in her wheelchair somewhere her instinct would pull her to, in the back, next to the counter, close to the entrance doors, or as she did for the first time that day, in front of the bakery.

***

Žanet was sitting in front of the bakery, like an animal, acquainting her eyes to her surroundings. Then, a giant vehicle stopped in front of the bakery, and a tall young man with playful brown hair reaching the tips of his shoulders started handing pallets containing all the needed ingredients for the bakery to Lea. Although Žanet was a shell of her former self, she could recognize the drops of light vibrating around her.

"We could switch," the young man said.

"There's no need," Lea paused. "Why do you think you're stronger than me?"

His lips extended into a gentle smile.

"Because I'm a guy," he shrugged. "That's perfectly normal."

Lea was quietly staring at him like she stared into every stranger's eyes with natural energy.

"I didn't mean to offend you," the young man came out of the vehicle. "You women are in many ways better than us."

Lea nodded.

"Something much more valuable hides in the absence of physical strength, you know?" he asked her.

"No," she shook her head. "I don't know."

"Tenderness," he blew a rogue lock of hair off his forehead.

Lea stared at him silently as if sniffing his presence with her eyes.

"Tenderness is not the absence of strength," she shook her head, "it's just the other face of it. But I am not tender."

The young man was quiet as the smile on his face started broadening once again. This time gently and slowly.

"Yes, you are," he nodded, "I can see it."

"You're just a guy who brings us ingredients once a week," she shook her head again. "You don't know anything about me."

Unlike Žanet's rapacious one, Lea's nature kept a secret: it wanted to be tamed.

What happens to people who want to be tamed? They are approached by a hand in which they can sense peace, belonging, and admittance. That sense often extends through their whole life, wrapping it with familiarity. Sometimes, the hand that offered to tame them becomes the same one that would chase them off again into the wilderness of their loneliness. A hand that would distort them into an abandoned being. The secret of abandonment lies behind a deceptive curtain. Only a tamed thing can be left. That offering hand was precisely the hand of the young man with playful hair, and Lea's peace broke into thousands of glass pieces with only one reflection morphing in them: abandonment.

The fruit of that short-term peace and the silent trace of taming had a name: Nadja.

Limits

JANUARY, 1984
PARIS

She fell asleep lying on the couch. The book *Personality and the Development of One* by Nikola Rot moved on her chest according to the rhythm of her breathing as the TV illuminated the room around her. The doorbell startled her out of her sleep as if wanting desperately to be louder than the TV.

She knew that her mother should be returning from her dance classes at this hour, and with that knowledge, she hoped that it wouldn't be Bošnjak, his nephew, or both behind the door. Clacking her heels sluggishly on the wooden flooring while rubbing her eyes to sharpen her sight, she approached the door and looked through the peephole.

Three. Am I still dreaming?

Two. Reality is better than lovely memories.

One. It's really him.

Warmth started accumulating in the corners of her eyes as she turned the key with a shaky hand. Joyously opening the door to her dreams, inviting them into her reality.

"Always?" his voice was trembling, and his lips tried hard not to let out the lump that visibly sat in the back of his throat.

Three curious dark curls peeked out from under his gray wooly hat. Mine, she thought warily. Mine, stars danced around her stomach. Mine, she stared at his shoulders as if staring at the skeleton of her existence. Not being able to resist the melody that her inter-world had started playing, she jumped into his arms. And she was home.

"Always," she muttered.

***

"I thought it would be bigger," Zair looked around the fairly small hallway.

"I hate this place," she poured water into the coffeepot, "but the balcony is great."

"You must write there a lot," he leaned on his elbows on the small counter separating them.

"On the balcony?" she put the pot on the stove. "When I have time, which is rare."

"How's that working out for you?" he now leaned on his hands, his gaze glued to her figure. "College?"

She thought she heard a hint of envy in his voice.

"Good," she leaned on the kitchen counter and gazed into his eyes. "I guess."

"I can imagine you," he sat on one of the chairs carefully, like he was afraid of the room surrounding him.

"As a student?"

She removed the pot from the stove and with trembling hands, added a teaspoon of sugar and two teaspoons of coffee to it.

"As a teacher."

Nadja filled their cups with black coffee and placed them on the table in front of him. It's unusual how much-unexpected beauty there is in the bits of reality that we previously plant into our dreams. She sat in front of him, uneasily watching him from above as he sat in the chair. She felt like she held him in the pit of her palm.

"Before we feed you..." she removed the hat from his head, freeing his curls. "It's been too long since I've seen them."

***

The night was starry, infallibly recalling Mr. Bošnjak's story. They sat along the iron fence of her balcony, cuddled under a blanket on a small rug, drinking hot cocoa. Sometimes, some people touch our lifeline so gently, all the while humbly making us younger.

"This is so strange," Nadja ripped the soft cloak of silence that was wrapped around them.

"Strange?"

"You and Paris," she took a sip of cocoa. "It's strange."

"I don't think we go together," he glued his eyes to the stars. "Paris is a luxury."

"And you're not?"

Her heart danced in her chest, tangling the net of scattered thoughts in her mind. He belongs where I belong. How does he not understand that?

"I'm poor," he replied silently.

"Zair," she shook her head. "Stop it."

"No," he shook his head a tiny bit more decidedly. "Trust me."

“Always?” she asked.

“Always,” he pulled her head into his lap.

She felt his fingers marching gently towards her lips, across her neck. Always. Always. Always. It was a sardonically unforgettable and unforgivably whole touch. Mine, mine, mine – she could almost hear his touch uttering those words. How gently, instinctively, and skillfully did he own her? He owned her soul to its tiniest, smallest, most delicate part. She turned her head towards him and, through the hairs of his sweater, spotted his eyes that were already fixated on her.

Always on her. Never. Never. Never. She would never be able to belong to this world entirely. This genuine mixture of hidden and loud reality, if someone else was to take his place beside her; if he wasn’t the one to fill that place with his body, his mind, his soul, and his presence. Some presences have a blessed curse in them. They’re bigger than all the others, as if they hold a part of ourselves that is irrecoverably necessary to us. She touched his thin beard with her short fingers and gently ran them over his chiseled jaw – she liked to believe that only he had a jaw like that – as if she were painting a starry path that led straight home. Like a faithful companion, the streetlight touched his light eyelashes while his eyes closed under her touch. She felt a lump in her throat as she watched the beauty of their relationship illustrated ever so humbly by that one blink of his eye.

“Nadja,” he uttered silently as a thick tear rolled down his gently rounded cheek.

There is something in the letters of our names: something that playfully reveals itself when the right person says them out loud. After almost forgetting how much of her joy she had placed inside him, she closed her eyes and felt his wide lips on hers.

Ten. Always.

Nine. Each one is like the first one.

Eight. Each one is like the last one.

Seven. As if the whole world could fit in it.

Six. Evil does not exist in the world.

Five. This is the limit between their two souls.

Four. The limit disappears. The limit does not exist.

Three. Forever is awfully too short. Cheap. Used.

Two. The touch becomes gentler. Slower.

One. He presses his cheek on her lips.

Zero. Pure, infallible joy. A joy that welcomed his words. The words that held the power to block every path that they could have taken.

OCTOBER, 1968
OSIJEK

She stared at the infinite perfection of the sky – blue, blue, and blue. There was not a single drop of gray, as though the night would never come. She could almost smell death in the beauty of the fresh air. Coming to get her as she decided to sit in that boat and sail far away. Away enough. The little girl merrily and loudly ran around as her golden locks swayed behind her, pulling Žanet into the realm of the living.

"Pretty, isn't it?" she heard her husband's voice.

He took the little girl in his arms, pointing his elongated finger at the airplane doodling on the blue sky.

"Plane!" the little girl yelled.

"Plane, yes," he placed a peck on her forehead.

"Take me on a plane," she leaned her head on his as if she were resting.

"Really, now?" they watched the line in the sky fade. "That's what Nadja wants?"

Nadja nodded, grazing Žanet with her gaze.

"Then we'll make it so."

***

The place in front of the bakery became her lair. She would always sit there when the fragile snowflakes fell around her, the rain poured down from the gloomy sky, and the sun stretched out its stubborn beams. That big world that offered lots was far too cheap regarding her wishes. Was that its simple answer? An eye for an eye, a tooth for a tooth? She believed it was. And in that far too big a world, she found a corner far too small but suitable for her withered self.

JANUARY, 1984
PARIS

"Nadja," his chiseled jaw convulsed. "There's something you should know."

"No," she moved her head from his lap, slowly shaking it. "No."

Silence reigned between them as if it toyed around; one moment with hope, the other with disarmament.

"What is it?" she asked. "Tell me."

"It's that," he sighed. "The thing you don't want to hear."

Her lips were wide open, and she had no intention of closing them. It felt as if a thick fog was coming out of her mouth, leaving her dry and empty. She was relieved but empty. But emptiness sometimes has a strange tendency to be whole. And sometimes, only pain is appropriate enough to fill it.

"I thought," her lips merged in a tremble, "it wasn't possible."

She stood on a thin line separating and simultaneously uniting her dreams and reality. She could almost feel the friction underneath her feet. Narrowing that line to a point beyond recognition, the point of inexistence.

"That what wasn't possible?"

Once again, he dove into her eyes. This time with a gaze full of pain.

"To replace me."

"And it isn't," he cupped her cheeks with his palms, turning them towards him. "Of course, it isn't."

She felt the warmth of his hands soaking into her cheeks. Mine. Mine. Mine? Sometimes, only a few defiant words leave a question mark on our strongest beliefs, leaving us ambivalent between what we truly are and all that our life threw at us.

"Stop it," she moved his hands off her cheeks as if separating herself from herself. "How can you even say that now?"

"It just happened," he placed his lonely hands in his lap. "You weren't there."

"I wasn't there?" she dove into his eyes, feeling banished from them for the first time.

"So, I have to be there so that someone wouldn't take my place?"

"No," he said snippily, not knowing who he was angry at.

"Then what?"

She could feel her heart arguing with itself. Mine, or taken away?

"It didn't mean anything," he shook his head, staring at the loneliness of his lap. "But it happened."

Her head turned into a vastness that echoed with his voice: but it happened.

"Is she beautiful?"

"Yes."

What is beauty? You are beautiful. I have to be beautiful. We were beautiful. Were.

"I am sorry," he exhaled.

He pressed his forehead against her shoulder, and the heavy silence between them filled with his sobs and tears. His sorrow. His weakness. His and hers. The inside of her whispered as though deciphering the hidden codes of his soul, exposing the secrets of his body language: every last bit. The universe never spares. It gives you a whole being with whom happiness multiplies and sadness breaks in half. Sometimes, however only sometimes, some souls end up possessing a supernatural power to break our hearts but without nicking even the smallest part of the love we harbor. It's precisely those supernatural souls of our lives that remember who we are in detail – even when we forget. When the curtains fall, and the mask slithers off of our weary face, and when the world goes silent, they recognize us because they unconditionally loved every bit of that whole that they inadvertently broke.

***

The walls of her room, with its low ceiling under which she spent so many moments thinking about him, turned from soft pink into all kinds of dark, rotten hues. Her bed, once soaked in trust and hope, became unrecognizably cold. But with his soul beside her that melted into that saddened environment, all of that could be survived. When the tears on their faces dried and the painful silence overcame their world, they were left with the only thing that always prevailed. Love.

"Nadja," her mother knocked on the door. "I'm bringing you a mattress."

Nadja opened the door and saw her mother with rollers in her thick black hair, wearing a purple silk nightgown.

"Somebody will have to sleep on the mattress," she held a small mattress in her hands. "Your bed is tiny."

"Alright," she took the mattress from her mother's hands. "Thanks."

"Good night, children," she blew them a kiss.

"Good night," Zair's voice surged through the air.

She placed the mattress on the ground, furiously pulled out a pillow from the upper shelf of her closet, took a blanket off the bed, and put it all on the mattress. She removed her clothes and felt his gaze sliding up and down her naked body. The threads of their souls had started tangling together again without a single touch. Just like that night on the roof of his building, which was now stuck inside the core of her throat like a memory that had a bitter shine. There exist intense moments that, even when we give up on them, remain burning somewhere deep inside us. Ever so adamantly rushing from one extreme to the next. From the simplicity of happiness to the rigor of sadness and vice versa. She hurriedly dove into her silk nightgown as he pulled the mattress out of the frame of her bed, laying it on the floor next to his.

"If this is the last night where you're mine," he lay on his mattress, "lie next to me."

"I don't want to touch you," she felt her insides rebelling against her words, "I can't."

"I won't touch you," he shook his head. "You have your mattress. I have mine."

She kneeled on her mattress and defied the pain she felt, lay on her back, gazing at the open window above them. With her peripheral vision – which usually catches the most important corners of our moments – she glanced at his figure that turned towards her, propped up on his elbow. Besotted by the mixture of pain and stars and wrapped with a sense of hope that the morning would bring unpredictable salvation, Nadja drifted off to sleep.

Wobbling on the thin line between her dreams and the reality – where she would eternally belong to him, and he would stay hers – she felt his lips plunging into her cheek.

"Always," he uttered in an almost nonexistent voice.

Like a goodbye, a farewell, a tear or eternity – she plunged her head into his chest and fell asleep there, with the rhythm of his heartbeat. When the sun extended its tentacles, chasing away every last breath of night, Zair left, never to return to Paris again.

Touches

FEBRUARY, 1984
OSIJEK

She stared at the broken piece of the doctor's glasses.

"Listen," he exhaled, "Mrs...."

"Tabita," she added hastily.

He nodded, taking a moment to soak up her name and hastiness.

"His current condition is," he spread his arms in front of him as if calling out for appropriate words, "solid."

She dug her sweaty palms into the small leather bag warming her lap.

"Current, yes," she cleared her throat. "But what will happen later?"

"Tabita," he dove into her eyes. "There's a significant possibility that it will remain this way forever."

But there's also another possibility that it won't.

"Multiple sclerosis is an unpredictable disease," he spread his arms again, "but we can try our best to keep it in its current state."

"What are the worst possible outcomes?"

"It's hard to say," he cleared his throat, "because this disease has many faces."

"What does it mean for his soccer career?"

"We can try our best to keep his life the way it currently is," he tilted his head gently as if trying to give her some of his strength. "But the disease sometimes defeats the will of the doctor."

And the patient.

"We'll begin with lighter medications," he placed a few sheets of paper in front of her. "Then we'll see how things go from there."

***

She had to purify her thoughts, wash them out, crumble them up, destroy them, chase them away, leave them to the wind. She walked through King Tomislav Park with its paths wide enough for her to be able to pour the sorrow of her being all over them. The trees, tall and rich seemed like a heart beating between the chest of the world, and with every movement of their branches, they talked with her sorrow. The sun shone in its full glory as defiantly as it could in contrast to the sun dying away inside her.

She could not stop the waves of her memories. A curly boy born out of our love. They lined up in her mind as if painting a paradox of enormous potential. Blue jerseys. A camera. Thick tears started rolling down her face. 1973. Soccer field. The world around her fell silent as it tried to let her know that in no way did the past belong to the present moment. Tiny soccer players. Excitement. Energy. Health. Joy. Her mind filled itself with thoughts, like some dam that tried to keep the strong river at bay, but to no avail. What would happen with that dam? The river keeps flowing, not wondering for a second whether the dam can take it. She stayed there for a few hours – right next to the river Drava – listening to the way it caressed the riverbank, gazing at Baranja's rich forests on the other side – not aware how much sadder that same Baranja was going to be only a few years later.

***

They sat at the table in the small kitchen. The same kitchen where she, twenty years earlier, couldn't utter the words that she was pregnant. That she was carrying a child – Zair.

"Tabita," he said with a calm, deep voice. "It's about time you told me what's going on."

She sat there in the shell of the small wooden chair. Still wearing her shoes, still in her pale denim jacket, and her purse hanging from her shoulder. The kitchen echoed with the sound of her sniffles.

"You're worrying me," Marko exhaled. "Just tell me already."

How do I tell you this? I can tell you anything but don't make me break your heart. Sometimes, some things are not in our power. She placed the stack of his medical records on the table.

"You were at the doctor's," he looked at the papers pensively, "I didn't even know."

She stared at his marble-like eyes dancing up and down, soaking it all up – all the things that shouldn't be soaked up.

"I don't understand," he shook his head. "What is this?"

She shrugged. It is what you see.

"Shit, Tabita," his eyes glinted as he stared at her widely. "This is crap."

***

Tabita and Marko were one of those couples whose affection never faded but gently blended with its environment, keeping its consistency safe like a chameleon. They did not have to spend every waking moment together, nor did they have to touch all the time. Love was always there. Calm, loyal. But, that night – when the image of Zair in a wheelchair was the only thing filling their minds – a touch meant more than anything else in that vortex of a world.

APRIL, 1984
PARIS

She bounced from one leg to the other, waiting for her turn to go to the toilet, until the door finally opened, and out of it walked a skinny woman with a dry brown mane on her head. Above her thick lips lay a mole that, through Nadja's eyes, as if through a portal, could easily belong to one of the characters from the newest novel she was tirelessly working on. She slipped through the space between the woman with the mole and the doorframe, swiftly taking her pants off, and only then, feeling a few pounds lighter, started looking around the toilet. Its turquoise blue tiles, the rotten wooden door, and the sticky floor her Startas shoes glued onto. Sometimes, however, the most vital details could not be touched with the eye but smelled with the nose. She wondered whether it stank so much in the men's bathroom and found herself searching for an answer only a few minutes later.

"Does it stink in the men's room?"

"Excuse me?" he turned around casually, briefly stopping his conversation with one of the assistant directors.

"Does it stink in the men's room?" she placed her lips against his ear and asked him again.

As though stopping the world with his stupefied delight, Patrik placed his lips against her ear.

"I haven't been yet," he exhaled with a gentle smile, "but I believe it does."

She nodded her head, content with the answer.

***

Patrik's short comedy shooting was, at least for Nadja, tiresome and pointless. She read the script before it became a movie; a married couple fighting. That was it. Two people, love, marriage, kids, and monologues. All that in just a few minutes. Nadja's mind restlessly moved around the set like a busy bee fluttering around a withered flower. Nadja's world, above all, always had a strong tendency to dive into the depths of the individual as much as the pair, as well as the depths of all that surrounds them and all that they create. Placing something like love and marriage in a mere couple dozen minutes was, in her world, absurd. Sometimes, however, the absurd of our world is the most apparent logic in someone else's. She wasn't enchanted by the actors either. Especially the twins who played two leading roles. The husband and his brother, who spent a lot of time with his brother's wife. They were too milky, slow, and empty.

But every time her instinct surfaced, a piece of the sensibility in her would let out a sound: what is actually the most important thing? Then she'd complacently answer her own question as if it spoke with a voice of some higher reason: that the creator is happy.

***

The tradition remained the same. Tuesday was a day for walking around the magnificent Paris, Saturday was for the fancy dinners, and Sunday was for their Croatian stomachs. That Sunday, with their bellies full and their heads already tired in advance from the upcoming week, Nadja and Patrik went to Patrik's apartment to skim over the scripts for the upcoming shooting.

Patrik had been living alone in his apartment for a few months, two floors above Nadja and her mother. It was on the last floor of the building, its balcony seemed like a glade of the world, and the interior was much more luxurious than the one Nadja and her mother lived in. The furniture was made from fine brown leather, table and chairs from heavy varnished oak, and the walls were painted a dark olive-green color, covered in black and white photographs with brown frames – perfectly aligned about six feet from the ground and a foot from the ceiling. Each photo had a man and a woman in it. She was strangely beautiful, and he looked awfully like Patrik. Or did Patrik look awfully like him? She did not ask questions. Even though she wasn't sure whether they were his parents, she was sure of one thing: it's always tricky to ask about the people that passed away.

"I don't feel like drinking wine," he said. "I have a lot to do anyway."

"No wine then," she glanced around the kitchen they had arranged together a few months earlier.

The kitchen was also made from fine varnished oak, and the elements looked like little windows. You could see inside them through the seamlessly clean glass.

"But I feel like drinking coffee," he opened the kitchen cupboard. "Would you like some?"

"I can always drink coffee," she replied.

"You can begin," he gestured towards the desk with his chin, "this won't take a minute."

A massive desk stood in the corner of that kitchen and living room, separating them with a mere counter. It looked like it grew out of the wall and into it simultaneously. It was full of papers written out with his wavy, playful handwriting. She could almost hear every wave calling out to her in its special voice, "read me."

Patrik was an interrupted constant following the line of her life silently and impartially, but she barely knew anything about him. She was not sure whether it was because of her running away every time they would start to deepen their acquaintance even remotely or because of the humble mystique he radiated. She took a paper from the top of the stack. It was one of the parts of the script they were currently working on. She skimmed through the letters already well-known to her and then placed the paperback. That was not it. That was not the voice that echoed read me. Something else spoke to her as though calling for her to find a lost treasure. She reached for the next sheet of paper. It was messily written out in a hurry, almost completely struck out with disgruntled lines. She knew that feeling very well. Many stuck-out letters exist on every writer's hidden sheet of paper. It seemed she was getting closer to that sunlit golden touch as she heard the call more clearly: read me. She reached for the next piece of paper. It was written out with the same wavy handwriting but more tidily, devotedly, fluidly – like the letters reigned over his mind and his hand. By then, all the hidden, calling voices had started merging with the letters she was reading.

Short golden hair. The letters poured one from the other as if glued together by a special magic every man succumbs to. The words hid strange magic in them like they held the power to pull the whole reality into their chamber. The dimple on her cheek awakens an insatiable thirst. These words were nothing like she'd ever read before in his works. It was so good. So good that every other story of his seemed a mere shadow of this one. She reached for the next one, written out with the same devoted handwriting. The magic continued. The iron fence hides me from her view. She paused briefly, wrapping these words into the veil of reality while she eats the apple. She could almost feel the taste on her tongue – the taste of the apple and the taste of the memories. The hunger of that devoted and fluid handwriting pulled her into a vortex that, in a glimpse, changed the hues of her reality. Dorothy. Dorothy dances under; Dorothy writes. Dorothy. The untouched metaphoricity of her mind touches the whiteness of the paper. Dorothy.

"I see," he placed the cups on the desk and stopped the clamor of her thoughts. "You've managed to find your way in this."

She placed the papers on the desk and dove into his eyes as her cheeks radiated. His eyes seemed awfully, frighteningly familiar now. Then, with a quick glance, he grazed the sheet of paper that she had put down.

"It's not finished yet," he cleared his throat. "That novel."

She nodded her head, still staring into his flustered pupils.

"I've been writing it for years already," he scratched the back of his neck, "and I'm not sure if it'll ever be good enough."

Good enough? It's perfect.

"You never told me about it."

"I'm telling you," he waved his hand towards the desk, "it's not finished."

"The writing style is much better," she turned towards the desk again, "better than anything else of yours that I've read."

She touched one of the sheets as if touching the surface of boiling water in a pot.

"That novel, it's important to me," he uttered tentatively, "and that's why it's never good enough."

She soaked in the written words: The untouched metaphoricity of her mind touches the whiteness of the paper. The last letter in the sentence seemed to melt.

"Dorothy," he uttered again insecurely, "she is..."

"Me," she turned around, interrupting him nervously.

A straight line rose between their pupils. For the first time, she gazed into his eyes – the mirror of his existence – and saw them. He was silent as an untamed fear before her gaze danced around his heart.

Ten. Her lips touch his lips.

Nine. Effort. Strain. Excitement.

Eight. Spark.

Seven. Shy butterflies tickle the pit of her stomach. Shyly, but they tickle.

Six. His dry palm touches her neck. Gently, hardly noticeable.

Five. Her fingers run through his hair. Thick, but dry... Dry.

Four. The smell of his perfume fills her nostrils and travels down her throat.

Three. His lips nimbly and passionately suck on hers, causing bitter guilt.

Two. Her teeth bite his lower lip, hoping that roughness will evoke passion.

One. The hope is shattered.

One. Her hands let go of his neck, and her fingers find their way to the buttons of his shirt.

Two. The shirt disappears.

Three. The firm paleness of his chest under her fingertips.

Four. Her waist in the shell of his palm.

Five. His hands lift her.

Six. Her naked skin touching the cold wooden table.

Seven. Her dress completely disappears.

Eight. Rough needles pick on her scalp.

Nine. Her body becomes his, and her soul follows in disbelief.

Ten. Everything begins, and everything falls apart.

Curtain

JULY, 1985
PARIS

Her ear scraped against Patrik's shirt as the musical voice of the culinary show's TV host echoed around the room. It was the first play she'd brought to an end and the first play that someone had read, other than Ilir and her mother. She could see it in his eyes. He pinned his unstoppable hopes into her script, and he'd give his best for it to be performed on an actual stage, portrayed by refined and well-rehearsed actors. The air smelled like the beginning of her dreams coming true, as if everything was possible. Fairies, witches, trolls, deep magic forests, dragons, and cyclopes; truly everything. Everything was achievable, close, and tangible.

She loved watching Patrik read her works. She knew he was a solid critic able to look at them from various angles and evaluate their worth. The sole action of his approval of her words meant success for Nadja. And she never thought, not even for a moment, that it could merely be proof of the unfaltering love he felt for her. The love that frequently felt like a withdrawal crisis where we stop at nothing to get our hands on our chosen vice. The vice that kills, but gently and mellifluously. However, all vices hid a simple truth in their essence: their tragic adversity was always a consequence of the addict's choice, without which the tragedy couldn't ever reach its peak.

Patrik and Nadja became a team. Every show of his was her show as well. They skimmed through scripts together, chose the actors, coordinated the people behind the stage, sat in the front row, and watched their embodied magic on the stage when all was ready. They were like two minds merged into one. But the mind was always a foot separated from the soul, which – unlike the pliable and curious mind – always searched for the same pattern of taming, like a tiny, wild creature.

Mother and Mr. Bošnjak adored their romance more so than Nadja herself. Their romance and the life filled with creations that twisted around her were, above all, the product of her mother and Mr. Bošnjak's passion for that thought; the thought of Nadja and Patrik strolling through life together, sharing their dreams, strengthening their mutual ambitions and conquering the world with their creations. Patrik was a shade of that big idea, a mere blind child whose dreams were extended on the palm of his hand, while Nadja, the subject and the essence of that whole affair, silenced her dreams and underestimated the power of her soul's voice. She lived for the present day as the adventurous spirit grew inside her. She was not as fragile and conquerable anymore. Her appearance was like an astonishingly intriguing shell that kept a timid, shining pearl hidden from the whole ocean. What kinds of secrets do the pearls inside of us keep? The deepest ones, indeed. One palm always hides the pearl inside us – as though awakening all our strongest senses and immeasurable values – and the shell remains tightly closed until the next touch, no matter how many other palms try to get ahold of the pearl in the meantime. Our heart always faithfully remembers whom it belongs to, even when the mind cunningly forgets.

The kitchen echoed with the blunt sounds of the knife hitting the wooden counter and her mother's sniffles. The water she left running to suppress the urge for tears was not much use. The sound of the phone ringing filled the room, interrupting all the other sounds – the knife, the sniffling, the television that Nadja abruptly turned off.

“Oui?” the mother picked up the phone, a dishrag hanging from her shoulder.

“Oh,” she exhaled joyfully, “Ilir.”

“All is well,” she smiled, “all is well. How are you?”

The smile faded from her mother’s face, and a blunt grimace replaced it.

“When did they take her away?”

Žanet. Nothing new.

“I’m so terribly sorry,” the mother grabbed the phone with both hands as though trying to hug Ilir.

“We were planning to come either way, so we will definitely see each other.”

She nodded her head gently.

“As soon as we can, you can be sure of that,” she paused, seemingly interrupted by his speech.

“Hang in there.”

She hung up the phone, inhaling deeply. She looked like she was angry at herself and at the world at the same time. Still holding her palm on the phone, she spoke.

“Žanet is sick.”

“Žanet has always been sick,” Nadja straightened her back on the sofa.

“Nadja,” her mother scolded her with her gaze, “it’s serious; she has cancer.”

Nadja's heart raced. She was never close to Žanet, but that woman was an irremovable part of her, and a part she was not ready to say goodbye to.

"What kind of cancer?"

"What do you think?" her mother threw the chopped onions onto the hot pan. "Lung cancer."

"When are we leaving?"

She could feel Patrik's gaze full of fear sliding all over her face.

JULY, 1985
OSIJEK

It was right there where she left it. Spread out alongside the river Drava, passionately making love with her stream and all her turmoil, magnificently gazing at Baranja, like a silent lover, every night as the unstoppable force of the river separated them, gazed back at it with a warm nostalgia in its gleaming eyes. Seemingly joyous for their return, Osijek welcomed Nadja and her mother with open arms, lighting up from the sun. Intent on keeping the tears right where they're stuck – encased at the sole bottom of her throat like a hard and heavy rock – she decided to focus on her mother's sorrow. She glanced at her pretty, elongated face, searching for signs of salted water on her face and in the corners of her eyes, but her mother became immune as well. Her pearl remained locked up a long time ago.

The bakery, just like the city, was right where they left it. But it looked as if it were hibernating, even though summer played around it with its sunbeams. Nadja rested her soul gazing at the wooden cupboard in the corner, still able to see herself clearly. A tiny girl whose feet dance above it, reading whatever they shoved in her hands. But, instead of that, there was now a black-and-white photograph with a red frame.

A tiny Nadja sitting on top of the wooden cupboard. Ilir holding a cake in his hands, his smile lit up by seven shiny candles, while Nadja, with a wide grin, presses the brown leather notebook tightly to her chest.

There was another one, framed in black, right next to the photo of Nadja's birthday.

A black-haired boy with a toothless smile sits with his legs crossed with a beautiful red-haired woman next to him. The boy holds a small bottle with an even smaller ship in his hands, and around them – on the high shelves of the narrow hallway – a multitude of ships in bottles.

Nadja was not entirely sure where the similarity between the little boy and Ilir lay. But it was there, and it was unquestionable. Maybe in the warmth of the boy's smile that hid inside his eyes.

"He told me to just bake one bread," her mother was already tying the apron that looked ever so elegant, magnificent, and natural on her waist, "and then to turn off the oven."

***

The hospital reeked of its usual smells; sickness, people, drugs, death, life, bitter disinfectants, and people's breaths. And the weariness of the human body. The weariness of souls, mostly, Nadja thought.

While Nadja and her mother – like silhouettes isolated from the monotonous hospital dynamic due to their health – slid across the hospital hallways searching for room 11 of the cancer ward, a small boy blocked their path. He bumped into Nadja with his small body and, frightening himself, fell on the ground rolling, and his glasses – like a crystal rain – broke into a million shiny pieces. His one eye – the one that was hidden behind a colorful patch on his glasses – was covered with a white bandage.

"I'm sorry," Nadja crouched beside him, picking through her bag. "Maybe this can be of use to you."

The boy watched her with his big eye.

"Their diopter is +2," she handed him her thin, black-framed glasses. "Have the doctors check if they'll be a match for you."

The boy's one free eye glanced at the glasses on her palm as though sniffing them.

"I only use them for reading, anyway," she brought the glasses closer to him. "Come on, take them."

The boy, breathing excitedly and revealing his two separated front teeth, took the glasses off Nadja's palm and marched in the other direction, merging with the crowd.

"Are you crazy?" her mother asked as their feet continued searching for room 11. "God knows how much Franjo gave for those."

"You know what, mom?" she grazed her with a soft glance. "I don't care."

Nadja knitted a fragile ball of hope inside her – that the boy was merely a visitor and not one of the patients. He only had a bit of dust in his eye, which was unrelated to their ward. She concocted a hope that would never be placed in one of the existing worlds of truth and untruth. Given the fact that she'll never see the boy again. Or maybe she will? Sometimes, the world is much smaller than we could hope for.

***

Žanet was sick. You could see it in her weary, blunt gaze and devoid of ideas. But Nadja knew that Žanet was ill long before her current diagnosis. Something had metastasized inside her for decades, but Nadja was never brave enough to ask Ilir about her secret. Now, as she stood before his figure, ready to jump into his embrace, it wasn't important anymore. Nothing was important except closeness and connection.

"Dear, dear," he embraced her with his big body and arms, "finally, I see you again."

She could feel how puny he became. He was still a plump man, but plump in a much wearier way, hidden behind a fluffy blue sweater.

"Ilir," her mother stole him from her embrace, "I'm so glad to see you."

Then there was silence. The silence faced them with two uniting facts: Žanet was perishing, even though nobody wanted that. Nobody but her, perhaps.

"What did they say?" her mother pulled Ilir to the side, her face filled with compassion.

"They just said she was dying," Ilir shrugged.

"Well," her mother uttered anxiously, "how long does she have?"

"They aren't sure," Ilir shrugged again, "but they know there's not much time, and they can't help her."

As their voices faded in the distance of the foggy reality, Nadja sat next to Žanet. She watched her chest tremulously rise and fall as her dry hair diffused all over the whiteness of the pillow. She seemed peaceful, even though the shell of her being knew only pain and sorrow.

***

After a two-hour phone call with Patrik, Nadja lit a cigarette at the bakery. The evening had a strange crackling to it as if it were trying to whisper something in Nadja's ear. She felt a bitterness of guilt in her feet because she now heard only partly the whisper of her city. She gazed at the blackness that diffused over the sky as if trying to find the codes that could translate a long-lost language. Just as she was about to give up on the translation, she saw her there, in the shy corner of the sky – a single star. I named her Iris. And I'm giving it to you. Lit up by the old memories that bring new understandings, she could see the parking lot in front of the bakery more clearly now. As well as the three trees on the other side. Osijek. I am here.

Her defiant soul was already there – inside the walls of his room – owning his every thought, gesture, movement, and touch. On the other hand, her body was merely an occasional servant to her soul and found itself there half an hour later. It was 10pm. Had she rung any other doorbell, she'd probably fly back down the stairs, rushing out of the building like hell. But now, only a tiny drop of discomfort grazed her throat, and her body – in that unstoppable intention – waited.

"Nadja," Marko was standing at the door with messy hair.

"Good evening," she uttered insecurely.

Now – when she could look at herself from foreign eyes – she could feel how French her pronunciation had become.

"Come on in," he waved his hand, "I had no idea you were coming."

"How are you?" she glanced around the well-known hallway, content because not much had changed. "How is everyone?"

"Great," he shrugged, "Tabita is already asleep."

She nodded her head, feeling a strange envy towards them feeling great.

"And Zair?" she uttered silently.

"He's not here," Marko shook his head.

What do you mean he's not here? Where is he sleeping? She nodded silently as her heart started beating fiercely in her throat.

"Nadja," he placed his palm on her shoulder, "I'm just messing with you."

The fast heartbeat in her chest paused for a second, silent in front of the double stupefaction she felt.

"He's in his room," he gestured towards the door with his hand, "where you left him."

Left. Walking towards the door, a question skyrocketed in her mind: is it truly possible to leave behind those that never really left our souls? She fixed her freshly cut hair – that was, at the time, the same length as the last time he'd seen her – and walked up to his room. The end of the hallway then left – right next to the living room, where she could see the silhouette of tiny Zair rushing around in all directions, kicking the soccer ball.

Darkness ruled over his room, broken up by only a few spots of pearlescent moonlight touching the tips of all his things. So pearlescent that, for a moment, it seemed utterly unreal. Unreal, just like that whole night which would remain carved in her memory like a dream that never actually happened. Zair's wooden-framed bed stood in the right corner of a small, long room, separated by a high wooden window. Moonlight touched the edges of his elongated eyelashes, diffusing over his dry lips, vigorously delineating his already chiseled jaw. She could hear him breathing and see his broad chest spreading and relaxing. With a magical movement, she took off her white knitted shirt and stiff jeans as though treading through a world awaiting her return for so long. Then she removed her white lingerie, carefully gazing at her pale shoulder. As a final note, she took off her black sandals, unfastening one belt at a time.

She did not sit next to him, she did not explain herself, and she did not utter a single coherent word. Feeling supernaturally potent over his being, she just stood there – until he gently and half-asleep opened his eyes and saw a line of her body – now even more narrow, like a snake. She watched him watch her, without breath or any idea what to do, and full of guilt that, in unprecedented shades, merged with love. Wake up from the dream, or indulge in it? He strode with his gaze across her thighs, her thin waist that maleficently curved into her hips, and for the longest time, he gazed into her two big eyes.

Ten. Like it's the first and the last time.

Nine. And it is.

Eight. His lips touch her neck, diving into her breasts, walking the line that leads to her navel.

Seven. His velvet skin under her teeth and the silk sheets under the awakened skin of her back. She knows she'll feel this forever.

Six. The world does not exist. Paris, Osijek, Patrik – they do not exist. Everything is made out of the two of them – the cause and the effect.

Five. The warmth of his shoulder shines into her lips as he immerses his fingertips into her skin.

Four. They dive in, then resurface again, without end. Cyclically. Entangled in the warmth of their breaths.

Three. His fingers ran through her hair, and hers immersed into his. It's not dry. It's not dry. It's not dry...

Two. Everything ends. Everything ages. And with that – it seems to come alive again.

One. The last moment of the last time. Just like the end of the most vicious show – the curtains ruthlessly close.

Zero. The last lyric of the song. The last tone of the composition. The final stroke of the brush.

Mailbox

JANUARY, 1986
PARIS

The salty river tickled the edges of her eyes as she sat in the front row – close enough almost to smell the actors' sweat that embodied the fruit of her imagination. Applause. Thousands of sweaty palms uniting, reacting to the show made according to her principles. As the crowd united their palms, she could only feel one thing: gratitude.

"You did it," Patrik whispered into her ear.

His red hair was lit up with the intense light of the reflectors as his eyes absorbed every last bit of her show – as if watching his creation – doubling her happiness.

"We did it," she placed his hand on his, watching the actors taking a bow, "we."

"We have to celebrate this," he got up and took her hand. "Come on."

"Congratulations," the theater director approached them, "Madame."

"Thank you," she blew a rogue lock of hair off her nose, trying to speak French as fluently as possible, pulling her leather gloves on. "I'm thrilled."

Their hands clasped in a firm handshake.

"You are talented," he smiled with his tiny eyes.

"Now that I hear it from you," she took a slight bow, "maybe I'll finally believe it."

"Congratulations to you as well," he shook Patrik's hand, "for digging out this one-of-a-kind."

***

They would go to a pub to heal themselves from too much sophistication and stiff habits. It was an inn, albeit strangely neat. Upon arrival, they would take two shots of tequila, and sometimes even more – when Paris became too big of a burden on their poetic backs. Their conversations at that wooden bar would last for hours. Made of senseless but at the same time nimbly thought-up word games. Both were so gently but fiercely making love with the whole world, touching it with their words, decorating it with imagination, leading it towards a playful absurd that gave meaning to every small man's story, even the most ordinary one.

"I knew you could do it," he raised his glass. "I've always known that."

He spread the tequila quickly over his throat, swallowing it awkwardly to hide the disgust on his face.

"I didn't," she raised her glass back at him, swallowing the burning bitterness.

She did not like strong drinks because they always boiled sharply in the pit of her stomach. But strong things had two sides to their magic. They burn us, but at the same time, they burn all those parts of us that need to be burned.

"My uncle is proud of you more than he is of his nephew," he smiled gently.

"Eh," she nodded playfully, "if you were as good as I am…"

His eyes laughed. She loved that about him – the way his eyes laughed, even if his lips stood still. He was always invincibly happy around her. And never, ever, in the whole history of their relationship, has there been a word or a thing she could not say or do around him. She was utterly idealized in his eyes – he adored every part of her sexuality, every dash of her joy, every slightest bit of her sorrow, and every flash of her anger. He loved her in every way, unconditionally. However, every idealized love raises a stubborn question. How much would they genuinely love us if we stepped out of the fog of their intimate fascination?

MARCH, 1986
PARIS

By then, Nadja knew how to satisfy her hunger while walking to the giant university building. Holding onto the door of her apartment, she put on her high heeled black boots and carried a paper bag with croissants under her arm. Then filling her mouth and stomach with the pastries' softness, she bounced hurriedly down the long spiral stairway, leaving behind the echo of her heels touching the concrete. Her blonde shoulder-touching ponytail bounced behind her in a thick wave, and her golden fringe fell down her right cheek, barely touching that single dimple.

The day was sunny and promising. Through the high window on the mezzanine of the building, she saw the morning sun shyly making its way through, like a barely screwed-on light bulb that was being carefully turned on. On her way out, she automatically opened the mailbox, her mind already immersed in her class and her brain entirely dedicated to theater and detached from her past and hometown. Then, like Deja Vu, all those buried memories, the muddy hallways of her soul, the silenced dialogues, and the evaporated smells were again rediscovered.

Sixteen. A well-known field, and the perspective as well. Three sunbeams are peeking out in the upper right corner of the photo behind a thick cloud.

On the back of the photograph: I believe you're familiar with the field you're looking at – Olympia.

Seventeen. The photo's upper line shows the sky's whiteness, and the center is divided by a greenish fence separating the small concrete bleachers from the bare field.

Eighteen. A big field takes up the whole photo with its avid greenery. The sun is bright, seemingly without a source, and the lower right part of the photograph shows a few small plastic chairs on the bleachers.

Nineteen. The center of the photo shows a man - older, greyish, and balding - turned with his back and wearing a ragged ash-gray undershirt. White smoke twists in the air above his balding head as he stands with his elbows leaning on the bar that separates the players from the field.

On the back of the photograph: This match did not end well.

Twenty. The lower right corner of the photo shows three of Zair's teammates - two of them in a lively conversation, the third one smiling widely at the photographer - as the upper part of the photo shows the blue sky.

Twenty-one. Mediocre-looking bleachers without chairs take up the lower part of the photograph, while the upper part is painted with the grayness of the evening. A parking lot gently breaks the monotony of the grayness.

Twenty-two. A big, muddy soccer net fills the photo's upper part as the field's greenness stretches out below it. A single thin vertical bar of the fence looms over the right edge of the picture as though accidentally caught on camera.

Twenty-three. The sky takes up the whole photograph - the deepness of its blue color is reminiscent of the sea dappled with white lines. Only a tiny part of the lower edge of the photo shows the tip of the long concrete bleachers.

On the back of the photograph: I couldn't resist – the sky was prettier.

She placed her cold, trembling palms on her forehead, summoning herself to reality. The sun now strongly hit directly into her eyes, making its way through the yellow window of the entrance doors. Not even knowing where she was running off to, but knowing that she had to run, she rushed across the wide busy road, bumping into a middle-aged woman walking a badly shaved and overly small dog. In the café – whose proximity and usefulness she had not noticed earlier – she ordered a black coffee-to-go and headed to the nearby park with her thoughts stuck in the past and her soul back on those bleachers. She approached the first unoccupied bench, chasing away three playful sparrows that flew away as she sat down and blended in with the branches of the trees. She took a big sip of her coffee, lit the last cigarette she had on her, and pulled out the rest of the photographs.

Twenty-four. An extremely small and desolate field. The photo is split in two by a thin yellow fence. A ruinous white door of the dressing rooms peeks out above it.

Twenty-five. The soaked grass of the field takes up the whole photo with its glowing raindrops. A wet soccer net fills the upper edge of the picture as though trying to hide the sky.

Twenty-six. A larger, fiercely sunbathed field takes up the center, while the bleachers stretch over the photo's right and left edges like some safety fence. An index finger peeks out from the upper right corner, gesturing towards the clean white soccer net.

Twenty-seven. The photo is divided into four parts – horizontally, with the fence separating the field from the spectators, and vertically with Zair's teammate standing sideways, smiling at the photographer.

Twenty-eight. Taken from a very low angle, touching the rail and reaching the soccer net. Next to it, a soccer ball sits abandoned.

Twenty-nine. One raindrop in the upper right corner of the photo shatters the grayness above the wet field.

Thirty. Once again, a rainy photo. The upper right corner shows a tall, thin trash can, and the image is divided by fence rods that look like two parallels playing in the rain. The dressing rooms sit in the distance behind the field.

On the back of the photograph: The one thing that hasn't changed nor diminished is my hope that you're finding happiness every day.

***

When she sat all by herself on that tiny balcony illuminated by the starlight while hearing the squeaking of an unknown critter, they thought moved in somewhere under the wooden bench her mother painted white, as well as hearing the howling of the wind through the sleepy, desolate streets showered in darkness. When she gazed into that luminescent glow of the streetlamp, which, like fierce sunlight, seemed to spread infinitely all around, she could see his silhouette standing on the glass balcony doors, skillfully projecting itself from the anxiously locked up hallways of her soul. Our peripheral vision sometimes catches glimpses of the most important corners of our moments, while sometimes – during our getaway – brings the things we miss the most.

Nadja missed quite a few things. A black hole lay in the shell of her chest, and her fingers – as though showered in black magic – rotted away under the emptiness her mind would produce. In the first circle of her inner hell, like an introduction to some more pungent depths, she missed her father. She missed him bluntly, sneakily.

Zair was a special kind of missing – like a ripped-off part that belonged to her, ripped off from a mutilated whole that even she had been ripped off. The whole that belonged to her unconditionally, above every earthly power. She did not miss the touch, without it, everything was quite the same because that kind of belonging did not depend on the simple essence of touch. In the silence that she heard that night – as the darkness softly caressed the air around her, giving her world a masked perfection – she missed the tone that he gave to the silence. She missed the way he ruled over it, and she missed his breath that crawled through that unique universe – only ever known to the two of them.

She sat on the right side of the bench, lit the last cigarette of her life, feeling a piercing emptiness on the left– an emptiness that felt like a whole other and strange world – like nothingness without sound, idea, or concept. For a moment, it seemed like pieces and atoms of his existence accumulated next to her. She felt a memory: his dented forehead on her shoulder filled with his sobs, the smell of his skin that her essence would forever be drawn to, and the touch of his existence that – according to the most precise calculations of all the existing constellations – nimbly and unerringly intertwined with hers.

She put out that last cigarette and went inside the four narrow walls of her room. She silently approached her tiny desk in the corner and opened the brown leather notebook where she wrote her first story – dedicated to him. The one in which she skillfully trapped that humble wish for them to catch their first snowflakes together. A desire hindered by the vortex of the hasty world, therefore never coming true. In that same notebook, she wrote her last words about him, embodying her pain that would – like a song that stubbornly stays engraved into our souls – spread united along the line of her existence.

Shadows

APRIL, 1986
PARIS

He loved Lea's adventurous spirit. If not for that, she would never have decided to go to Rome with his uncle to a premiere of his new play, allowing him to observe Nadja's figure undisturbed – the way she lies in the bathtub, hidden under white bubbles.

The coldness of the floor tiles pierced his feet as he sat on the bathtub's edge, observing how she reached for the thin glass of wine with her soapy hands. That was, to be fair, the third glass that she'd been reaching for – which anyone would be able to notice even not having witnessed her drink the previous two, seeing as she was far too merry. Almost every second word of their conversation was now followed by her drunken laugh, which to him, felt like Turkish delight with roses that he and his uncle sometimes had with coffee – adventurously gentle and sweet. He found her toes captivating and interesting – how they stuck out on the other end of the white bathtub surrounded by a foamy white liquid. The dent next to her collarbone, like a trough that her neck flowed into, was like the Bermuda triangle for him – dangerous, sly, and playfully mystic.

***

He loved her sleepy, immersed in dreams, although her dreams hid something terrifying, hardly reachable to him. He would see everything but himself on her low forehead and big, closed eyelids. She dreamt absently, as though she ran away to another world he didn't belong to. He could watch her without a pause. That hint of ingratitude in her towards him and his carefully tender love fed him with inexplicable madness.

He loved making love to her. All men love making love, and all men hide an overwrought sexual drive underneath their skin which had to be directed, but Patrik loved making love to her. Just to her. He loved touching her soft, fluidly formed body. Even though he was merely a writer, playful in the world of letters, her naked body awoke his appetite for the paintbrush that would be able to record the milky ways of her body on canvas. He loved the soft touch of her lips which brought him immense sorrow but at the same time filled him with great joy. Joy because Dorothy, the inexhaustible meaning of his creation, was truly there – in the shell of his palms. She became the core madness of his art. All the other parts of his creation would become mere shadows – refined, but shadows – was she removed from his mind for only a second?

***

"I know you want to come in," she splashed him, holding her fourth glass of wine.

"Actually," he smiled, "I just want to watch you."

"Dorothy is taking a bath," she tilted her head gently, "Dorothy is drinking wine," she took a sip of her wine, calling him in with her gaze.

He wasn't sure whether it should offend him, like a writer of some absurd little story.

"Dorothy is pretty," she leaned on the edge of the bathtub.

"Nadja is pretty," he drew his face closer to hers, touching her cheek gently with his palm.

"Her – I love," she whispered.

"Her – I love," he confirmed.

He could feel the lightness of those words that came out of him, caressing his lips as they passed.

APRIL, 1986
PARIS

"I don't know, Patrik," she kept re-reading the Latin letters scattered all over the paper, "if I tell her this..."

"There's no 'if,'" he shook his head, "you have to tell her."

He stood there – just like every time, blending in with the moments of her lifeline – her guardian angel.

"This is impossible," she shook her head, her gaze still immersed in the paper.

"She has the right to know, Nadja,"

"Then explain it to me," she moved her gaze away from the paper, pointing it towards him, "How do you even say something like this to a person?"

They were standing in the silence of the cloud of worry surrounding them, encircled by the traffic noise.

"I don't know," he lowered his gaze, his hands restlessly fidgeting in his jean's pockets, "but I know you have to."

She glanced once again at the paper, then at him.

"The doctor would tell her anyway," she shrugged her shoulders gently, "sooner or later."

They continued to walk towards the building.

"Writers surround her," he exhaled deeply, "maybe we can remember her name."

"You're telling tales again, Patrik," she shook her head anxiously, "and this is the real world."

"Nadja," he squeezed her upper arm tightly and pulled her before him. "I'm right here."

He cupped her face with his palms as her green eyes glimmered with tears. Tears that did not touch her cheeks but being too dense remained in the corners of her eyes, glistening with an intense gloom.

"I'm here," he pulled her into his embrace.

***

Nadja was standing on the balcony doors, watching her mother drink coffee, and gazing into the distance over the high treetops of the park below them. She thought of all the things her mother had forgotten by now as the stubborn lump stopped in her throat again at the thought of how much of her childhood would die away, together with her mother's memory. In the true sense of those words, she and Ilir were the only witnesses of her whole existence – like a jigsaw connecting her present with the details of her past, giving full meaning to everything.

"Today is a great day for painting," the mother nodded affirmatively, her fingers wrapped around the thick mug.

Nadja stepped onto the balcony, wearing only socks on her feet.

"Are you alright?" she sat next to her mother, gazing into the same distance she was staring at.

"Are you alright?"

No, of course I'm not. How the hell did you know?

"Mom," she exhaled, "you know I have something to tell you, right?"

Her mother always served as a comforting mailbox in which you could put your bad news. Using her secret formulae, she knew in advance at least half of the envelope's contents.

"I know, darling," she nodded, her gaze still fixed on the distance in front. "It's bad, isn't it?"

"Maybe not," Nadja shrugged as she got a fierce urge to escape inside herself, "for you."

"What do you mean?" she glanced at her.

"You know," she tried desperately to restrain the incoming river of tears, "that feeling when you experience something awful," she swallowed a thick cluster of her saliva, "so awful that you simply know it will leave a giant mark on you for the rest of your life?"

Her mother kept quiet, but Nadja knew she was waiting for her to continue.

"And all you want to do is," she sighed, "just forget that it ever happened?"

She could feel a crystal sorrow clustering inside her mother. A sorrow she so faithfully kept hidden for all these years.

"To forget," she added, "and just to be able to be that pure, undamaged person," she smiled softly as her voice almost gave into the tears, "the child in you."

"Yes," her mother sighed, "there have been many of those moments."

"You see, that's what you'll be able to be," she gazed softly into her still undeniably beautiful face. "You'll be able to be that magical."

She swallowed hard once again, hoping that the river of tears wouldn't start flowing just yet.

"So," her mother swallowed a lump in her throat, seemingly out of the same reasons, "it's bad."

"There are pills," she glanced at the treetops.

"They only delay the inevitable," her mother added monotonously, "I assume."

"Yes. They just delay the inevitable."

Watching her mother straight in the eyes and telling her everything would be alright was impossible for Nadja. Her mother was the strongest woman she'd ever known and the strongest one she ever would meet, and you can't sell a 'happily ever after' to strong women.

OCTOBER, 1987
OSIJEK

She loved her new gray coat that extended to her knees, covering her spindly thighs and revealing her tiny stiff calves that hid under a pair of black tights. Pressed against the university building on Lorenz Jäger Street, Tabita watched her brown sky-leather boots soaking in the wet grass. The vehemence of the wind assumed a gentle rhythm, and her ears caught a glimpse of the remaining leaves that swayed up and down like hands on an old antique grandfather clock. A plastic cup filled with a bitter coffee-to-go warmed her palm as she waited for Marko to leave.

At last, his silhouette appeared in front of her. She watched the black-framed square glasses on his nose. Even though glasses were – in the world of the ordinary – a symbol of aging, in her eyes, they exuded some completely different symbols. Watching him that way, for a short and sweet moment, she painted a picture in her mind: him, naked – with only those glasses on his nose – standing in front of their bedroom window while she lays on their new iron bed, waiting for him.

"And?" she asked.

"I don't know," barely stopping, he continued walking towards Croatian Republic Street. "I don't know if they even liked me."

"Well," she picked up her pace, "what did they say?"

"The usual," he ran his fingers through his hair. "My lifelong writing and the magazine didn't seem to faze them."

But that's the only thing you ever really did.

"What did you even talk about, then?"

"That's the problem," he shook his head. "I don't have any teaching experience."

"What about others?" she threw the plastic cup into a trash can. "How did the other candidates seem?"

"Young," he nodded his head insecurely.

"Alright," she inhaled the freshness of the October air. "That's a plus for you."

"A plus for me?" he frowned questionably.

"The older you get, the wiser you are," she uttered with a musical tone of voice, "that's the old saying, right?"

She knew that in a world of complex possibilities and almost certain failures, she should be feeling guilty for not showing much care for Marko's job interview, but she didn't feel it. She was not worried, she didn't even try to be concerned, and she didn't feel even a pinch of guilt about it. She knew they'd manage somehow. She knew that the two of them – two imperfect, crazy, and sometimes outlandishly silly beings – would always find a way out – which would turn out to be a new entrance. All those labyrinths, filled with their colorful financial problems, next to him seemed to take the form of an adventure. Their team life had always been a unity – of black and white, rain and sun, night and day, twilight and dawn – and she loved every part of it immensely and infinitely.

***

She was sitting in the living room, stretched out on the sofa. Their apartment started smelling like varnished wood and baked nut rolls. She entertained herself with the idea that it was because they were becoming one of those older people who sit in their living room reading newspapers, watching TV, and enjoying the monotony of their life, ingraining the smell of their old age into the walls. However, the dice of life roll, old age always has one virtue: it is a mathematical proof of accumulated moments. And what is truly worth more than a moment? Nothing. All that we own and all that we are lies precisely in the diameter of a moment.

She was drinking Divka with a lot of milk and watching Only Fools and Horses – the show whose episodes she looked forward to every day recently. Then, the phone suddenly rang, interrupting her laugh.

"Hello?" she heard Marko's voice coming from the hallway.

He cleared his throat.

"Sorry?"

The fact that he was so formal with the person on the other side of the line activated a fierce echo of her heartbeat inside her eardrums.

"And now?" his breath got faster. "Everything alright?"

She heard the muffled scraping of his jacket against his satin shirt, then the phone hanging up, followed by the irregular footsteps approaching her through the hallway. Then, he stopped in front of the living room doors, one shoe partly put on, the other one in his right hand, and just as the ceramic cup touched her lips, he spoke.

"Zair is in the hospital," he put on his other shoe. "Apparently, it was a disastrous game."

Lullaby

OCTOBER, 1987
OSIJEK

She could hardly keep her eyes open. It seemed like a heavy patch of time lay on her eyelids, sleeping heavily, never to wake up. Excruciatingly, she woke up that heavy load of time from its hibernation and saw the light of day touching the window glass of the hospital room.

With her shivering right hand, she ran over her left one and, feeling wrinkles under her dry fingertips and the disappeared flexibility of her skin, she wondered: when did it all fly by irretrievably? Now, years later, it seemed as though all of her dreams, along with the youth she ruled over, died overnight. She was not sure, however, which night. That far away one, where she heard the creaking of the orphanage gate? Or the one where she, pressed against his shoulder, fell asleep waiting for the phone call? Or, perhaps, the one long before anything else – the one that erased the clearest figure of a soul mate she knew.

A nurse – the young one she somewhat liked, with her hair tied in a messy, firm ponytail – tiptoed into her room and approached her bed to see whether she was sleeping.

"You're not asleep," she lowered her palm onto hers.

Žanet shook her head.

"How are you feeling today?"

She did not answer, trying to remember the last time she even answered someone's question. As though already expecting the absence of her reply, the nurse soon continued her monologue.

"You look better," she smiled softly. "I know it's cramped and busy in here," she caressed her hand as though trying to transfer a part of her life to her, "but a couple more tests, and you'll be back in your room."

She fixed the needle pinned into the turquoise line of Žanet's vein that became somewhat of an integral part of her. A metal part of her strangely aligned with the essence of her heart and then left the room, depriving it of life again. Gray clouds, seemingly heavy and soaked with the world's tears, hid the sun and sprinkled the windows with a silver grayness. Cancer did not represent a medical term, diagnosis, sorrow, or nostalgia. For her, cancer was a critter, a crab that Petar often brought to her from the depths of the sea and took care of later in his room. A sweet, gangly critter. Above all, cancer was a symbol of death that she had been waiting for so long, for all these years. The only peace that could be offered to her in this deadly, stifling world. Gazing into the grayness and the sun's mutual embrace, she drifted off to sleep.

***

"He was told," she heard the wheels turning on the hospital bed, "of course, he was told that he wouldn't be able to play again."

The shortness of the doctor's breath lured her into the waking world. It took only a few seconds for her vision to clear up, for the fog of her dreams to disappear from her pupils so that she could finally see. The conversation between a skinny doctor with short, red hair and an elongated nose and the young doctor that pushed a hospital bed. Her old anxieties reminded her of her existence, clustering together playfully into a well-known lump in her chest. On the hospital bed next to her lay a young man with a chocolate complexion, and his dark soft curls diffused all over the whiteness of the pillow. No. Not in this room. Her lungs started enduring an even worse pain with every inhale, and the whole room spun like an uneasy ballerina. The nurse's palm touched her forehead as the needle dug into her other arm, making her doze off again.

***

She was not sure how long she had been out. The mumbling opened the door to reality, and she knew: everything was still physical, the sickness was still holding her tightly in its grip, and her heart was still beating underneath her chest – even though she was sure that death had come to take her.

She gazed into the whiteness of the ceiling, knowing that Heaven couldn't possibly be so monochrome. For a moment, she embraced the thought of Heaven – that hidden world of eternal peace – but then abruptly stopped her thoughts, firmly believing Heaven was not waiting for her. The mumbling of the hoarse voice summoned her gaze, and she turned her heavy head as her eyes drifted off to sleep again.

Three, two, one. She opened her eyes, and the image in front of them seemed clearer than ever.

One. A small iron chair without a backrest.

Two. It's placed between her bed and the bed of the young man with a chocolate complexion.

Three. A skinny woman sits on it.

Four. Her complexion is a shade of bronze.

Five. Her hair – dry, curly.

One, two, three. She closed her eyes and rested – from the light, from the mortal world. Three, two, one. She opened her eyes again.

Five. The woman speaks with a hoarse voice.

Four. "You have to stop," she tells him.

Three. "Can't you see it's bad for you," she adds.

Two. The young man turns his head towards the window, the curls on his nape squashed from the pillow.

One. "Zair," she squeezes his hand, "please."

Zero. Zair. It's not possible. The biggest craving of her life – dead for decades already – now lies young on the bed next to hers.

One, two, three. Her eyes closed as if the world of the living had become much too crowded, not ready to retain her being.

Three, two, one. She opened them again. A gray-haired doctor opened the hospital room door, glanced at them and around the room, then closed the door. As if lured, the bronze-skinned woman turned towards the open doors. Grayness in her eyes. It was the most beautiful grayness she had ever seen in her life. The same one that she got rid of years earlier. As if there wasn't a single moment separating the past times from the present ones, she could again feel, see, and hear: the chubby cheek pressed against her shoulder, a small mouth completely open, and her heavy trumpet-like exhales. Entirely naturally – like a fair and pure river – the song started flowing from her lips, followed by a coarse cry.

Three golden jackdaws

Singing louder than me.

A painful cough interrupted her and conjured their gazes. She cleared her throat, building a shield that would protect her from the fierce hits of the sickness for a short time, then continued singing, trying to be as intelligible as possible.

Three golden jackdaws

Singing louder than me.

Again, the same painful cough interrupts the song.

One, two, three. Her eyes were closed. Her body was hastily taking over her mind. The cold river of tears – that seemed to evoke lots of things –flowed down her dry cheeks in a relentless stream, touching her trembling lips. As though recognizing that the song was addressed to her, the bronze-skinned woman sat on the edge of her bed.

Three, two, one. She opened her eyes again.

"Ma'am," she dove into her eyes with her gray orbs, "is everything alright?"

She invested all the strength that she had left in her into a nod of confirmation.

One, two, three. Her eyes closed again, but her voice did not betray her.

Three golden jackdaws

Singing louder than me.

Three, two, one. She watched the grayness above her – that pretty, sophisticated, and refined grayness nesting in her pupils – and the few small wrinkles south of it that looked like beautiful scars. The whole world seemed to stop in those two gray eyes – the whole world, except her. Except for Žanet. There was no memory of Žanet in that skinny woman's gaze who, despite all those years, still strangely looked like that little girl that lay asleep on her shoulder.

"Ma'am," her voice traveled towards Žanet's ear, "I can call the doctor."

Again, she invested all her strength into her head – shaking it. The room assumed the shape of an anxious ballerina, and Žanet – for the first time resisting the symbols of death – swallowed her thick, bloody saliva. With her blurred gaze, she locked onto the woman's gaze once again. That gray gaze she had not seen in decades but had loved for all eternity.

Three golden jackdaws

Singing louder than me.

She felt her bony arm caressing the dryness of hers. Then, prompted by that warmth, tears flowed down her cheeks again – like some holy wave that would wash out all sins.

"It's alright," she squeezed her twiggy hand, "everything's alright."

Her hoarse voice sounded exactly the way Žanet thought it would. As if catching the rhythm of her body, a magical silk danced in her throat, luring her toward the golden clouds. Intoxicated by the silky dream, she dove into the soft gray eyes for the last time – the eyes that were telling her that everything would be alright – and she sang the whole lullaby.

Three golden jackdaws

Singing louder than me.

Three little jackdaws

Playing hungrily

As three silent rivers flowed

And now I have to leave you be.

He was there. He did not lie. The magnificent, blissful, and immaculate – l'Eternità. It was just the way he promised it would be. The sky glimmered confidently – like millions of jewels – and they were there. Petar and Ilir. Sitting on the ship, their giant smiles widened – as it befitted them – calling out to her. The sound of their voice that had always been her favorite melody. The palm of the gray-eyed woman gently and painfully caressing hers looked as if it were giving her approval: get on the ship. Freed, she took a step forward, and the sound of the waves crashing started rising above every bitter voice of the past. Petar's slender figure got up, untied the knot, and let the ship sail. The wind – so naked, nimble, and freeing – caressed the sails of their eternity, imprinting her essence into the eternal world.

As they set sails, she left behind a monotonous sound and a thin line on the small monitor beside the hospital bed. A line gently engraved into the gray-eyed gaze. It was a picturesque sight of her death that she had been waiting for so long, which will never affect that skinny, dry-haired woman. That little girl with gray eyes, as much as it would have, only once in her life, felt the warm touch of a mother's love. The lack of some joys always reduces some sorrows. During her whole life, Žanet was – for her – just a dead memory, never having been born.

MAY, 1991
PARIS

She was sitting on the edge of the sofa with her knees pressed against her chest, correcting one of the many essays next to her. She was an assistant teacher - only a glimpse of the thing she wanted to become. Their apartment smelled of chocolate cake and burnt coffee - burnt with the magic wand of her mother's forgetting. She left the coffee boiling and then, naturally, forgot that she did. The television broadcasted a report under the guise of a giant surprise.

"Twelve Croatian policemen killed in Borovo, right next to Vukovar."

The sentence echoed in her mind a few times as she scrubbed the stove. Twelve Croats.

"What will this come to..." her mother's eyes were palely fixed on the screen.

As if wanting to stir up the flame of distrust and anticipation, the doorbell rang. She wasn't sure whether she felt at ease because of Patrik's arrival or felt a forceful disgust because of Bošnjak's. Nadja opened the door wearily and saw the always damned happy look on Mr. Bošnjak's face. For a moment, she felt like he was the culprit responsible for the tragedy striking Croatia. In her eyes, Franjo Bošnjak was always both guilty and responsible for everything at the same time.

“What a surprise,” she smiled bluntly.

She wasn’t sure whether she was joking sweetly or being fastidiously ironic.

“You always are to me,” Patrik kissed her forehead.

“Is there something burning here?” Bošnjak started casually strolling down the hallway. “Or am I wrong?

“Burnt,” she passed by him, countering his cadet-like step. “Past tense.”

“Oh, I see,” he smiled, glancing at Patrik excitedly.

“What’s with him today?” she asked Patrik under her breath, gesturing towards Bošnjak with her gaze.

“He’s just excited,” he smiled at her restlessly.

Just as she was getting ready to ask him why, the answer had found its way into her mind: dinner, Patrik, and Nadja. His question. And her answer.

The Golden Tooth

13 April 1983
Osijek

Dear Mr. Smith,

I'm so glad to have finally met you – and only a few funny moments after I had tasted her lips for the first time – her wet, full, soft lips – and absorbed the sweet smell of her skin.

I have experienced something unbelievable, Mr. Smith, her affection. I never even dared to think that a being like her – a being that ruthlessly reigned over my soul – could be so blissfully gentle. I have kissed many girls before her, and I'm as proud of that as any young man; thus, it is a very relative feeling of pride. Many of them were so pretty that it made my heart stop. I didn't know how to arrange the thoughts in my head. But no one had left a trace as deep as she had – with that single kiss.

Some of them, Mr. Smith, was even prettier than her. They did not have the same funny gestures that made them crudely less attractive, and many laughed more feistily than her. Many of them, My Friend, kissed me more nimbly than she did. But... all of that – now – seems to fall into oblivion. That youthful taste I had been building up for all these years seems to hold no value anymore. It seems I had been doing it all blindly. It appears that everything before her was just an illusion.

I'm not a man of letters – never was. But, not too long ago, I was forced to read 'Anna Karenina' for school. One hell of a thick book, that I can tell you! It's one of the rare ones that my eyes read when my hands reached for it. And now I can understand it better. At least some parts. For Levin, all the world's women were divided into two groups. All the women of the world, with all their virtues and flaws, belonged to the first group. The second group was only the one – Kitty. She was above all the other women of the world, above all the human world. What do you think Kitty would be called if I were to take that book in my hands again? By her name, of course.

I know that you, Mr. Smith, know very well the answer to my every question. That's how damn well you know me. But what you may not know is how fulfilled I felt today, having finally met you, squeezed your coarse palm, gazed into your tiny eyes, and smiled at you. Now, as I remember, Mr. Smith, just how covetously you admitted that you had watched my first match, I could laugh for hours. Ah, you Old Fart, how had I not noticed it? Your golden tooth amid the crowd. It must've shone brightly, lit by the sun burning in the sky that day. I wonder, Mr. Smith, how come I hadn't smelled that funny stench of your unburned cigarette? My Friend, I must have been very blind.

Thank you for the encounter today.

Yours,
Zair

25 May 1991
Osijek

Mr. Smith,

I'm writing this letter as my palms tremble. This time, it is not my sickness that's causing it. This time, she serves as the sickness that pushes me towards the abyss more than any other disease medicine could explain.

Today, on that paper – which I painfully predict will never be torn apart – she vowed to be someone else's for the rest of her life. She agreed to lie down with the wrong man. To birth him children – he who will never know her quivering in the middle of the night as much as I can – deeply and strongly – recognize it time and again. I would recognize her, Mr. Smith, in the deepest of crowds – like a torn-out part of myself.

She agreed to smile at one another until her very last breath. May I be damned, Mr. Smith, because I wish she'd never smile again now, as she smiles in front of someone who will never truly recognize the actual, frightening value of her smile. She agreed to smile to another man, sing to another man, and create her stories next to another man. All letters are damn good stories with her.

Does she not know, Mr. Smith, how wrong of a choice she has made? Does she not realize where all her inspiration lies? All her pain, hatred, warmth, love, life, and eternity? Did she not realize yet, My Friend, that all of that lies in me? Does she not understand that you can't fight against that? You can run away and hope, sometimes even be sure of it, but in the end, everything except the two of us will always be a lie.

Write to me, Mr. Smith, so that I know you're still breathing.

I need you.
Zair

Carousel

MAY, 1991
PARIS

The night before the wedding - after an eternally long standstill of dreams - she fell asleep. It was a strangely tangible and present dream, almost like any other piece of sheer reality.

She was sitting in the middle of an empty house surrounded by playful, orange-colored walls. It appears the color evaporated out of them. An almost fully melted candle smolder stood in the wooden cupboard in the corner, painting a yellow core of the orange canvas with its flame. Anxiety overtook Nadja's chest, and her breath became dense, hard flowing.

A fine melody from the outside reached her ears. An index finger hit the smooth piano key. She heard the arrogant lovemaking of the violin string and its lustful bow, while the belligerent sound of the cello stimulated fear in them, causing them to sin, but sin blissfully.

She couldn't breathe. Creamy, fickle shades crawled around the room, and she had to get out. Yes, she had to, the melody was alluring. She got up, her footsteps easy as if she didn't weigh a pound. She stepped towards the sound, almost levitating, as the melody became stronger, its magnificence boiling out of it like coffee in a kettle wanting to get out and show its bitter beauty to the world.

She got out from under the orange walls and entered the twilight dappled with blue, green, and purple. As though wrapped in those cold shades, a forest appeared in front of her. Light reached out of the woods like a thermal nucleus, while in the back of her mind, she heard the echo of her mother's voice, reading a bedtime story.

She was breathing more easily now. Cooled from the wind that, like a breeze that stirred up the summer air, traveled throughout her lungs. The nature around her moved as she – seemingly motionless, unstoppable, and greedy – traveled. Everything was but a simple uninterrupted sound. The sound of nature erasing the limit between the inside and the outside. She traveled, felt, and arrived there. Then, she stopped.

A lake. A crystal lake painted with the reflection of an infinite amount of stars. The beauty inebriated her, and the wooden boat called to her. There she saw Him – ginger, humble, lost, reckless – smiling at the sky. She sat into the boat, put her restless palms into her lap, and watched him from behind, besotted with beauty. As though called out for by her presence, he turned around towards her, steadily happy and content.

She looked up at him, trying to locate the source of his joyful gaze. She found nothing, and the nothingness created a storm inside her; the fear of the unknown, the anger because he didn't share this feeling with her, and her ignorance of the magic his eyes fled towards. She knelt on the ground and placed her hands on his knees. His eyes were glistening like the finest of wine glasses. There lay – she saw the reflection in his irises – the cause of his intoxication. A reflection of a thousand lanterns. And in them the lights were out. The lights were out. The lights were out...

JUNE, 1991
PARIS

"On the 27 June, a tank of the Yugoslav People's Army runs over fićo," an eerie voice was heard from the radio station.

She was sitting on the sofa in front of a freshly bought TV box that skillfully showed the scenes of the tragedy that had befallen Croatia, her homeland, that streamed silently in her veins. At the same time, she was trying to finish up the script for the upcoming play The Miracle Chaser – a play that she and Patrik shared. The tenuous sound of the phone ringing, still coming from the same corner next to the balcony door, blew away the last drops of her inspiration, making her jump on her feet.

"Great," she heard an anxious voice on the line, "you picked up!"

"Mom?" her heart started racing abruptly. "Everything alright?"

"I'm just..." the silence was filled with antsy sighs, "I was just walking, and" she chuckled softly, almost ironically, "I'm not sure which turn I should take."

Without an introduction or a gentle announcement, boiling tears started rolling down Nadja's cheeks as she listened to her mother's lost tone of voice.

"This Paris," she chuckled lightly again, almost embarrassed, "it's such a big place, like a labyrinth, and" she sighed, "I don't know how to get home."

"Mom," she exhaled.

"I'm not even sure where I was before this conversation," she interrupted anxiously.

"Mom," Nadja squeezed the phone as if she were squeezing her mother's shoulders, "calm down and look around, please."

Everything went silent for awfully too long.

"Just tell me the street name," she sighed. "Just read what it says on the sign, and I'm coming."

***

Nadja's life was filled with absurd, sad, and factual news for the next few months. She did not know where to aim her hatred more – the radio station, the sound that kept them updated on all the catastrophes, or the phone ringing. The ringing could bring two possible outcomes: Ilir's life or death. Sometimes, it also brought the third possibility – her mother getting lost in reality.

Her head became a mash of bad news. Baranja falls in a whisper, occupied on the 22 August. That same Baranja that made love with her hometown without ever touching it. Vukovar, with its weak defense of only 1800 poorly armed soldiers. YPA heavily armed, with approximately 36 000 soldiers. Her brain convulsed as she calculated the immense difference in their numbers. On the 18th of November – Vukovar falls. Hundreds of Croatian soldiers and civilians were massacred, around 31 000 deported from the city and its surroundings.

The wheel of her thoughts always silently stopped at the same question, where is Zair now?

SEPTEMBER, 1991
PARIS

As the whole world revolved around her as if she were on a carousel whose speed made her inexplicably nauseous, she was thinking about the pills on her mother's nightstand. The drugs were supposed to maintain her sanity, preserve her memories, and that was – as it seemed – only a one-sided shell. The doctor's foggy but piercing voice cut her thoughts into small, fragile pieces.

"Your mother," he exhaled gently, "she is alright."

In that half-nightmare brought upon by reality, she noticed Patrik in her peripheral vision, wiping his sweaty forehead with his trembling hand.

"Even though the pills gave a solid result," he scratched the nape of his head, staring at the paper wriggling in his hand, "her memory is significantly damaged."

She thought that the learned sense of empathy in the doctor's voice was borderline arrogant.

"Unfortunately," he nodded his head, as though confirming her agony with a simple gesture, "the stroke left significant repercussions – the same ones we were trying to avoid, given her Alzheimer's."

Nadja then knew sometimes, the thread of fate finds its way to push through. The easy way, or the hard way.

"It's very likely that her mobility," the doctor continued, "as well as her functioning routine to date, will change significantly."

"And that's it?" Patrik asked anxiously.

"Surely," the doctor continued insecurely, "the possibility of her remembering something from time to time and functioning normally is not excluded."

"Can we see her?" Patrik asked as the gloom in his voice became almost odorous.

"Of course," the doctor nodded, gesturing towards the door with his hand. "She's sleeping now."

The pure white doors of the hospital room opened perfectly without a single creak. Greedily, almost as if the whole sequence of those events had been undeniably right. For Nadja, it was considerably hard to accept that many things born with her mother were slowly disappearing from the face of the Earth.

The room was filled with greenish light unacceptably reminiscent of happy days as she lay there under the whiteness of the fragrant hospital sheets. That pretty woman – gently piercing, slender and strong – was now just a sorrowful memory of her former self: sickly, skinny, hollow-faced, her weak hair dyed in black, with her elongated nose and purple-green bags under her eyes. Nadja tiptoed in, silently and frighteningly checking to see if she was breathing. Patrik placed his frightened, filled with his erratic heartbeat palm on her shoulder.

"I'm here," he whispered.

They stood above her bed with their gazes fixed on her weary eyelids. In them, Nadja could see that she didn't remember anything. Not one morning, lunch, or the alluring smell of the early morning bread coming out of Ilir's bakery. Not one cup of coffee on their balcony that she playfully adored, and not a single bedtime story.

***

The sound of the kettle coming from the stove called her in and wanted her to move, but she was still trapped in the thoughts of her mother's freedom. Can she be free if her mind keeps her trapped somewhere far away?

"It's difficult for us all," Patrik removed the kettle off the stove, "trust me."

I understand. But what does it change, exactly? As though placed in a labyrinth without existence, she realized that some sorrows could not be cut in half. Or rather, it can only be cut in half with some people.

"But they'll surely take better care of her," she heard Bošnjak's unforgivably rigid voice.

Why don't you take care of her? She imagined her mother detached from both the world and herself. She was good when she was your keychain. Yes, that's what she was good for.

"It can't be," Bošnjak was adamant, "that you don't believe my judgment?"

I couldn't care less for you or your judgments.

"Look," Bošnjak got up and sat at the table across from her, "we can visit her whenever we feel like it."

He outstretched his wide, dark palm and placed it on hers. The touch of a traitor. She withdrew her palm and scratched the back of her head anxiously, avoiding his gaze.

"I don't know," she replied.

Faked Deaths

30 May 1991
Osijek

Dear Mr. Smith,

Today was my last match ever. It was the longest but the shortest ninety minutes of my life. The longest because all of me, my dreams, ambitions, tears, and sweaty smiles can fit into this one sport. The shortest, Mr. Smith, on the other hand, because 5400 seconds is too cramped a number to represent the accomplished potential of my body's instinct. The same as my soul's, my dear Mr. Smith.

The last goal, the winning one, was mine. Just like it was at my first match while my bearded coach smoked his unfiltered cigarette and the second most beautiful woman in the world sat on the bleachers, watching the sun hit my back, and the warm sweat slide down my forehead. The same scenario played out today. It's funny, Mr. Smith, at the same time, I felt like both a boy and an old man, while truly, I am neither of the two. Or, I'll be damned, maybe I am both of them.

Moving into a defensive position, placing that loyal ball into the net, I touched my long-lost beginning and felt its end – that fiercely disgusting end of my beginning. I guess that's the way it goes, Mr. Smith. The beginning and the end are like two sides of a coin stretching out into a regular, meaningful line. But those two green eyes, my Good Friend, make me think that some lines are constant. Some stories – like melodies that keep playing even when the dancers give up on the podium – arrogantly refuse to end. And then their tones tirelessly remind us that the melody is still playing and will continue playing for as long as we live.

After that last goal, the crowd roared from the bleachers. Some had even called out my name, having it safely tucked away in some corner of their mind. I was not a world champion in this sport, Mr. Smith, but it was an unbreakable part of my world. At that moment, tears started rolling down my face. They were tears of pride, tears of joy, but also tears of sorrow, quite difficult to explain.

Ah, the times you've faked your death. I wouldn't be surprised if you were playing out that same scenario this time, My Friend. I wouldn't put it past you. But still, I write to you. I write to you because today is the end of my beginning and the beginning of my end. Despite being so young according to the numbers, Mr. Smith, my body is rotting away like an old man's, and my soul follows. Some new generations will step onto the fields I used to rifle through. Some new kid will set foot on my path and win the prizes I once won. Then cry joyfully at the end when he scores his final goal.

I guess that's the way it is, Mr. Smith – everything has its time. There's always a gentle beginning, the introduction leading us into the story. Then we slide across some tumultuous paths: we conquer, we lose, we cry, we scream, we sigh, we smile. Then, as we dive profoundly into those depths – the end starts emerging, as sweet as it is bitter. And nothing else but that. She asked me once – I remember it as if it happened yesterday, even though it's been over a decade – what does it feel like to play soccer? I did not know how to answer it then. Maybe I know now when it's too late to answer all of her important questions.

Life is truly like a soccer game. You come onto the field with so many people side by side, soaking up the last unobstructed gaze of your opposing teammates before the start. You're hoping that the collective touch will encourage you enough. Then, without any special introduction, the game begins. You're entirely ready, untouched, undamaged. You can't be sure what will hit you from that moment on and when. So many types of injuries can befall you on the field. Sometimes, they happen in the first minute, sometimes in the middle of the game, and sometimes they avoid you altogether.

When someone elbows you for the first time, you feel dizzy, but you hold up well. Because… what else can you do? Well, the game had just started! You run rampant, arranging your atoms into an invincible figure of bravery and let the game lead you. Once the game has you in its hands, you get overwhelmed by strength. You become wise when you need to be. You become a shield where it needs shielding, a shooter when you need to aim, the bullet itself when it's time to shoot it out, and the peace when the situation requires it. Only sometimes, you're reckless when you need to be methodical. But then there's always someone – maybe on the other side of the field – who will embody the peace and soothe the storm. Life is a web, My Dear Sir, just like the game itself. Never, not even in our wildest mistakes, are we ever alone.

Sometimes – besotted, as if in a half-dream – you see a bright red or yellow card. And you stare at your teammate – as they break his leg, arm, nose, or as he walks up to the bench himself. But sometimes – which is maybe the greatest torment of them all – you are the one who's hurt. The one who – of your own culpability, or someone else's, it doesn't truly matter – sits on the bench and watches the rest of the game.

In that case, My Friend, you can't do anything. You want to close your eyes and give no thought to it, but the outcry of your teammates provokes you to look at their tragedy or leadership. And, of course, if it's leadership, you don't know whether to cry or to laugh out loud. Cry – because you're not there, and you're not responsible for the goal. And if a tragedy happens – loss or injury, you're not there to stop it, to fight alongside them.

But that's only the "maybe" hiding behind the playful power of those colored cards. Let's continue the story, assuming we're still playing. Besides, every life story is based on the assumption that we're still playing. The game, however life-like and spry, starts coming to an end. The ones that carefully followed your steps from the bleachers – outside of the fire you were thrown into – are as restless as you are, maybe even more. You know it's the end, but the beginning doesn't seem that far away either. Everything happened in a flash, and if you gave it your best when you needed to and in the moments that mattered to you, the cliché of victory doesn't play an important role anymore.

Then, Mr. Smith, comes the magnificent ending. Then, My Good Friend, and only then, I don't think that the sole lucky few are the ones that carry the victory on their backs. No, I don't think so. In that moment, My Dear Mr. Smith, I believe that we are all the lucky ones. Everyone that played. In the end, nobody asks you what you've won. They ask you what you got from it.

Am I wrong? Please write me with your wisdom because I need to be wiser to assess your answer.

Don't stay absent for too long.
Zair

Daughter

FEBRUARY, 1992
PARIS

She despised the unforgivable smell of the fresh white hallways that led to room 79 – her mother's. She couldn't take the creaking of the wheelchairs that held powerless human figures stuck in their pasts, detached from reality. But maybe more than anything, she hated the insensibility of the white coats that monotonously danced on the medical staff's bodies. That morning – which was far too spring-like for a winter month – her stomach seemed loaded, as though someone had placed a ton of rocks in it. The tiny being inside of her was becoming less and less patient.

"Your mother is in the exercise hall," the nurse uttered indifferently while stacking her mother's closet.

"Exercise?" she felt her hormones raging to the surface. "She's in a wheelchair, for crying out loud."

"She still has muscles though, ma'am," the nurse gave her a sour smile.

***

The sun lit the exercise hall, reminding her of a pavilion in the middle of her dreams, touched with supernatural light forces. A couple of older ladies were stretching as per the orders of a slender young man in front of them. She placed her right hand on the softness of her gray shirt – stretched by her stomach – and sat against the wall full of windows. Right next to her sat thin silhouettes of gray hair. Her palms rested peacefully in her lap, and her head was aimed toward the bright source of the sunlight. A convulsed smile widened on Nadja's face as she placed her other hand on the enormity of her stomach.

"Hello," she touched her gentle wrinkles with her gaze.

Her mother turned her weary face towards Nadja with a slow and trembling movement, gazing into her eyes foggily.

"Hello," she nodded her head and returned her gaze to the sunlight.

"Lea Silvia, is it?" Nadja asked.

The unsure look on her face – that momentary fogginess even at the sound of her name – frightened Nadja intensely. Least of all, she wanted to scare her.

"Can I help you?" her voice sounded gentle.

"So," Nadja smiled, "you're the one."

She nodded her head, clenching her jaw insecurely.

"I saw one of your paintings," her gaze joined her mother's staring into the bright sunlight, "and I wanted to meet you."

"My paintings?" she frowned.

"Yes," Nadja nodded her head decisively. "One of your works, and I especially liked the one of the balcony."

Her mother's eyes lit up as though letting a piece of memory pass through. Seemingly flattered, she nodded her head.

"I think your paintings are truly beautiful."

Her dry lips formed a weakly smile, shyly painting the joy on her face.

"And she?" her mother asked.

The end. The moment is lost. The memories – drowned.

"Who?"

She smiled forcedly, wanting so badly to keep at least a piece of her mother in the present moment.

"Your daughter."

Nadja lowered her gaze toward her stomach. Even though she fiercely wanted to know how her mother knew that she was having a girl – even though neither she nor Patrik wanted to know – she gave up on trying to find that out and sailed into the conversation that her mother had tailored.

"She too," salty water stung the corners of her eyes, "she too thinks your paintings are beautiful."

"You're very kind," she nodded, smiling softly with her eyes, "you and your daughter."

Silence reigned over them. A silence that reminded them that there were no surviving memories left inside her. Then, taking the form of a consoling touch, her mother spoke.

"You know," she gazed at the disappearing sun. "I've never seen a pregnant woman prettier than you."

Shivers danced down Nadja's spine. Starting from her heels, they rushed towards her calves, over her thighs, then curiously settled on the tips of her shoulders.

"Sorry?"

Her mother stared right into her eyes as her head trembled lightly.

"I said," she cleared her throat and smiled widely for the first time after a long while, "I've never seen a pregnant woman prettier than you."

Nadja felt the earthquake of her lips which couldn't resist the trembles, as the old, well-known lump stuck in her throat.

"Would you like to feel her?"

She reached gently for her mother's skinny hand and placed it on her belly.

"Sometimes she kicks really hard," she gazed into the dark bags under her mother's eyes. "Seems she'll be feisty."

"She'll be a strong girl," her mother smiled softly and placed her hand back into her lap.

"Like her grandmother," she tried hard to keep the river of tears at bay.

"Sometimes," her mother nodded, "grandmothers aren't as strong as everyone expects them to be."

Nadja felt her mother knew what she was talking about. Somewhere, in the utmost depth of her being, her mother knew they were talking about her – about the strongest woman she'd ever known. But – they both knew – her mother's brain could not discern between its knowledge and the feelings from every other imaginary thought. But Nadja knew both sides of the mirror of reality always hold on to some bits of truth.

FEBRUARY, 1992
PARIS

Dorothy was not the same anymore – that peculiar, mystical, wanting magic. She became much more tangible and clearer. Her calamitous invincibility took the mask off its face, and Patrik knew that the calamity was never a part of her but rather a part of him.

Her calamity always lay in one clear but intolerable fact: she will always be a step ahead. Always close enough to make him want to touch her, own her, but far enough never to be tamed in his anxious lustful embrace. She was his support, his strong defense from everything that attacked his spirit. Meaningfully and decisively, she was his protector who was, at the same time, making him stronger. She was there, omnipresent in every part of him.

He wanted to be the lust that made her groan strongly in the middle of the night when the moon lit up her pale breasts. He wanted to be the shoulder she would lay her head on while her hair was wet and the warm sweat flowed down her face, which looked sublime. He wanted to be the shoulder she would lay her lips on and, maybe, etch the words on his skin with her tongue that she'd never love anyone as much as she loved him. In those tiniest moments, in the failure of her not placing her head on his shoulder but instead just lying next to him and drifting off to a distant sleep.

He knew that the belonging was not mutual. More than anything, he wanted to be the object of her instinctual desire and the definition of her weaknesses and at the same time, iron support. But in every movement of hers, he could read out that it wasn't so. And it never truly will be.

That was why she was his worst nightmare. He knew everything he wanted her to think of him was everything he thought of her. And precisely there lay buried the eternal mistake of their marriage. But, it was a mistake that he decided to live with because she filled his whole strange universe with life. The love inside of him was often borderline insane – now adopted the peculiar warmth of some new shades. Dorothy was now eating for two. Two inevitable souls – irreplaceable to their essences – that gave his giant world meaning.

***

He bit his lower lip as he entered the room anxiously so as not to crush the tenuous castle of her dreams with a creak of the floorboard. He could hear her breathing heavily but rhythmically.

The moonlight dove into their bedroom as if it were also dreaming or seducing. She lay with her back turned towards the window as the moon's silver blueness touched her cheek. Trying to make his footsteps as easy as dry leaves in autumn or the pollen that flows through the air in spring, he stopped the moon's flow as he reached the sight he yearned for: she, with the fruit of their peculiar love inside her. Her hands poured over the black sheet of their double bed, and her golden hair – thicker and longer than ever – diffused all over the black pillowcase.

Every curvature of her hair glowed merrily like a star – accidentally transferred into the mortal world from the skies. Her eyelids were a bit chubbier, seemingly weary, and her forehead still hard and absent, while her lips – probably for the first time– didn't seem so rich. They were trapped in the dark shadow, pressed against the hard mattress of the bed. The space around her, filled with joyful expectation and unbreakable hope, smelled of the future. He smiled and curled up next to her. Gently and fearfully – as though touching a butterfly's wings – he placed her sleepy head on his chest. At that moment, as if detached from everything else that may have been important earlier, he belonged to that one single world: the world of her warm breath and her moist palms. Everything that fulfilled him then and there was her and the moonlight.

Estuary

SEPTEMBER, 1996
OSIJEK

Setting foot on those city grounds – of the city that rose out from the ashes of the ruins like a dirty limping soldier – she felt guilt. Guilt because she wasn't there in some cold cellar, caressing his hurried heart while he wept and fought for all that belonged to him. But that layer of guilt was covered by another, much thicker one; the layer of pride. With her whole being, she was proud because her people fought back with a bold shriek to every whisper that marked a fall.

She firmly squeezed Ema's little hand in her palm, which served as an elixir to the pain that filled her chest. They were standing at the end of Lorenz Jäger Street – not that far away from the Franjo Krežma Elementary School where Nadja got a job as a teacher – as a strong wind swayed their hair, seemingly ready to blow it all around and mixed it up skillfully. Nadja's smooth, golden locks with Ema's auburn dry curls. Ema wore a denim backpack on her tiny back. A gift from Nadja in the name of the grandfather Ema never got to meet. Nadja's other hand firmly squeezed her royal blue suitcase, worn out by time, as her locks played in the wind and danced under a black hat. The same black hat that she left her city in that bygone year of 1983.

***

It didn't take long for her to fall in love with the house on Lorenz Jäger Street. It had a view of the passage that led into the parallel street through the diner Breskvica. On the right side, Lorenz Jäger Street led to the European Avenue – a hallway of joy and adventurous energy. The European Avenue was woven out of tall and proud buildings from the Secession era. Buildings that seemed to disperse and dance around the street at night when no one was looking like every dream ever dreamt there suddenly came alive. Like some presumptuous ill-tempered fairies whose souls were made out of gold.

She loved that house like it was a part of her, even though there was no trace of her childhood in it. She loved the cramped hallway where you could only make about three steps and that it strangely smelled cold. She loved the big, and at the same time, puny door that led to the living room. The living room – always so boldly cordial – merged into a big dining room, and the dining room was, as though thirsting for light, opening a view towards the garden with one whole wall. The garden they shared with a few other tenants and the usual parking space for their Renault 5. Right below the magnanimous windows, there was a deep brown colored chest of drawers, and on it – slowly swimming in three separate tanks – lived Ema's turtles. In a humble desire to feel more needed in her life, Nadja sometimes wished that Ema would forget to feed them so that she – the mother, the indispensable pillar of support – could do it instead of her. However, in that carefree motherly life that Nadja led, Ema's conscientiousness was often slightly frustrating.

The small hallway hid another door. It was on the left wall, right next to the dark wooden shelf filled with a variety of Ema's shoes. The door was creaky, with a yellow window that opened the view towards the kitchen. The kitchen was not big, and its preciousness could only be measured in time. All the elements were valuable antiquities given to them by Franjo Bošnjak on the occasion of one of their many anniversaries. Although enriched with time and some long-lost secrets, the kitchen was poorly lit. Only an elongated black-framed window crossed with two black wooden diagonals was letting in some of the daylight. Next to the last antique shelf on the right side was a door leading into the dining room, facing the quiet home of Ema's turtles.

It was precisely there that she would correct her students' exams, at the massive dining room table. Although her back would be facing the windows, she loved feeling like the night sky of Osijek was watching her. At the same time, she occasionally raised her gaze from the sheets of paper, pointing it towards Ema and Patrik, curled up together on the black leather sofa, staring at the TV. Their curled-up positions were rarely usual. And they usually end up with someone's toe almost poking into someone else's nose. That made her laugh and sometimes even turn a blind eye to some of her students' mistakes.

The living room was – although small – spacious enough, separated from the kitchen by a simple hall without walls that curved left behind the living room. That curve – as though refusing to get separated from its roots – housed a square hole that looked like a window and again faced the living room. Continuing forward, it finished – bravely and widely – in an estuary leading into three different rooms. The middle room was Nadja's study, where she had just finished the last part of her trilogy, which was now waiting for reviews and getting ready to publish. The room on the right belonged to Ema's world, while the left door, like an essence, emanating parental light, led into Nadja and Patrik's room. Small but spacious. It was the one where she adored taking off her clothes and teasing the gentle sexuality of his lust that he was saving only for Dorothy, over and over again.

That bedroom – as if yearning for vastness – hid the entrance to an oblong white bathroom with a long pearly white bathtub in the middle. At that moment in her life, Nadja couldn't decide whether she was more passionate about the ritual of her morning coffee or the extended and silent moment of diving into the dream world as the cluster of white bubbles touched her breasts and spread all over her body. Through the arched doors that were her last visual stimulus before falling into a bubbly sleep, you could enter the hallway with the living room on the left and the dining room on the right side. Before the dining room – as though hidden between the world of cleanliness and food – there was a long and narrow hallway. On its very end, it led to the bathroom on the right side, while the other side – as if inviting them to play – led to the garden. To their Renault 5, rose bushes and iron table and chairs.

The room Nadja loved more than any other was Ema's room; the right branch of the estuary. There she would, at night, just as her mother used to, sit on the edge of her bed and read her a bedtime story she chose. Even though she wanted to give her daughter freedom more than anything, she knew one thing: every generous parent tells their own stories to their child and then lets the child form their own story from all the bits and pieces they accumulated. Ema's wooden bed – which Patrik and Nadja painted white – was so tall it reached the high, elongated window. Precisely there – with her head right next to the window, and her mind in another, utterly detached world – Ema would fall asleep every night.

Nadja would still read her the whole story until the very end. She knew very well that bedtime stories echo across our dreams as well and follow us throughout our entire eternity. When she'd finally say goodbye to the story she was reading, she'd get lost in Ema's dry curls, soaking up the interlocking of orange and red on her head, which unambiguously echoed with Patrik's name. Then – with a smile whose honesty she felt deep inside her chest – she'd kiss her daughter good night and turn off the stubborn, yellow light of the night lamp.

Silhouette

OCTOBER, 1996
OSIJEK

The clacking of Ema's shoes on the concrete ground in front of the bakery was the sweetest sound he had heard that day. That sound seemed to chase away every other bitter taste he had encountered. Watching Ema run into Ilir's arms, he thought about Nadja being angry because another day had passed, and Ema's fiery hair was still not washed.

"Mom said I could," Ema uttered silently, pressed into Ilir's arms.

Ilir glanced at him, searching for approval, and he responded with a surrendering smile.

"Daddy doesn't know," she whispered to Ilir, almost inaudibly.

But, a parent's ear sometimes strongly tends to hear the inaudible.

"Daddy doesn't know?" he approached them, barely keeping his laugh in.

"No," Ema shook her head as her curls swayed in all directions, "he doesn't."

He knew she was teasing him, the same way her mother used to do many times before her. He knew that a risky desire lay in her. The desire to have him hold her in his arms, to tickle her and nibble on her cheeks up until she started screaming. So he gave her the same answer he used to give her mother to every provocation of hers. He took her in his arms. He tickled her tiny armpits and watched her cheeks grow into a wide grin.

"Alright!" she screamed. "Alright, daddy, enough," she laughed unstoppably, gagging sweetly from all the laughter, "stop it!"

"Chocolate donut," Ilir handed him a paper bag with a donut in it.

"What do we say?" his gaze dove into her glistening eyes, "I'm listening."

"Thank you," a wide smile formed on her face.

"Don't mention it," Ilir replied, giving her a half-toothless smile.

Seeing Ilir nursing unconditional love towards Ema and Nadja, he knew that orphans like him were not sentenced to a lesser quantity of love. And he also knew that blood, in the end, was not as powerful a liquid. A blood connection to him seemed merely a tool with the help of which life makes us love someone despite it all. Despite all their flaws, failures, and malice. To love them despite everything. Now, enriched by this blood connection – but also full of scars etched into him by the hand of the world ignorant to his roots – he realized that you could always love someone despite it all. But also that people are often too lazy to invest their sinful souls into the sinfulness of another one. Ilir – that weakly old balding and graying man with his body wrapped in an apron, without a single front tooth and legs now already as thin as two twigs – was one of the rare proofs of human unselfishness.

***

"She's at work for so long," she touched the surface of the tank water with her small fingers.

"That water is filthy, Ema," he skimmed through the newspapers, his peripheral vision fixed on her movements.

"So what?" she shrugged. "People are filthy, too."

"I agree," he smiled lightly." And I think it's time we got a bite to eat."

"We could wait for mom," she placed her tiny body in the chair across him, "so she could get a bite to eat with us."

"When mom comes," he exhaled, "it will already be..."

The blunt doorbell was heard as though saving him from the apron and the need to prepare something to eat. A skinny figure in a gray coat, ragged on the sides, stood on their doorstep. His hollow face was standing here, hidden under a greasy, shoulder-length hair, his skinny neck barely connecting to his body, and his duped blue eyes stared at Patrik beseechingly.

"Can I help you?"

"You," he cleared his throat clumsily, then spoke with his hoarse voice, "You're Mr. Bošnjak?"

"Indeed, I am," he nodded.

The stranger's eyes steered clear of Patrik, luring him to turn around. Ema stood in the living room, curiously watching the slender figure at the door.

"Wait for me in the kitchen, Ema," he scratched his scalp, torn between his daughter's hunger and the sudden visit, "I'll be right there."

The stranger's blue eyes glistened, seemingly filled with tears.

"Sorry," he cleared his throat, his body becoming uneasy, "But are you sure I'm the one you need?"

He continued staring at the empty space behind him, which Ema had filled out mere seconds ago.

"Look," he uttered, now increasingly uneasy, "I don't know why you knocked on this door..."

"You shouldn't be frightened of the yearning look I'm giving to your daughter," the stranger interrupted him.

He could feel fury and disgust accumulating on the sole edge of his throat. Just as the vortex was almost ready to spring out of him in ways not even he could anticipate, the stranger interrupted him again.

"She's as much my blood as she is yours."

A magnificent sort of sorrow, almost crystal-like, shone over the stranger's face.

"Excuse me?" Patrik asked, almost inaudibly.

"Let me," he pulled his veiny hands out of his pockets, "let me introduce myself."

They shook hands warily – each for his own reasons.

"Mr. Silvia," his gaze avoided Patrik's, "A pleasure."

That can't be. Their hands were still up in the air as they shook, and Patrik's mind produced a vortex of mixed thoughts and feelings.

"So, what do you expect of me now?" he pulled his hand back.

"I want to," he cleared his throat again, covering his mouth with his trembling hand, "I want to see her."

"See who?"

"Nadja."

"Nadja's not here," he shook his head, lowering his gaze towards his feet.

"Where is she?"

Not like it's any of your business.

"She's at work," he dove into his blue, shameful gaze, "She's a teacher."

"A teacher," he nodded. "That's imaginable."

"Mm," Patrik nodded, growing unstoppably anxious by the minute.

"Please," he sighed nervously, stammering. "If you'll allow me to wait for her..."

"What makes you so sure Nadja wants to see you?"

"I want to see her."

A couple of moments passed, filled with silent stares. He was unsure which evil was the lesser of the two: to let in a man who broke Nadja's heart. Or to chase away the man she missed her whole life, the man that was never within reach but has now finally appeared? There was no right choice. Each of the options seemed wrong in its unique way. But there seemed to appear a spot of light in all that, a speck of the right that spoke: only Nadja has the right to choose which evil is the lesser one.

"I hope I won't be sleeping on the couch because of this," he gestured at him to come in.

***

"My mommy taught me how to sew," Ema was sitting on the living room floor, unaware she was watching her grandfather sitting rigidly in the armchair, "but just the essentials."

"Your mommy must be a hard-working woman," he nodded, smiling softly.

"I could sew your coat," her big eyes stared right at the tears of his coat. "I could try."

"Ema," Patrik sipped his cold coffee, "Behave yourself."

"My mommy is a teacher," she proceeded, uninterrupted by Patrik's words.

"A teacher?" his eyes showed a peculiar glow as if they were torn off from the rest of his weary body.

"Yes," she nodded confidently, "She has many children other than me."

"But I'm sure," he leaned on his bony knees, "That you're her favorite."

"I think so, too," she curled the locks of her hair around her fingers. "Did you know my mommy?"

"Not as well as I could have."

***

The closing of the entrance door and the sound of her shoes coming off made his heart race and triggered the thoughts of the lesser of two evils. His peripheral vision caught onto Mr. Silvia running his fingers through his greasy hair. His fussing was silently interrupted by Nadja's figure that appeared on the door of the living room. A golden lock had escaped her high ponytail contributing to the evergreen beauty she had in her. Her black leather handbag stood firmly on her left shoulder as she embraced Ema's tiny body with her right arm and kissed her forehead softly.

"I told him I could fix his coat," she pointed at Mr. Silvia.

"Did you eat?"

Without interruption, Nadja stared into her father's eyes.

"Yes," Ema giggled, "But the turtles didn't."

"Go feed them, then," she ordered with her gaze still locked onto his.

"I know," Mr. Silvia inhaled deeply, "I know...."

"You don't know a thing," she interrupted him.

"Please," he put his palms together anxiously, "Have coffee with me."

"Coffee that I'll pay for, by the looks of it," she glanced at him from his head to his toes.

OCTOBER, 1996
OSIJEK

The café seemed like a peculiar illusion – and so did the people in it, while he was the only irritating reality. Her father – already older, filthy, seemingly very poor. But, most of all, undeserving of her presence, sight, and hearing.

"You were much more respectable the last time I saw you."

She stared at his greasy locks of hair, her insides fighting between sorrow and enjoyment.

"Much more," he nodded as his palms fidgeted with one another.

"Why now?" she shook her head. "You have nowhere else to go, so you turn to me? I'm your last choice?"

"It just looks like you're my last choice," he tilted his head softly as if his thoughts seemed unclear, "but you're the first right one."

They stayed silent, each of them drowning in their sorrows.

"You're completely right," he inhaled, breaking the silence, "I'm the..."

"Don't start," she interrupted him. "I know I'm right. Of course, I am."

"Nadja," his voice adopted a peculiar shade of wakefulness, "Forgive me."

"Don't worry about it," she sipped her cappuccino. "I'm one of the ones that forgive as soon as the deed is done."

He was speechless, appalled, one moment looking at her, the next at the cup she held.

"But you don't forget something like that," she added. "The absence. You missed my wedding, as well as Mom's funeral."

He replied with a sigh – a tenuous and frightening sigh.

"Funeral," she leaned over the table, her eyes wide open, searching for his humbly bowed head. "Dad!"

"I made the wrong choices," he shook his head. "I chose the wrong people in life, Nadja."

"Yes, you did," she nodded and took another sip.

"Nadja," he exhaled, "I'm sick."

She placed the cup on the plate abruptly.

"You're fascinating," she chuckled ironically, "After everything, you come to seek pity."

"No," he shook his head strictly, "No, I don't deserve pity."

They stayed silent, both trying to decipher the other's gaze.

"My diagnosis doesn't leave me much time," he ran his trembling fingers through his greasy hair. "I have a couple of years left, maybe less."

Nadja's thoughts could not be put into words. They moved around her mind, morphing from panic into pain.

"Let me," he exhaled, as if giving up, "Let me spend that time with you, with all of you."

She still could not turn her thoughts into words or sentences. That same absent father was now a clear vision in front of her. And he had an expiration date.

"She's beautiful, Nadja," he sipped his cold coffee. "I can see so much of you in her."

She could almost see the love pouring out of his gaze. Then she wondered: is it truly possible? To love, but to be blind to it the whole time? Blind to your primordial instincts?

"Nadja, please," he continued, "You don't have to talk to me, you don't even have to look at me, but allow me to be a... a silhouette in your life."

As the world in Nadja became soundless, the room echoed with the melody of a well-known song.

Beauty I've always missed

With these eyes before

Just what the truth is

I can't say anymore

At that moment, memories started stubbornly overflowing her mind: her mother's small car. The cassette player. The cassette. Always the exact same cassette.

"You're lucky we're so different, you and I," she uttered silently. "Do you know why we're so different, Dad?"

He bowed his head, expecting the answer.

"I was never able to leave you hanging."

Chocolate Complexion

SEPTEMBER, 1997
OSIJEK

A single pearl earring was enough to mess with her patience. It seemed like it had a pair of legs because it was nowhere to be found. Not on the shelf next to the bathroom mirror, not on the cupboard in the dining room, not in a single drawer in their bedroom, nor Ema's room. Her thoughts were frozen with a question: How do you show up in front of all those people – wearing only one pearl earring?

Not even remotely trying to hide the mixture of excitement and thrill that had overcome him, Patrik peeked into the bedroom and glanced at her in the mirror.

"We're ready."

"Well, I'm not," she frowned. "My earring's missing."

As if he could feel her mood throughout the air, he approached her and cupped her flaming cheeks into his hands.

"Hey," he caught her gaze softly, "We're professionals. To hell with the earring."

"That's easy for you to say," she smiled shyly. "You're a man."

"Come on," he kissed her forehead, "We're waiting for you."

She stared at his reflection in the mirror as she joyfully pulled away from the bedroom, courageously rushing into her special day.

"It's not like you have another dozen pairs of earrings," he winked sarcastically, then disappeared from the door.

Just as she reached for the jewelry box, thinking about a worthy substitute for the pearl earrings, he peeked into the bedroom again.

"The golden ones are fantastic!" he yelled happily. "Hurry up. We're waiting for you in the hallway."

***

The chairs were still empty, and that big gym – where she usually did exercises with her class – now assumed a completely different purpose, a seemingly frightening one. The publisher, Patrik, and a few other writers were going through her book's promotion plan once again. At the same time, Ema ran around the gym tirelessly as her limping grandfather – visibly enjoying every moment – tried to catch her.

"Ilir?" Patrik whispered into her ear, softly burping, smelling of goulash. "Where is he?"

"There," she smiled and gestured towards the entrance to the gym.

He truly was there – the faithful companion when it came to her works and the sponsor of her first leather-covered book. A plaid French hat rested on his head, and a collar from a neat and freshly ironed white shirt wrapped around his slender neck, making way for a bowtie. Even though he missed that front tooth, he kept a firm, warm smile. Ema rushed into his arms, and he picked her up and kissed her hard forehead just like he did with a golden-haired girl some decades earlier.

"When does this spectacle start, Bella?" he asked as he approached the stage, holding Ema in his arms.

"Soon," she nodded nervously, trying to form a warm smile. "You sit there," she pointed her finger towards the first row. "The first row is yours."

She watched as they approached the chair – it seemed like in slow motion. The three of them – the two fathers of her life, each holding a miniature little girl's palm. And she knew that sheer happiness was enclosed in a moment, ruthlessly unrepeatable and unique.

***

An untouched bottle of water stood in front of her with a poorly washed glass next to it. She was ready to drink out of it if everything was going according to plan. The plan where all those people would be lured towards her words and softly intoxicated by the letters of her stories. There was an invisible but perceptible difference between French promotions and the one she was doing here. We always somehow tend to enchant one of our own. And that act always leaves us strangely astonished.

She went into one of the kids' dressing rooms and, in the reflection of a small mirror, dove into her own eyes – frightened, anxious, and happy. Golden suspenders on her shoulders firmly led the way towards a golden evening dress that reached down to her quivering pale knees, blending in with her body's playful contours. She glanced at her hair as well – just as any other lady in a toilet would, even though she rarely defined herself by that word – which was tied up in an indestructible bun right on the top of her rounded head. Everything except her eyes and her shoes was golden.

Then, seemingly with a finger snap, one of her career's most important events started. The commotion stopped with the buzzing of the microphone, and Patrik began to with the introductory words, filled with pride and a familial, almost idyllic glory. She was listening to his words absently, at the same time gazing into Ema's glowing eyes that silently spoke: mommy, you're winning. And she was right. The writer always wins. Because a writer never competes and very rarely gambles.

***

She was tired from all the signing, expressing admiration, sweaty palms, and tireless smiles. The Franjo Krežma Elementary School hallway was filled with women in loud high heels, men in dark suits, professors, and other teachers with whom she shared the teacher's lounge. Only on her way out did she realize how damn hard it was to walk in those stubborn shoes that had been squeezing her feet the whole night long.

The commotion of the crowd that listened to her talking about her trilogy tirelessly for a whole two hours rounded up like sardines in front of the school building and, as if they were on some red carpet, waited for her to take photographs. The camera flash pinched her eyes as Patrik's proud arm pressed her closer to him. They smiled at the camera whose operator tried to, as acrobatically as possible, catch as many photos as he possibly could, and her eyes escaped towards the crowd. The women bounced in one place, softly intoxicated by the coolness of the evening hours, the men in suits lit their cigarettes, waiting to go home finally, and children running around.

The cause of her shortness of breath. He was in the middle of the crowd that pushed into him and swayed him left and right. The well-known chocolate complexion. Not a single curl under a hat, only half-placed onto his head. The same two sleepy eyes were lurking under the bare forehead, a bit wearier than before, and the arms – that once formed the strongest and a gently selfish embrace – were now leaning on crutches as his legs touched the ground unsteadily. A gaze happened as if the whole symmetry and the harmony of the world depended on it. One single gaze you could cram an eternity into.

***

The crowd magically disappeared. Only one woman remained, seemingly waiting for her ride, and two men were immersed in a political conversation. Ilir, as promised, took Ema to get a chocolate donut, and her father wished to walk home this time, leaving them – the two spouses – alone. Feeling a strong desire to break something, she let her tight bun loose and put on her gray coat, hiding the bits and pieces of a wearily woven happiness.

"I'll drive," she said, her gaze fixed on her shoes touching the ground.

Patrik silently took the passenger seat as her golden locks gave way to the wind and touched her eyelids – whispering to her, calling to her for one last gaze. Again – him. The weight of his body leaned onto the crutches as if creating some alternating melody: legs, crutches, legs, crutches. The melody seemed to go on and on. Just as if nature refused to accept the forgetting she longed for, the wind – cunningly ruthless – filled her nostrils with the scent of a well-known man. The figure of love, the silhouette of pain. Out of rage – towards herself or him, even though it didn't matter anymore – she got into her vehicle without a word and slid onto the road.

Boomerang

DECEMBER, 1997
OSIJEK

The crowded Christmas fair reminded her of denim backpacks, stories of evil stepmothers, and her mother reading the newspaper in the kitchen in their old apartment on Ivan Gundulić Street. But Ema was like a broom for all the dust that fell into her life and made it filthy as it traveled through time, smelling of the past. Ema was fascinated by the crowd around them, and Nadja – intoxicated by her joy – fell in love with every corner of her old memories, building some new chambers on top of their foundations.

One of the many careers that come in the same package as family, and which we have no intention to build ourselves, is precisely shopping for Christmas presents. She was not great at it. She did not like stores, and stores – in a strange way – did not like her in return. They pushed through the crowd, bumping into all kinds of people, breathing in the dense air of their mutual intimacy. She thought about getting new Christmas lights for their tree, a kitchen toy set for Ema, a new winter shirt for her father, Harry Potter and the Philosopher's Stone for Ilir, and a set of leather-covered notebooks for Patrik. A writer can never have enough notebooks, she thought.

As her thoughts swarmed all over, and the song *Walking Home for Christmas* played in the background, broken up by the people clamoring, she suddenly felt a hollowness in her right hand. An uneasy, empty, and horrible light feeling. Kitchen set. Kitchen set for Ema. Ema. Ema! She could almost feel her heart breaking anxiously, one half flying up her throat while the other traveled down her stomach, and in the echo of her scared heartbeats, she could hear the sole core of her brain. Where is she, damn it?

Polite pushing through the crowd was not on the menu anymore. She didn't bother if she grazed someone with her elbow or how loud she called out for Ema. Nothing mattered anymore except Ema's figure, which was nowhere to be seen. And her voice did not respond to Nadja's cries. She placed her body into Santa's armchair – whom she'd seen having a smoke outside – and dove into her sweaty palms, feeling the boiling tears flowing down her cheeks. A gentle palm touched her shoulder, intruding into her sorrow.

"Ma'am," a humbly gentle voice was heard, "is everything alright?"

Like a child caught in a sob that desperately wanted to hide, she wiped her tears with an abrupt movement and then looked up. A slender young man with a narrow face and dark, neatly cut hair stood before her, his eyes hidden behind sunglasses. For a second, she wondered why anyone would wear sunglasses in the middle of a Christmas fair, but the thought of Ema – the thought of her lost little girl – stopped her from thinking more about it.

"No," she replied tremblingly, "It's not."

"Can I help you somehow?"

His plump lips revealed his separated teeth as he spoke.

"I came here with my daughter," she looked around, searching for those red curls in the crowd, "And now I can't find her."

"How old is she?" he crouched in front of her. "Maybe she went into a shop she found interesting."

"No," she shook her head, "She's young, too young to be by herself."

He looked around as though searching for her, even though he didn't know what she looked like.

"Alright," he inhaled deeply, "This fair isn't the Bermuda triangle."

He patted her on the knee, and she replied with a fragile smile.

"We'll find her."

***

She watched him approach the doorman's booth as he explained what happened, gesturing calmly. Although seemingly absent, the doorman approached the microphone.

"Ema, if you can hear me, come to the doorman's booth," he glanced at the young man, then continued almost as if reading his lips, "Where your mother's waiting for you."

The doorman repeated those exact words a few times, expecting to see the little girl appear in front of the booth. In Nadja's eyes, every sound of a child's step belonged to her, every shade of red or orange hair was hers, and every word that even remotely sounded like mom seemed as if it were coming off Ema's lips. Then she realized how astonishing it was – how powerful hope was to make the inexistent come alive.

"Come on," the young man approached her, "Let's circle around the fair."

She felt his gentle touch on her rigid back, as easy as the wind.

“God,” she kept turning around, her vision getting foggy, “It’s been so long already…”

“About half an hour,” he stood before her and smiled softly, “But I’m sure everything’s fine.”

They pushed their way to the Christmas tree where they found a woman practically stumbling over her bags. A ragdoll with a frozen smile peeked out of one of the bags. Denim backpacks. Dolls. Ragdolls. Stepmothers. Stepmothers and sisters. Half-sisters. For Nadja, those two concepts – half-sisters and stepmothers – were equal to characters in a fairytale. Those memories did not have a dash of sweetness to them.

“Alright,” the young man widened his gaze, still looking around, “She’s not here, is she?”

Only then did she realize that the young man was searching for a girl without a face.

“No,” she shook her head.

“Come with me,” he gently placed his palm on her back again, “We’re going back to the doorman’s booth, and if she still isn’t there, we’ll check out the parking lot.”

“A red-haired little girl,” she followed him, “Curly hair. So you know who we’re looking for.”

***

They went out the big entrance doors, far too old and rusty, and the cold touched her nose as the sky, filled with her fear, seemed awfully too empty.

“Catch some air,” he nodded, encouraging himself, “Then we’ll continue.”

“You always did shop for too long,” a sweet voice was heard.

She couldn't turn around for the first couple of moments, not ready to face the possibility that the same hope she felt earlier was now creating illusions again. She closed her eyes and then sucked in the coldness of the winter air.

“Isn’t that the young lady we’re looking for?” the young man asked.

Ema. She was sitting on the freezing concrete entrance stairs, carefully petting an unsightly kitten that was wrapping around her legs.

“You scared me, Ema,” she crouched beside her, pressing her into her arms.

The freshness of her smell was like the beginning and the ending of everything she needed at that precise moment.

“Does that mean you’re angry at me, and I’m not allowed to keep Kiwi?”

She dove into the dryness of her hair with her short fingers, and with her lips pressed against Ema’s scalp, she whispered.

“That’s an awful name for a kitten, and you can keep him, but he’s going under the tree first.”

The young man, with a gentle smile, stood leaning on the big iron door. His white sneakers with a perfectly tied bow made Nadja smile.

“Thank you,” she got up and approached him, unsure how to even thank him properly. “I don’t understand why you’d waste all this time. People are...”

“Busy,” he interrupted her, “I know,” he nodded his head gently and removed his sunglasses.

“When you’re only ten years old,” his strongly humble smile turned into a generous opposite line, “And when your whole world is falling apart, you remember all the faces that stand out in the crowd and help you."

Hospital. Little boy. Glasses.

"And I have to admit," he bowed slightly, "That you've made it quite easy, you don't seem to have aged a day."

She nodded her head, returning the grand smile. Then she realized again what she'd always known, the good deeds you do are like a boomerang that knows precisely when to return.

Wounds

MARCH, 1998
OSIJEK

Dreams. A source of many hidden possibilities. Premonitions, fears, hunches. Sometimes, however, dreams can be a source of death. She lay in the solitude of their bedroom, infinitely gazing at the dark ceiling, and wondered: what was the last thing he'd done? Maybe turned off the lamp on his bedframe? Or perhaps he woke up and coughed for a second or two? And then passed away. Maybe he drifted off into eternal sleep looking at the pictures on his nightstand? Which of them was the last one he looked at? Petar? Žanet? Nadja herself? Or maybe her red-headed spawn?

It was the first time - after her mother - that death had touched a mortal part of Nadja's existence. A part that unconditionally gifted her with smiles and love while completely devoid of any blood connections. The sheets were cold, and the iron of their costly double bed let out a creak, as though it grieved with her. She closed her eyes, but all those stars that used to live inside her darkness were now extinguished. They went silent. Her darkness was now an ethereal blackness stretching out into the abyss.

The stiff lump in her throat stung hard that day and continued to sting for hours. Days. Months. Up until the day, seemingly all of a sudden, that lump became a burden. A burden she learned to live with. It became a perfect part of her that had always existed.

***

Watching her little girl grow up, she adopted one of the most honest truths about time reasonably quickly; it always has a hard time resisting harmony while giving as much as it takes away. Sometimes, however, we realize that we would rarely exchange what comes for that which has escaped. And we realize that nothing is truly ever taken away. It remains deep inside us.

As the years lined up on her back and her spawn metamorphosed from a child into a girl, Nadja was discovering all the secret instructions for life. The ones belonging to the grownups – mothers, grandfathers and grandmothers, fathers, uncles, aunts, godfathers, and teachers. There was not much to be revealed, in all honesty. The instructions were simple: walk. Walk through life.

Time has nimbly but slowly taught her that all the lives get extinguished sooner or later. Tragedies befall one's life as if that were precisely where they should be, reeking of cold but simple harmony. Observing the tragedies mixed with joy that blended with her life, she realized that the wounds we get from them are inevitable. Every time – as if it were the first – a wound gets created. A wound that never truly heals. A wound that one learns to live with because life keeps creating them. The fresh ones that call out for you to bear with them. The old wound doesn't seem so scary anymore – because you've been living with its pain for too long. You coalesce with it.

She realized that it was us. Us – people. A cluster of wounds. Beaten up beings with so many things to forget but so many things to remember, as well. Something to discover, to perfect to understand. And when we get a little bit older, all we have left is to understand all that we had always known anyway courageously but have been too scared to admit to ourselves.

***

To Nadja's immense surprise, Ema was not a copy of her parents. She was somewhat of a jewel. She did not reveal herself in the world of letters or reach for the pencil and paper. Moreover, when the school would ask it of her, she'd ask her parents to do it for her. Unsuccessfully, mostly.

Her nose had grown elegantly, trapping the memory of Lea Silvia in itself, and her hair became more red and curly by the day. Gently revealing the traces of Patrik, as well as the woman whose eyes Patrik would still sometimes see in the world between his dreams and the reality. Her body was developing into a pretty slender figure, and her skin assumed a pale shine – merging Patrik and Nadja's world into one. A cluster of freckles formed underneath her green eyes, delineating once again Patrik's reflection, but her gaze was of a completely different sort: Nadja's. Her temperament gently revealed the inheritance of Nadja's lively nature – nothing went past her, and she went past no one.

She finished high school in the same building in front of which her parents exchanged their first gazes and their first letters. She was an excellent student, and her passion flew towards science – having magically escaped from the literary world she grew up in – and took her before the doors of the Faculty of Medicine in Osijek.

MAY, 2016

Tiny and plump palms kept relentlessly touching his cheek. He did not resist because they were funnily wondrous. Awaiting Ema with two cups of tea, he observed the toy cars thrown around their living room. One was missing a door, one was upside down, and one was getting ready to zoom towards the kitchen.

"...Pa'!" a tiny voice was heard.

He looked at his hair, all sweaty and golden, standing up stubbornly in the air. Then he glanced at his forehead – smooth, small, and low, as well as his chubby cheeks and brown eyes – larger than the biggest ones, as it seemed to him – staring directly into his.

"Pa'?" he repeated after him. "Or grandpa?"

With pride underneath his chest, he gazed at his grandson curiously, digging through his mind, searching for the right answer.

"Grandpa," he bowed his head shyly.

"Mommy," he played with blocks in his miniature lap.

"Mommy is making tea," he glanced towards the kitchen, "She's been there for too long, if you ask me."

"Tea," he repeated after him in a pensive voice. Patrik could not restrain his laughter.

"Tea," he nodded. "That's right."

"Why is mom still working?" Ema asked, followed by the sound of the cups bouncing on the tray. "It's seven already."

"Parent-teacher conference," he replied.

"Right," she sat on a footstool across from him.

"Tin decided to clear the entrance from the snow."

"And you didn't have to force him?" he teased her.

"He's well trained," she took a bite out of the crisp cake, "He knows how to do it himself."

"I don't doubt it," he smiled lightly, "You little spitfire, you."

"Dad," she swallowed, "Do you think it exists?"

"What?"

"That," she flailed her hands around, then reached for her tea. "That kind of love."

Ilir's random and tenuous sounds interrupted their conversation as they glanced first at him, then at the blocks in his lap, then again at each other.

"Sometimes, I have a feeling it's only..." she continued, "Only some sort of light refraction or something."

They were silent, and her chewing of the cake loosened the tension of the conversation topic.

"And then," she shook for a second, elicited by a small cake piece that bounced onto her shirt, "It seems that it creates an illusion of something beautiful and magical."

"What's an illusion but the only reality a man knows?"

"Ugh," she waved her hand at him, "Artists!"

He replied with a smile.

"I'm so smart," she swallowed the last bite of the cake, "But I can hardly understand what you're talking about."

"It exists, Ema," he finally answered her question, feeling both a heavy and a sweet load of pain in his chest. He reached for the cup of tea, preparing himself for the words he was about to utter.

"Before I begin with my artistic speech," he took a sip, "It would be useful to mention that your mother will be home soon, and we're nowhere near using coasters."

As quickly as the breeze, she ran to the kitchen and returned with a few randomly picked coasters.

"Come on," she clapped her hands, eyes wide open excitingly, "Artistic speech, please!"

"Love exists, surely," he nodded as if making peace with his truth. "It's the most beautiful illusion I ever had the pleasure of knowing. Even though I always, somehow, knew I was toying with the untruth. But I, nonetheless, over and over, always chose to believe in that illusion. I chose to pretend that it was the only accepted reality."

"What do you mean untruth?" she wondered.

"Your mother is magical," he smiled blissfully, "Do you know that?"

She nodded like a little kid endlessly in love with its mother.

"But I was never her magic."

She started fidgeting, seeming like she wanted to escape this moment, escape these new layers of reality that her parents kept hidden very skillfully.

"She loved me," he emphasized, interrupting her fidgeting, "She still loves me."

She nodded, seemingly calmer.

"That was never the question, but," he was suddenly frightened of his words. The words that finally admitted the things that they kept denying for all these years, "She was always my magic, unquestionable and unavoidable, but to her, I was just a chosen reality."

A couple of moments filled with the well-known, intimate silence. Then, Ema's voice broke through the particles of that thickly dense air.

"Maybe that's the magic, dad. That she chose you."

She tilted her head sweetly as her red curls gently fell over her shoulder.

"Every day," she whispered.

Tango

24 April 2018
Osijek

Dear Mr. Smith,

This is the last letter I will write to you. I know that time has left its grand mark on the last letter you read. But I feel bound to write to you one last time. Even though I know you'll never get to read it, My Deceased Friend.

The letters I wrote to you will keep all my memories of her alive. With that, they'll keep me alive as well. And all that I used to be. Let this be the last written memory of her.

I sat in my wheelchair yesterday next to the wooden bench of the well-known park facing the health center. I had just finished with one of those senseless medical exams – that somehow seem to keep assuring me that it's a miracle I'm still alive – and I was listening to the rippling of the fountain when a young man sat on a bench right next to me. I felt ashamed for a moment because a ragged blanket covered my atrophied knees.

We didn't say a word for a while. Maybe so that both of us could find our own world inside the rippling fountain, and then he let out a sound. I am not entirely sure what those first words were that united our two seemingly incompatible worlds into one, but I remember that I started talking about her.

I did not mention to him that I used to be healthy or ran as fast as an arrow, leading a ball throughout the field. That was not of importance. I told him about her. It was painfully wonderful to relive our story for the last time, to assemble it into a rich whole, seemingly without an ending. He listened carefully to my every word. It seemed like the notion of true love was completely alien to him. I told him a lot about her stubborn nature. But my memory still serves me well, Mr. Smith, so I found some reasonable boundaries and told him about the tenderness she gifted me with – me and the whole Universe. In the end, he didn't say much.

"I don't know," he scratched his head uncertainly, "It seems that you were always somehow the first one she'd take it all out on and the first one she was so strangely arrogant towards."

I smiled, surely. What else could I have done, My Dear Friend? You would have smiled too, knowing full well the nature of our story.

"Yes," I nodded. "That's true. But I was also the first one she'd hug when she felt down and happy."

To my surprise, he smiled at me – how someone who understands the essence of your words would smile at you. He tapped his knee with his index finger a few times. He was wearing pale blue jeans tightly wrapped around his muscular legs. The kind of legs I used to have once, My Friend. He seemed so inexplicably alive. Full of excitement and unstoppable ambitions. I pondered whether to ask him what he was doing there – alone with an older man in a park on such a joyfully beautiful day. But I kept quiet – it seemed distasteful for the both of us.

And it was good I did so Mr. Smith, because at that precise moment, his phone rang. He muttered something in his deep voice, then returned the phone back into the pocket of his jeans.

"Cheek to cheek, it's too early for a bow. All of this should be lived through once more."

He recited the lyrics of a song that keeps playing on all the radio stations, then got up and told me he had to go. I listened to the cracking of the small stones below his feet. It reminded me of the river Drava flowing peacefully. If I'm not mistaken, the song he'd recited was 'Tango' by the band Vatra.

Yes, Mr. Smith – so help me, my shiniest star Iris – all of this should be lived through once more. It has been immeasurably beautiful knowing you.

Until we meet again,
Zair

P. S.

I would have loved it, Mr. Smith, if someone had told me the secret of life a bit earlier. The secret of youth and expectance. Life has this silly tendency to rip us from our roots, give us wings, and then teach us to fly. When is it best to fly, Mr. Smith? When you're young, of course. But something is not quite right here...

I always believed that the youth was destined for flying, and that's where I was utterly wrong, My Old Friend. Yes, we spread our wings in our youth, but our whole life is destined for flying. All of it. And then I wondered, how do we fly when our wings are destined to unite?

We don't fly alone, Mr. Smith. That would be too boring. We fly in pairs. I wish someone had told me that simple secret much earlier: we fly in pairs.

Yes, life tends to rip us from our roots, give us wings and send us off into the heights. But youth... youth can sometimes tear us from our own hearts. It enchants us with its blinding promises and makes us forget about our flying partner for a short while.

And then – if we are blind enough to spread our big wings without checking to see where our partner in crime is – we remain alone. Sad and alone. Then it truly doesn't matter anymore, Mr. Smith, how many pairs of wings we touch in that sky if it isn't our partner in flight. It's only that one pair of wings that can keep up with us in sync. No matter how powerful we are or how many expectations we fulfill, no matter how many slopes we touch with our bare hands, we remain empty.

And forever we wonder, will they peek out from behind some cloud? Those two giant eyes where we laid our torn-off heart?

Snow

DECEMBER, 2018
OSIJEK

The scent of cold was surprisingly rigid that day. Ilir was bouncing around together with the ball of yarn on his new green hat, and you could already see Zrinjevac. She focused on his soothing voice that sang a Christmas song, although she wasn't sure which one.

"I don't know that song," she lowered her gaze towards his miniature figure. "Teach me."

He ignored her remarks. He casually, as his mother tended to do, continued his way. The bouncing made his voice hack as his squeaky voice uttered the words.

"You better not cry, you better not cry," he didn't mind her loud laughter, "you better not cry, I'm tellin' you why!"

"The little spitfire learned how to sing," she squeezed his tiny palm, "Better than granny Nadja, who's a tuneless oaf!"

"That's your own fault!" he proudly exclaimed, having only recently learned the meaning of the word 'fault.'

***

The sky morphed into a dense combination of gray and purple. The night was preparing to chew the last signs of dawn into pieces so that it could produce a new one. Seen so many times, but still unique as ever.

Ilir was restlessly running around the bench she was sitting on, his hands spread as if he were a plane, still singing that same Christmas song. She decided that she and Patrik should teach him some new ones, just in case. She rubbed her palms, listening to the creaking of her leather gloves, thinking that her almost five decades of life were never friendly towards the cold days. The meadow she used to play on was now turned into a playground, and there were only two boys – because of the cold, she assumed – playing on it. Each on his side of the teeter-totter.

"Daddy is slow," Ilir remarked.

"He's on his way," she fixed his hat, "And then he'll take you to see Santa Claus."

"I see him!" he tore himself from her hold.

Tin was crossing the sidewalk on Adam Reisner Street and coming towards Zrinjevac.

"Close your eyes, grandma," he placed his fingers on her eyelids, "And count to a thousand, so you'll never guess in which direction I went!"

"Deal," she covered her eyes with her palms.

"To a thousand!" he pressed his palms onto hers once again as if he wanted to make sure she didn't see anything. "Three," he counted down, "Two," his tiny voice was pulling away, "One!"

You could hear his boots tapping, and a moment later, Tin's muffled voice addressed him.

Ten. A white seagull leading to Ilir's bakery.

Nine. A purple boat with a single sunflower chained on its sail.

Eight. The pot with Ema's unsuccessful goulash and the smell of Ilir's gummy bears.

Seven. Cesar kissing the silhouette of a beautiful black woman that her mother used to read to her about a long time ago.

Six. Cleopatra.

Five. A thousand orange, glowing lanterns.

Four. Her father's ragged shirt.

Three. A giant phone factory. All of them keep ringing, but no one's picking up. The smooth screen reads out – Life calling.

Two. A star dies. Falls. Disappears. As if it never existed. Even though it did. Of course, it did.

One. Again, a thousand lanterns, the years pass through the hourglass. The lights in the lanterns went out. The lights are out. The lights are out...

Zero. A shiver. What is he doing here? Beside her, his hands leaning on the wheelchair handhold – as if he were invited, completely calm and strange to his core – sat a man with a chocolate complexion and a black hat partly resting on his head. She gazed into his smile, strange and familiar, then his bearded cheeks – graying with hints of black – and the soft wrinkles in the corners of his eyes. He pulled something out of a small pocket of his coat on his chest.

"This is the first field I ever photographed," his hand trembled lightly, "A couple of minutes before my first game ever."

Without words, she took off her right glove with her teeth, then with her right hand, she took off the left glove, and – in the wintery twilight, the streetlamps not yet turned on – she saw a faded photograph. A pretty photograph. Very faithfully showing that moment, that Saturday of that August of the year 1973. Very faithfully – the first soccer field.

Thirty-one. A sunbeam in its infinite line of blinding light touches the soccer net that is facing the dressing rooms sideways, then the tips of the little field grass and the cap of the coach of their small team strolling across the field, with a no-filter cigarette between his lips, holding his one hand on his stooped back. A short fence – that single barrier separating the players from the fans – obstructs the complete view of the field.

It was clear that Zair's perspective was a frog's one and that on the other side of the camera stood a boy that found himself there only moments before his very first game ever, on that strange wavy lifeline. She smiled as she felt a hot, intense sting on the nape of her head and her cheeks. It was life and all the beauty of the pain that synchronized with it. She returned the photograph. Her gaze pointed towards the peculiar man with chocolate complexion that was sitting next to her, observing her uniquely and carefully.

"Keep it," he nodded his head peacefully as a soft, warm smile formed, "It's the only one I hadn't sent to you."

She nodded and placed the photo into her pocket, frightened not to break it – so fragile but so valuable as it was.

"Run," he gestured towards the playground in front of them with his chin.

She dove into his gray gaze, protesting with herself: am I dreaming?

"Why?" salty drops started forming in the corners of her eyes.

"Because you're bored," his voice trembled as if he were skillfully and humbly painting out the biggest fears of his existence.

"And how do you know that?" her shivering voice seemed to unite with the emotions in his naturally.

"Everything that you know," he paused calmly as though revealing a secret that can't save anyone anymore, "I know too."

She shook her head softly as a thought crossed her mind – some secrets are better left untold because their magic is too strong. And people… people rarely ever know how to handle magic.

"Come on," he gestured towards the playground again, "Run, and I'll catch you."

Truly, she listened to him. She stepped onto the meadow of the playground and started running, defying the wind, breathing fast and strongly. She turned around to check how close he was to her. Like a stubborn child – with a wide smile, he turned the wheels on his wheelchair, not taking his gaze off her, not even for a second. The grass screeched underneath the soles of her shoes, and her heart raced violently because it was not often that she ran like this – and she was not as young as she once was. In those abrupt moments – the short and incomplete moments when she turned towards him – she could almost see those big old curls flying through the air as he, enjoying every moment of his rush, fixated his gaze on her, following her every move. When she finally stopped – there, in the middle of the former meadow – and placed her palms on her belly, his wheelchair had finally reached her.

"I knew I'd catch you."

He read her soul with his gaze, regardless of the ciphers and layers she secured herself with throughout her life.

"You can't run forever," he added with a smile.

The words did not seem to be able to come off her lips. So she – as if returning the treasure to a treasure – just stood there, kept silent, reading his soul with her gaze.

"I could chase you forever," his voice shivered from the strain.

Just then, when she started feeling like she had to finally say something – the first snowflakes began gently falling from the sky. They gazed into the sky towards the purple light of the evening winter sky, and the streetlamps turned on – as if they knew what they were lighting up and how important it was. They started laughing in unison – vigorously, unbreakably synchronized. The freed child in her stuck out her tongue, hoping to catch a snowflake on it, and he – she knew it, she felt it on the surface of her skin watched her, still assuring that her inner child would have a safe stay in this crazy world.

Just then – after a long, long time that had silently slipped through her fingers – the bliss of the enlightenment landed on her eyelids, enriching her with the truth. A fragile snowflake was dying, singing songs of the cold, touching her cheek that was not so chubby and rounded anymore. And with those distinct tones told her the most silent secret of them all that she, like a mute witness of that colorful nature, always kept hidden somewhere underneath her skin. When time finally catches up with your body – the one that served you tirelessly and that you were, sometimes, for all those years, a slave to – you stop yearning for conquering the world, or the changes that would save it. Right then, a tame moment happens when you realize that love cannot be made. It cannot be gained. Love is a connection between the seed and the fertile soil. And once the seed is thrown – on the single fertile soil made precisely for it – it can never be canceled.

That leaves only one question, have we been brave enough? Did we dedicate our whole life to burning up the sun so we could feed it, then calling for rain so that we could cure it? If we did, our final purpose is written somewhere in those foggy starts, and its echo will touch the eternity of the whole illusion of time.

But had we not been brave enough – had we not seized that one true power given to us long before our bodies were even created –then we destroyed that godlike flower. We did not kill it – because that flower does not know death – but we cursed it to a life without purpose, just like we did ourselves. And every other flower we curiously tried to nurture later in life grew to become a weed.

A weed that may hide behind a dry red hair, sweet freckles under the eyes, the magnificent choice of words, and coherent creative passions. Maybe. But on that path, we had forgotten one thing: that same weed – had we only not tried to nurture it so selfishly on our fertile soil that belonged to a completely different flower – could have been a rose rooted into a different soil, akin to its essence. After the final verse of that fragile snowflake's song. She knew love cannot be gained, and there only, truly, ever exists, only one rose. All the weeds grow in vain...

Meet the Author

Matea Čvagić Prašnjak is a writer from Croatia. 31 Fields is Matea's debut novel and the first one published in English. As the owner of the Croatian publishing house LUX NOCTIS, Matea is the originator of a unique combination of services in Croatia, called individual online writing consultancy, as well as the manager of form-specific and record-breaking Croatian creative writing workshops. She was born on October 6, 1996, in Osijek, and she began her literary journey as a fifteen-year-old, winning first prize in the Mali Galović competition after which she published her first book.

Matea is currently working and living in Croatia with her husband.

Printed in the USA
CPSIA information can be obtained
at www.ICGtesting.com
LVHW020054091123
763425LV00006B/146

9 781088 036327